THE HOPE CHEST

BRIDES *of* LANCASTER COUNTY | BOOK 4

WANDA E. BRUNSTETTER

New York Times BESTSELLING AUTHOR

Print ISBN 978-1-62836-134-6

eBook Editions:
Adobe Digital Edition (.epub) 978-1-63058-494-8
Kindle and MobiPocket Edition (.prc) 978-1-63058-495-5

All scripture quotations are taken from the King James Version of the Bible.

All German-Dutch words are taken from the *Revised Pennsylvania German Dictionary* found in Lancaster County, Pennsylvania.

This book is a work of fiction. Names, characters, places, and incidents are either products of the author's imagination or used fictitiously. Any similarity to actual people, organizations, and/or events is purely coincidental.

For more information about Wanda E. Brunstetter, please access the author's website at the following Internet address: www.wandabrunstetter.com

Cover design: Müllerhaus Publishing Arts, Inc., www.Mullerhaus.net

Published by Barbour Publishing, Inc., P.O. Box 719, Uhrichsville, Ohio 44683, www.barbourbooks.com

Our mission is to publish and distribute inspirational products offering exceptional value and biblical encouragement to the masses.

Printed in the United States of America.

To my daughter, Lorine VanCorbach,
the recipient of my special hope chest.

With special thanks to my helpful editor, Rebecca Germany, for giving me the opportunity to revise and expand the four books in this series that were originally part of the Lancaster Brides collection. I also thank the following women who willingly offered their research assistance: Betty Yoder, Sue Miller, and Ruth Stoltzfus. As always, I appreciate and thank my husband, Richard, for his continued help and encouragement. Most of all, I thank my heavenly Father, who gives me the inspiration, strength, wisdom, and desire to write.

For thou art my hope, O Lord GOD:
thou art my trust from my youth.
PSALM 71:5

Chapter 1

Rat-a-tat-tat! Rat-a-tat-tat! Rachel Beachy halted under a giant birch tree. She would have recognized that distinctive sound anywhere. Shielding her eyes from the glare of the late afternoon sun, she tipped her head back and gazed at the branches overhead. Sure enough, there it was—a downy woodpecker. Its tiny claws were anchored firmly to the trunk of the tree, while its petite little head bobbed rhythmically back and forth as it pecked away at the old birch tree.

Hoping for a better look, Rachel decided to climb the tree. As she threw her leg over the first branch, she was glad she was alone and that no one could see how ridiculous she must look. She'd never really minded wearing long dresses. After all, that was what Amish girls and women were expected to wear. At times like this, however, Rachel wished she could wear a pair of men's trousers. It certainly would make climbing trees a mite easier.

Rachel winced as a piece of bark scratched her

knee, leaving a stain of blood that quickly seeped through her dress. It was worth the pain if it would allow her to get a better look at that cute little wood-tapper, though.

Pik-pik-pik! The woodpecker's unusual call resonated against the trunk. *Rat-a-tat-tat!* The bird returned to the pecking process.

"Such a busy little bird," Rachel said quietly as it came into view, two branches above where she straddled the good-sized limb. She and her older sister, Anna, had gone to the river to get cooled off that afternoon, and Rachel had been the first one to head for home. Now she wished she had left the water sooner so she could spend more time studying this beautiful creature God had created and knew everything about. She was reminded of Psalm 50:11: "*I know all the fowls of the mountains: and the wild beasts of the field are mine.*"

Rachel lifted one leg in preparation to move up another limb, but a deep male voice drew her attention to the ground. She halted.

"Hey, Anna, slow down once, would you, please?"

Rachel dropped down so her stomach lay flat against the branch. When she lifted her head a bit and peeked through the leaves, she saw her older sister sprinting across the open field. Silas Swartley was following her, his long strides making Rachel think of a jackrabbit running at full speed.

With his hands cupped around his mouth, Silas yelled, "Anna! Wait up!"

Rachel knew she'd be in trouble if Anna caught her spying, so she held as still as possible and prayed that the couple would move quickly on past.

Anna stopped near the foot of the tree, and Silas joined her there. "I–I really need to talk to you, Anna," he panted.

Rachel's heart slammed into her chest. Why couldn't it be her Silas wanted to talk to? If only he could see that she would be better for him than Anna. *If Silas knew how much I care for him, would it make a difference?*

Rachel was keenly aware that Silas only had eyes for her big sister, but that didn't make her love him any less. As far as she could tell, Silas had been in love with Anna ever since they were children, and Rachel had loved Silas nearly that long, as well. He was all she wanted in a man–good-looking, kindhearted, interested in birds–and he enjoyed fishing.

She was sure he had many other attributes that made him appealing, but with Silas standing right below the tree where she lay hidden, she could barely breathe, much less think of all the reasons she loved him so much.

Rachel looked down at her sister, arms folded across her chest, body held rigid as she stood like a statue facing Silas. It was as if Anna couldn't be bothered with talking to him, which made no sense since she and Silas had been friends a long time. Silas had been coming over to their place to visit ever since Rachel could remember.

Silas reached for Anna's hand, but she pulled it away. "Just who do you think you are, Silas Swartley?"

"I'm your boyfriend, that's who. Have been since we were *kinner*, and you know it."

"I don't know any such thing, so don't try to put words in my mouth."

Rachel stifled a giggle. *That sister of mine. . .she's sure got herself a temper.*

Silas tipped his head to one side. "I don't get it. One minute you're sweet as cherry pie, and the next minute you act as if you don't care for me at all."

Rachel knew full well that Silas spoke the truth. She'd seen with her own eyes the way her sister led that poor fellow on. Why, just a few weeks ago, Anna had let Silas bring her home from a singing. She had to feel some kind of interest in him if she was willing to accept a ride in his courting buggy.

Rachel held her breath as Silas reached out to touch the ties on Anna's stiff, white *kapp*. Anna jerked her head quickly, causing one of the ribbons to tear loose. "Now look what you've done." She pulled on the edge of her covering, but in so doing, the pins holding her hair in a bun must have been knocked loose, for a cascade of tawny yellow curls fell loosely down her back.

Rachel wished she could see the look on Silas's face. She could only imagine what he must be thinking as he reached up to scratch the back of his head and groaned. "Why, you're prettier than a field full of fireflies at sunset, Anna."

Rachel gulped. What she wouldn't give to hear Silas talk to her that way. Maybe if she kept hoping. Maybe if. . .

Rachel thought about a verse in Psalm 71 that she had read that morning: *"But I will hope continually, and will yet praise thee more and more."*

She would gladly offer praises to God if she could win Silas's heart. Truth be told, the verse of scripture she should call her own might best be found in the book of Job, chapter 7: "My *days are swifter than a weaver's shuttle, and are spent without hope."*

Rachel figured she would most likely end up an old maid, while Anna would have a loving husband and a whole house full of children.

"Sometimes I wish I could wear my hair down all the time," Anna said, pulling Rachel out of her musings. "Or maybe get it cut really short."

"Why would you want to do that?"

"Because I might look prettier if I. . .oh, never mind."

"Are you questioning the Amish ways? Now, what would your *mamm* and *daed* have to say about that?" Before Anna could answer, Silas added, "You've always been a bit of a rebel, haven't you?"

Anna leaned against the trunk of the tree, and Rachel dug her fingernails into the bark of the branch she was lying on. *What will my sister say to that comment?*

"My mom and dad would be upset if they knew I had mentioned cutting my hair short." Anna sighed. "Many things about the Amish ways are good, but sometimes I wonder if I might not be happier if I were English."

"You can't be serious."

"*Jah*, I am."

Rat-a-tat-tat! Rat-a-tat-tat! Pik! Pik!

"Say, that sounds like a woodpecker to me." Silas leaned his head back and looked into the tree where Rachel lay partially hidden.

She froze in place. If Silas should spot her instead of the bird, she'd be caught like a pig trying to get into Mom's flower garden. Anna would sure as anything think she had climbed the tree just to spy on her and Silas.

"Forget about the dumb old woodpecker," Anna said in an impatient tone.

Silas continued to peer into the branches. "Hmm. . .I know I heard him, but I don't see that old rascal anywhere."

"You and your dopey bird-watching. One would think you'd never seen a woodpecker before." Anna grunted. "Rachel's fascinated with birds, too. I believe she'd rather watch them eat from one of the feeders in our yard than eat a meal herself."

Silas looked away from the tree and turned to face Anna again. "Birds are interesting little creatures, but you're right. . . I can do my bird-watching some other time." He touched her shoulder. "Now what was it you were saying about wanting to be English?"

"I didn't exactly say I *wanted* to be English; just that I sometimes wonder if I might not be happier being English." Anna pointed to the skirt of her long, blue dress. "Take these clothes, for example. It might be nice to enjoy the freedom of not having to wear a dress all the time."

Rachel sucked in her breath. Where was this conversation headed? If Anna wasn't careful, she might say something stupid and maybe get in trouble for shooting off her big mouth. Especially if the bishop or one of their deacons got wind of it. Truth was, Anna had been acting a bit strange of late–disappearing for hours at a time and saying some mighty peculiar things. Her conversation with Silas only confirmed what Rachel suspected. Anna felt some dissatisfaction with the Amish way of life. It wasn't like Anna climbed trees and saw her dress as a hazard. No, Rachel's prim and proper sister would never climb a tree.

Rachel knew that a lot more than wearing long dresses bothered Anna about being Amish. Not long ago, Anna had mentioned to Rachel that she wished she hadn't been so hasty to join the church and was worried that she might have made a mistake. When Rachel questioned her sister about it, Anna had quickly changed the subject. It made no sense, because Anna had never suggested such a thing before or immediately after joining the church. Something had happened between last fall and this summer to get Anna thinking this way.

"What would you suggest women wear, then—trousers?" Silas asked, jerking Rachel's attention back to the conversation below.

"Maybe."

"Are you saying that you'd wear men's trousers if you could?"

"I—I might. I could do some of my chores a bit easier if I didn't have a long skirt getting in the way." Anna paused. "If I weren't Amish, I could do many things that I can't now."

Oh, great! Now you've gone and done it. Why can't you just be nice to Silas instead of trying to goad him into an argument? Rachel shifted her legs, trying to get a bit more comfortable. *Can't you see how much the fellow cares for you, Anna? If anyone should be wanting to wear men's trousers, it's me—Rachel, the tomboy. At least I've got the good sense to not announce such a thing. And suggesting that you might want to try out the English world is just plain stupid, especially since you already had that opportunity during your* rumschpringe.

"I, for one, am mighty glad you're not English," Silas said, his voice rising an octave. "And you shouldn't even be thinking such thoughts now that you've joined the church, much less speaking them. Why, if your daed or any of our church leaders heard you say anything like that, you'd have some explaining to do, that's for certain sure."

Anna moved away from the tree. "Let's not talk about this anymore. I need to get home. Rachel was way ahead of me when I left the river, so she's probably already there and has done half my chores by now. Mom let me have the afternoon off from working in the greenhouse, so I don't want her getting after me for shirking my household duties."

"Jah, well, I guess I need to be heading home, too." Silas made no move to leave, however, and Rachel had to wonder what was up.

Anna rolled and pinned her hair into place; then she put her head covering back on. Just as she started to walk away, Silas stepped in front of her. "I still haven't said everything I wanted to say."

"What'd you want to say?"

He shuffled his feet a few times, gave his suspenders a good yank, then cleared his throat loudly. "I. . .uh. . .was wondering if I might come see you one evening next week."

Rachel's heart missed a beat. At least it felt as if it had. Silas had been sweet on Anna a good many years, so she should have known the day would come when he would ask to start courting her. Only trouble was if Silas started courting Anna, then Rachel's chances would be nil, and she couldn't bear to think about that.

"You want to call on *me*?" Anna's voice came out as a squeak.

"Of course, silly. Who'd you think I meant– your little sister Rachel?"

That's what I wish you had meant. Rachel's pulse quickened at the thought of her being Silas's girlfriend and riding home from singings in his courting buggy. She drew in a deep breath and pressed against the tree limb as though she were hugging it. No sense hoping and dreaming the impossible. Silas didn't care about her in the least. Not in the way he did Anna, that was for sure. To him, Rachel was still a girl, five years younger than he was, at that. She knew he felt that way, because he'd just referred to her as Anna's "little sister." Besides, whenever Silas had come over to their house, he'd always spoken to Rachel as though she were a child.

"We've known each other for many years, and you did take a ride in my courting buggy after the last singing," Silas continued. "I think it's high time–"

"Hold on to your horses," Anna cut in. "You're a nice man, Silas Swartley, and a good friend, but I can't allow you to court me."

"Why not?"

"Because we're not right for each other."

"Ouch. That hurt my feelings, Anna. I always thought you cared for me."

Rachel could only imagine how Silas must feel. Her heart went out to him. How could Anna be so blind? Couldn't she see what a wonderful man he was? Didn't she realize what a good husband and father he would make?

"I'm sorry if I've hurt your feelings." Anna spoke so softly that Rachel had to strain to hear the words. "It's just that I have other plans for my life, and–"

"Other plans? What kind of plans?"

"I–I'd rather not say just now."

"You may think I'm just a big, dumb Amish fellow, but I'm not as stupid as I might look, Anna Beachy."

"I never meant you were stupid. I just want you to understand that it won't work for the two of us." After a long pause, she added, "Maybe my little sister *would* be better for you, Silas."

I would! I would! Rachel's heart pounded with sudden hope. She held her breath, waiting to hear what Silas would say next, but disappointment flooded her soul when he turned on his heels and started walking away.

"I'll leave you alone for now, Anna, but when you're ready, I'll be waiting," Silas called over his shoulder. He broke into a run and was soon out of sight.

Rachel released her breath and flexed her body against the unyielding limb. Hot tears pushed against her eyelids, and she blinked several times to force them back. At least Silas and Anna hadn't known she was up here eavesdropping on their private conversation. That would have ruined any chance she might ever have of catching Silas's attention. Not that she had any, really. Besides their age difference, Rachel was sure she wasn't pretty enough for Silas. She had pale blue eyes and straw-colored hair. Nothing beautiful about that. Anna, on the other hand, had been blessed with sparkling green eyes and hair the color of ripe peaches. Rachel was certain Anna would always be Silas's first choice because she was so pretty. *Too bad I'm not* schee *like her. I wish I hadn't been born looking so plain.*

When Rachel arrived home several minutes behind her sister, she found her brother Joseph replacing the bolts on an old plow that sat out in the yard. A lock of sandy brown hair lay across his sweaty forehead, and his straw hat rested on a nearby stump.

As she approached, he looked up and frowned. "You're late! Anna's already inside, no doubt helping Mom with supper. You'd better get in there quick, or they'll both be plenty miffed."

"I'm going. And don't be thinking you can boss me around." She scrunched up her nose. "You may be twenty-one and three years older than me, but you're not my keeper, Joseph Beachy."

"Don't go gettin' your feathers all ruffled. You're crankier than the old red rooster when his hens are fighting for the best pieces of corn." Joseph's forehead wrinkled as he squinted his blue eyes and stared at her dress. "Say, isn't that blood I see there?"

She nodded.

"What happened? Did you fall in the river and skin your knee on a rock?"

Rachel shook her head. "I skinned my knee, but it wasn't on a rock."

Joseph gave her a knowing look. "Don't tell me it was another one of your tree-climbing escapades."

She waved a hand and turned away. "Okay, I won't tell you that."

"Let Mom know I'll be in for supper as soon as I finish with the plow," he called to her.

As Rachel stepped onto the back porch, she thought about all the chores she had to do. It was probably a good thing. At least when her hands were kept busy, it didn't give her so much time to think about things—especially about Silas Swartley.

Silas kicked a clump of grass with the toe of his boot. What had come over Anna all of a sudden? How could she be so friendly one minute and almost rude the next? Worse than that, when had she developed such dissatisfaction with being Amish? Had it been there all along, and he'd just been too blind to notice? Was Anna going through some kind of a phase, like some folks did during their rumschpringe? But that made no sense, since Anna had already been baptized and joined the Amish church.

Silas clenched his fists and kept trudging toward home. *I love Anna, but if she's really the woman for me, then why is she acting so disinterested all of a sudden?* He still couldn't believe she'd suggested he start courting her little sister.

"Is that woman simpleminded?" he grumbled. "Rachel's still just a kinner. Besides, it's Anna I love, not her little sister."

As Silas rounded the bend, his farm came into view. A closed-in buggy sat out front in the driveway, and he recognized the horse. It belonged to Deacon Noah Shemly.

"Hmm. . .wonder what's up." He shrugged. "Maybe Mom invited Deacon Noah and his family to join us for supper tonight."

When Silas entered the kitchen a few minutes later, he found his folks and Deacon Noah sitting at the kitchen table, drinking tall glasses of lemonade. It didn't appear as if any of the deacon's family had come with him.

"Is supper about ready?" Silas asked, smiling at his mother. "I'm sure hungry."

Mom gave him a stern look over the top of her metal-framed glasses, which were perched in the middle of her nose. "Where are your manners, son? Can't you say hello to our guest before you start fretting over food?"

Silas was none too happy about his mother embarrassing him that way, but he knew better than to sass her back. Mom might be only half his size, but she could still pack a good wallop to any of her boys' backsides, and she didn't care how old they were, either.

"Sorry," Silas apologized as he nodded at the man who had come to pay them a visit. "When I saw your buggy, I thought maybe you'd brought the whole family along."

Deacon Shemly shook his head. "Nope. Just me."

"Noah came by to have a little talk with you," Pap said, running his fingers through his slightly graying hair, then motioning Silas to take a seat.

"What about?"

"Your friend Reuben Yutzy," the deacon answered with a quick nod.

Silas took off his straw hat and hung it on a wall peg near the back door. Then he took a seat at the table. "What about Reuben?"

The deacon leaned forward and leveled Silas with a piercing gaze. "As you already know, Reuben works for an English paint contractor in Lancaster."

Silas merely nodded in response.

"I hear tell Reuben's been seen with some worldly folks lately."

"As you just said, he works for the English."

"I'm talking about Reuben's off-hours." Noah gave his full brown beard a few good yanks. "Word has it that he's been going to some picture shows and hanging around with a group of English who like to party some."

Silas frowned deeply. "I see."

"You know anything about this, son?" Pap spoke up.

"No. Why would I?"

"Reuben and you have been friends since you were kinner," Mom reminded.

Silas shrugged. "That's true, but he doesn't tell me everything he does."

"So, you're saying you don't know anything about Reuben being involved in the things of the world?" Deacon Noah questioned.

"Not a thing, and it's probably just a rumor." Silas scooted his chair back and stood. "Now, if you'll excuse me, I'd best see to my chores before supper."

"Reuben's folks are mighty concerned that if he's involved with the things of the world, he'll never decide to join the church. So, you will let me or one of the other ministers know if you hear anything, won't you?" the deacon called as Silas headed for the back door.

"Jah, sure."

Outside, on the porch, Silas drew in a deep, cleansing breath. What in the world was going on here? First Anna acting off in the head, and now all these questions about Reuben. It was enough to make him a nervous wreck!

Chapter 2

Rebekah sat in her wheelchair at the table, tearing lettuce into a bowl, while her oldest daughter stood at the stove, stirring a pot of savory stew. They'd been working on supper for the last half hour and still saw no sign of Rachel.

"Are you sure your sister left the river before you did, Anna?"

"Jah, Mom. Several minutes, in fact."

"Did she say she was coming straight home?"

"Not really; I just assumed she was planning on it."

"Hmm. . ."

Just then the back door opened, and Rachel stepped into the room—her face all red and sweaty, her eyes brighter than a shiny penny.

"Sorry I'm late." She hurried over to the sink to wash her hands and face.

Rebekah wiped her hands on a paper towel and reached for a tomato. "Anna said you left the river quite a bit before she did. What kept you, daughter?"

"I. . .uh. . .did a little bird-watching on the way home, and Anna must have missed me somehow." Rachel picked up an empty pitcher and filled it with water from the sink. "Want me to set the table and fill the glasses?"

Rebekah nodded. "It seems as if you and Anna have been living in a dream world lately. Is this what summer does to my girls?"

Rachel shrugged. "I can't help it if I enjoy studying God's feathered creatures."

Anna turned from her job at the stove and frowned. "Sure is funny I never saw you on the way home. If you were looking at birds, then where were you–up in a tree?"

"What difference does it make?" Rachel's face flamed, making Rebekah wonder if up a tree was precisely where her daughter had been. Rachel had been climbing trees ever since she was old enough to run and play outdoors, always chasing after some critter, watching a special bird, or hiding from her siblings.

I wonder if I would have been a tree climber if I'd had the chance. Rebekah's thoughts pulled her unwillingly back to the past–back to when she'd been a little girl and a tree branch had fallen on her during a bad storm. The accident had damaged her spinal cord, and ever since then, Rebekah had either been confined to her wheelchair or strapped in braces that allowed her to walk stiff-legged with the help of crutches.

"What kind of stupid bird were you looking at, Rachel?" Anna asked, halting Rebekah's thoughts.

"It was a downy woodpecker, and it's sure as anything not stupid."

"Silas is such a *kischblich* man. He likes watching birds, too, but I think it's a waste of time."

"Just because Silas appreciates birds doesn't make him a silly man." Rachel moved over to the table with a handful of silverware she'd taken from the drawer.

"And speaking of Silas, I know he brought you home from a singing awhile back. Seems to me he might want to start courting you pretty soon," Rebekah stated.

Anna silently kept stirring the stew.

"Might could be that you'll soon be making a wedding quilt for your hope chest." Rebekah smiled. "Or would you prefer that I make one for you?"

Anna pursed her lips. "It was just one ride in his buggy, Mom. Nothing to get excited about. So there's no need for either one of us to begin an Amish wedding quilt."

"Why not be excited?" Rebekah set the salad bowl aside and turned her wheelchair so she was facing Anna. "Silas has been hanging around our place for years now, and your daed and I both think he's a nice enough fellow. Besides, you're twenty-three years old already and joined the church last fall. Don't you think it's past time you considered getting married?"

Anna moved away from the stove and opened the refrigerator door. She withdrew a bunch of celery and took it over to the sink. "I'm thinking the stew needs a bit more of this; that's what I'm thinking."

Rachel headed back across the room, removed a stack of plates from the cupboard, and brought them over to the table. She looked a bit disgruntled, and Rebekah wondered if the girl might be jealous because Anna had a boyfriend and she didn't. She shifted her wheelchair to one side, making it easier for Rachel to reach around her, then glanced over at Anna again. "I think a lovely quilt would make a fine addition to someone's hope chest, and if Silas is so sweet on you, then maybe you should–"

"I'm sorry if Silas thinks he's sweet on me," Anna said. "I just can't commit to someone I don't love."

Rebekah clicked her tongue against the roof of her mouth. "*Ach.* I didn't mean to interfere. Guess I jumped to the wrong conclusion, but seeing as how you and Silas have been friends for so long, and since you let him bring you home from a singing, I thought things must be getting serious."

"Anna has other things she wants to do with her life. I heard her say so." Rachel covered her mouth with the palm of her hand, and her face turned red as a cherry tomato. "Oops."

"When did you hear me say such things?" Anna turned to face her sister, leveling her with a most peculiar look.

Rachel shrugged and reached for the basket of napkins in the center of the table. "I'm sure you said it sometime."

"What other things are you wanting to do with your life, Anna?" Rebekah asked.

Anna merely shrugged in response.

"If I had someone as *wunderbaar* as Silas after me, I'd marry him in an instant." Rachel's cheeks turned even redder, and she scurried across the room.

"My, my," Anna said with a small laugh. "If I didn't know better, I'd think my little sister was in love with Silas herself."

"Rachel's only eighteen—too young for such thoughts," Rebekah said with a shake of her head. "Besides, I'm sure she wouldn't be after your boyfriend, Anna."

"How old were you when you fell in love with Dad?" Anna asked.

"Guess I wasn't much more than nineteen. Even so—"

The back door flew open, interrupting Rebekah's sentence, and her twelve-year-old daughter, Elizabeth, burst into the kitchen. Her long brown braids, which had been pinned at the back of her head when she'd gone outside awhile ago, now hung down her back. "Perry won't let me have a turn on the swing. He's been mean to me all day, Mom."

Rebekah shook her head. "You know your twin

brother likes to tease. The little *galgedieb*. I wish you would try to ignore that scoundrel's antics."

"But, Mom, Perry–"

Rebekah held up one hand to silence Elizabeth. "It's almost time for supper, so please run outside and call your daed and your *bruders* inside."

"Oh, all right, but if Perry starts picking on me again–"

"You'll just ignore him."

"I'll try."

Rebekah shook her head as Elizabeth went out the back door. "That youngest daughter of mine has a lot to learn about ignoring a tease." She clicked her tongue. "Why, I can't tell you how many times I had to endure teasing when I was a girl."

"Did your brothers and sisters tease you?" Rachel asked as she placed a napkin beside the plate nearest her.

Rebekah nodded. "Sometimes, but most of my teasing came from kinner outside my family–those who thought my handicap was something to joke about, I guess."

"Anyone cruel enough to make fun of someone who's disabled ought to be horsewhipped," Rachel muttered.

"I agree," Anna put in.

Rebekah smiled. She was glad her daughters felt that way.

Rebekah's husband, Daniel, and their oldest son, Joseph, entered the room just then, and Elizabeth and her twin brother, Perry, followed. Soon the family gathered around the huge wooden table, and all heads bowed for silent prayer. When it was over, Daniel glanced at Joseph. "Did you get that old plow put back together today?" he asked, as he filled his plate with a generous helping of stew.

Joseph nodded. "Jah, I did. Should be able to use it again tomorrow morning."

Daniel pulled his fingers through the ends of his full brown beard, now lightly peppered with gray. "No matter what those English neighbors of mine may think, I say you can't replace a reliable horse and plow with any kind of fancy equipment."

"Horses aren't always so reliable," Anna put in. "I've known 'em to be downright stubborn at times."

Daniel cast a curious look in her direction but made no comment.

"I've been wondering, don't you think we need to modernize a bit?" Anna continued. "I mean, working the greenhouse would go much better if we had a telephone. . .even one outdoors on a pole."

Daniel frowned. "We've gotten along all these years without a phone, so why would we need one now?"

Everyone fell silent, but as Rebekah watched her eldest daughter fiddle with her food, she sensed the frustration Anna felt and wondered if she should say something on her behalf. Before Rebekah could say a word, Anna pushed her chair aside and stood.

"I'd like to be excused."

Daniel nodded, but Rebekah felt the need to protest. "You've hardly eaten a thing, Anna."

"I'm not so hungry." Anna lowered her head, causing her long lashes to form crescents against her pale cheeks.

"Let her go," Daniel said. "Just might could be that going without supper is what she needs to help clear her head for better thinking."

Rebekah had never been one to usurp her husband's authority, even if she didn't agree with everything he said. So with a quick nod, she replied, "Jah, all right then."

Anna rushed out of the room without another word, and Rebekah released a sigh. Her oldest child had been acting a mite strange of late, and it had her more than a bit worried.

Rachel leaned against the back of her chair, her shoulder blades making contact with the hard wood. *Such a silly one, that sister of mine. She seems so dissatisfied with her life these days. Guess maybe she doesn't know how good she's got it.*

As soon as the rest of them had finished supper, Rachel cleared the table and helped her mother and Elizabeth do up the dishes and clean the kitchen.

"Many hands make light work," Mom said, as Rachel handed her a platter to dry.

Rachel nodded and glanced toward the hallway

door leading to the stairs. Too bad Anna was in her room sulking. If she'd been down here in the kitchen helping, like she should have been, they would probably be done already.

When the last dish was finally dried and put away, Rachel turned to her mother and said, "I think I'll go upstairs and see how Anna's doing. Unless you've got something more for me here, that is."

Mom shook her head. "Nothing right now. I was thinking about going outside to check on my herb garden." She glanced at Elizabeth, who was drying her hands on a terry cloth towel. "How'd you like to join your old mamm outside?"

Elizabeth wrinkled her freckled nose. "You ain't old."

Rachel noticed the smile that crossed her mother's face–that sweet, dimpled expression that made her so special. Even with Mom's disability, she rarely complained. From all Rachel had been told, their mother had been confined to a wheelchair most of her life. But Mom didn't allow her disability to hold her back much. It was Rachel's understanding that her mother had been quite independent when she was a young woman and had decided to open the greenhouse she'd named Grandma's Place.

Rachel smiled to herself as she thought of the stories Dad and Mom often told about their courting days and how they almost didn't marry because of some silly misunderstanding. Mom had convinced herself that Dad only wanted her because he loved flowers so much and hoped to get his hands on her business. It took some doing, but Dad finally made her believe he loved her most, not the plants and flowers. At last, they got married. They ran the greenhouse together, and a year later, baby Anna was born.

Mom had said she thought it was a true miracle, the way God had allowed her to give birth despite her partial paralysis. Rachel could only imagine how her mother must have felt when she kept having one miracle after another. Two years after Anna was born, Joseph arrived. Another three years went by, and Rachel came onto the scene. Mom must have thought she was done having *bopplin*, because it was another six years before the twins made their surprise appearance.

Five miracles in all, Rachel mused. *I would surely feel blessed if God ever gave me five children.* She drew in a deep breath and released it with such force that Mom gave her a strange look.

"You okay, Rachel?"

"Jah, I'm fine; just thinking is all."

"Were you daydreaming again?"

Rachel nodded. Daydreaming was nothing new for her. As far back as she could remember, she had enjoyed fantasizing about things.

"Say, how did you get that blood on your dress?" Mom asked suddenly, as she stared at the spot on Rachel's skirt where she'd injured her knee.

"Oh, just scraped my leg a bit," Rachel replied

with a shrug. No point in explaining how it had happened. Mom would probably lecture her about it being unladylike and dangerous to go climbing around in trees.

"Want me to take a look-see?"

"No, it's nothing. I'm ready to go up and see Anna now."

"Go on ahead. Maybe you can talk some sense into her about courting Silas."

Rachel winced, feeling like she'd had a glass of cold water thrown in her face. Surely Mom didn't mean for her to actually try and convince Anna to let Silas court her. If she did that and was successful in getting Anna to agree to do what Silas wanted, then Rachel knew the chance of him ever deciding to court *her* would be slim to none.

Anna lay on her bed, staring at the plaster ceiling and tumbling things over in her mind. She thought about her encounter with Silas and wondered if somehow Rachel could have been nearby and overheard what they'd said. She wondered, too, why Silas kept pressuring her to let him court her and couldn't seem to take no for an answer.

Her mind went over the conversation that had gone on at the table during supper, and she realized that her folks would have a conniption if they knew the thoughts that had been going through her head of late.

A soft knock at the door roused Anna from her musings, and she rolled onto her side. "Come in."

Rachel poked her head into the room. "Mind if I join you for a while?"

Anna motioned her sister into the room. "Why's Dad have to be so stubborn?" she asked after Rachel had taken a seat on the bed beside her. "Can't he see there's a place for some modern things? He's the reason I got so upset at supper, you know." A stream of tears trickled down her cheeks, and she swiped at them with the back of her hand.

"People often blame things on the previous generation because there's only one other choice," Rachel said in a near whisper.

Anna sat up, swinging her legs over the side of the bed. "What's that supposed to mean?"

"The other choice would be to put the blame on yourself."

Anna sucked in her protruding lip and blinked several times. "How dare you speak to me that way!"

"It's true."

Anna jerked off her head covering and pulled out the pins that held her hair in place; then she began to pace the room with quick, nervous steps.

"Are you unhappy being Amish? Is that the reason you've been acting so strange lately?"

Anna released a sigh. "Not unhappy, really, but if I weren't Amish–"

"But you are Amish, and you should be happy being such."

"Shouldn't I have the right to choose how I want to live and with whom?"

Rachel nodded. "Of course you should, but you're already baptized into the church, and if you were to go against the *Ordnung* now, you'd be shunned, and that's a fact."

Anna sniffed. "Don't you think I know that, Rachel?" She moved over to the window and stood looking out at the darkening sky. "What'd you come in here for, anyway–to pummel me with a bunch of questions?"

"Of course not. I just wanted to see how you were doing."

"I'm fine."

"Okay. I'll leave you alone then."

"*Danki*." Anna released a sigh of relief when she heard the bedroom door click shut. She wasn't ready to tell anyone her secret yet–not even Rachel, whom she knew she could trust.

Silas shielded his eyes from the glare of the morning sun as he strolled through the small village of Bird-in-Hand. He'd come in early today with the intent of speaking to his friend Reuben, who was supposed to be painting a new grocery store in town.

He found Reuben around the back of the supermarket, holding a paintbrush in one hand and a giant oatmeal cookie in the other.

"I see you're hard at work," Silas said with a grin.

Reuben chuckled and popped the cookie into his mouth. "I do need to keep up my strength, you know."

"Jah, I'm sure."

"What brings you to town so early?" Reuben asked, as he applied a glob of paint to the side of the wooden building.

"I came to see you."

"So now that you see me, what do you think?"

Silas shook his head. "Always kidding around, aren't you?"

Reuben's blue eyes fairly sparkled, and he pulled his fingers through the back of his thick, blond hair, which was growing much too long for any self-respecting Amish man. Silas had to wonder how come his friend wasn't wearing his straw hat, especially on a day when the sun was already hot as fire. He was about to voice that question when Reuben asked a question of his own.

"You heard any good jokes lately?"

Silas shook his head. "Nope. Have you?"

Reuben nodded but kept right on painting. "My boss told me a real funny one the other day, but I can't remember it now."

"How come you don't give up this painting job and go back to helping your daed on the farm? I'm sure he could use the extra pair of hands."

"I don't like farming so much anymore. In fact,

I'm thinking about starting a whole new life for myself."

Silas rocked back and forth on his heels, trying to think of the right thing to say. He had been helping his dad work the land ever since he'd finished his eighth-grade education. That was nine years ago and he was still happy staying at home on the farm. It was hard for him to understand why an Amish man, born and raised on a farm, preferred painting to working the land. But then he guessed everyone had different likes and dislikes.

"So, what's new with you?"

"Not so much." Silas shifted from one foot to the other. "Deacon Shemly was at our place yesterday. Said he'd heard some things, and he seemed to be kind of concerned."

Reuben stopped painting and turned to face Silas. "Things about me?"

Silas nodded. "Are they true?"

"Are what true?"

"Have you been running around with some English fellows?"

Reuben's brows furrowed. "You planning on telling anyone what I say to you?"

Silas shook his head. "Thought I'd ask, that's all."

Reuben grunted. "I haven't done anything wrong–just going through rumschpringe, same as you did before joining the church. I'm smart enough to know what I'm doing."

Silas shook his head. "One thing I've learned

is never to mistake knowledge for wisdom. One might help you make a living, but the other helps you make a life."

Reuben flicked a fly off the end of his paint-brush. "Let's just say I've learned that we only live once, and until I'm ready to settle down, I aim to have me some fun. I plan on keeping my truck for as long as I can, too."

Hearing the way his friend was talking put an ache in Silas's heart, the same way it had when he'd spoken with Anna yesterday. He didn't understand why some of the young people he knew seemed dissatisfied with the old ways. Well, he might not be able to do much about Reuben, but Anna was another matter. If he could figure out a way to get her thinking straight again, he was determined to do it.

Chapter 3

The following morning, Rachel awoke to the soothing sound of roosters crowing in the barnyard. She loved that noise—loved everything about their farm, in fact. She yawned, stretched, and squinted at the ray of sun peeking through a hole in her window shade. Today the family planned to go to the outdoor farmers' market, where they would sell some of their garden produce as well as a bunch of plants and flowers from Mom and Dad's greenhouse.

Before Rachel headed down the stairs to help with breakfast, she looked out her bedroom window and saw Dad, Joseph, and Perry out by the buggy shed, getting their larger market buggy ready to go.

The sweet smell of maple syrup greeted Rachel as she entered the kitchen a few minutes later, and she noticed right away that Mom sat in her wheelchair in front of one of the lower counters, mixing pancake batter. Anna stood in front of the stove, frying sausages and eggs, while Elizabeth was busy setting the table, which held a huge pitcher of fresh maple syrup.

"*Guder mariye,*" Rachel said cheerfully. "What can I do to help?"

"Good morning to you." Mom glanced up at Rachel, then back to the pancake batter. "You can go outside and tell the men we'll be ready with breakfast in about ten minutes."

Rachel nodded, then made a hasty exit out the kitchen door. Dad and Perry were still busy loading the back of the buggy, while Joseph hitched the brawny horse that would pull it.

"Mom says breakfast will be ready in ten minutes," Rachel announced.

"You can go get washed up," Dad said with a nod at Perry.

Rachel's freckle-faced brother pointed to the boxes of green beans sitting on the grass. "What about those?"

"You stay," Dad said, nodding toward Rachel, "and you go," he instructed Perry. "I'll see to the boxes."

Perry straightened his twisted suspenders and took off in a run. Looking at his long legs from the back side, Rachel thought he appeared much older than a boy of twelve. From the front, however, Perry's impish grin and sparkling blue eyes made him look like a child full of life, laughter, and mischief.

Rachel stood quietly beside her father, waiting

for him to speak. His shirtsleeves were rolled up to the elbows, and she marveled at how quickly his strong arms loaded the remaining boxes of beans. When the last box was put in place, Dad straightened and faced her. "Do you think you could do me a favor?"

Rachel twisted one corner of her apron and stared at the ground. Her father's favors usually meant some kind of hard work. "I–I suppose so. What did you have in mind?"

Dad bent down so he was eye level with Rachel. "Well now, I know how close you and Anna have always been. I was hoping you might let your mamm and me know what's going on with her these days."

Rachel opened her mouth to respond, but he cut her off. "Fact of the matter is Anna's been acting mighty strange lately, and we need your help finding out what's up."

Rachel wrinkled her nose. Was Dad saying what she thought he was saying? Did he actually want her to spy on her sister? If Dad thought she and Anna were still close, he was sorely mistaken. Here of late, Rachel and Anna didn't see eye to eye on much of anything. Rachel knew if Anna's talk about learning more of the English ways ever reached Mom and Dad, they would be very concerned. That was obvious by the way Dad had reacted last night when Anna suggested they should modernize some. Rachel didn't want to be the one to tell them what was going on inside Anna's stubborn head. Not that she knew all that much. Fact was she wouldn't have known anything at all if she hadn't overheard Anna and Silas's conversation while she was hiding in the tree.

"So what do you say?" Dad asked, scattering Rachel's thoughts.

She flicked her tongue across her lower lip. "What exactly am I expected to do?"

"To begin with, your mamm's told me that Anna has a suitor, yet she's not the least bit interested in being courted by that nice fellow."

"You must mean Silas Swartley. He's sweet as molasses on Anna, but she won't give him the time of day."

Dad glanced toward the front of the market buggy, where Joseph stood fiddling with the horse's harness. "Kind of reminds me of your mamm when I was tryin' to show her how much I cared."

Rachel listened politely as her father continued. "Sometimes a man shows his feelings in a strange sort of way." He nodded toward Joseph and chuckled softly. "Now take that big brother of yours—we all know that he's sweet on Pauline Hostetler, but do you think he'll do a thing about it? No way! Ever since Pauline returned from Ohio, Joseph's been making eyes at her, but he won't make a move to ask her out. That boy's gonna fool around, and soon some other fellow's bound to come along and win Pauline's heart. Then it'll be too late for my *bleed* son."

Rachel knew all about Joseph's crush on Pauline, as well as his bashful ways. He had been carrying a torch for Pauline ever since Eli Yoder had dropped her flat to marry Laura, the fancy English woman from Minnesota. The fact that Pauline was three years older than Joseph didn't help things, either. Rachel had to wonder if the age difference bothered Pauline the way it did her brother. It seemed rather strange that the twenty-four-year-old woman still wasn't married. Either she'd never gotten over Eli, or Pauline simply wasn't interested in Joseph. He sure wasn't going to take the initiative; Rachel was sure of that.

"Well, I'm thinkin' that if anyone can talk to Anna about giving Silas a chance, it would be you," Dad said, cutting into Rachel's contemplations one more time. "She needs to know that she's being foolish for snubbing someone as nice as Silas."

She swallowed hard. If her father only knew what he was asking of her. It was hard enough to see Silas hanging around Anna all the time. How in the world could Rachel be expected to talk Anna into something she really didn't want to do? Truth be told, Rachel would just as soon slop the hogs every day for the rest of her life as to tell Anna how stupid she was for snubbing Silas. But she knew her father probably wouldn't let up until she had agreed to his request.

Rachel let her gaze travel over their orderly farmyard for a few seconds as she thought things through. "Jah, okay. I'll have a little talk with Anna about Silas," she finally agreed.

"And you'll tell us if anything strange is going on with your sister?"

Rachel nodded, feeling worse than the thick scum that would no doubt be covering much of their pond by late August. "Okay, Dad. I'll tell you what's going on."

❧

Joseph cringed as Rachel walked away. He hadn't eavesdropped on purpose, but he couldn't help hearing part of Dad's conversation with Rachel. Should he say anything about it—maybe give his thoughts on the whole thing?

He approached his father cautiously, his mind searching for just the right words. "Say, Dad, I caught some of what you were saying to Rachel, and I was wondering if it's such a good idea for her to be meddling in Anna's life."

Dad whirled around. "If I want your opinion, I'll ask for it."

"Sorry, I just thought—"

"How much of our conversation did you hear, anyway?"

"Just that you were hoping she could talk to Anna about giving Silas the chance to court her."

Dad nodded. "I said that all right."

Was that a look of relief he saw on his father's face? Had he said some things to Rachel that he didn't want Joseph to hear? If so, what had he said? Could it have been about him?

"I like Silas. He's a hard worker, and I think he would make Anna a fine husband, don't you?"

Joseph shrugged. "I suppose. I just don't think–"

Dad gave his stomach a couple of pats. "I don't know about you, but my belly's sure starting to rumble. Let's go eat, shall we?"

"Jah, okay." As Joseph followed his father to the house, he wished it had been he who'd been asked to speak with Anna. Rachel and Anna had always been close, and if Rachel started butting into Anna's business, she might not take so kindly to it. Besides, Joseph and Anna were closer in age, so she might be more apt to listen to him.

The farmers' market where Rachel and her family were heading was eight miles from their farm. Today the trip seemed even longer than usual, and the cramped quarters in the buggy combined with the hot, sticky weather didn't help much, either. Rachel had felt a bit cross all morning, and now she was even more agitated.

Dad and Mom rode in the front of the buggy, with Elizabeth sitting between them. Two benches in back provided seating for Rachel, Anna, Joseph, and Perry. Behind them, they'd stashed the boxes filled with produce, plants, and fresh-cut flowers. Mom's wheelchair was scrunched in back, as well.

The temperature was in the nineties, with humidity so high Rachel felt her dress and underclothes sticking to her body like flypaper. When they finally pulled into the parking lot, she was the first one to jump down from the buggy.

Perry tended to the horse, while Joseph and Dad unloaded the boxes and carried them to the spot where they set up their tables. Elizabeth and Rachel followed, with Anna a few feet behind, pushing Mom's wheelchair over the bumpy terrain.

Everyone scurried around to help set up their tables, and soon the Beachys were open for business. People started buying right away, and whenever they were between customers, Rachel and her siblings were allowed to take turns wandering around the market.

Rachel took a break around noontime and headed for a stand advertising cold cherry cider. A tall, gangly Amish fellow waited on her. Freckles covered his nose, and he looked to be about nineteen or twenty. Rachel didn't recognize him and figured he must be from another district.

"It's a mighty hot day, isn't it?" he asked, giving her a wide grin.

"Jah, it surely is warm." She handed him some money. "I'd like a glass of cherry cider, please."

He bent down and removed a jug from the ice chest underneath the table, then poured some of the cider into a paper cup and handed it to Rachel. "Here you go."

"Danki."

Rachel drank the cool beverage quickly, then moved on to another table where Nancy Frey, the Amish schoolteacher in their district, sold a variety of pies.

Nancy smiled up at Rachel. "Are you here with your family?"

"Jah. We're selling produce and lots of flowers and plants from my folks' greenhouse." Rachel pointed across the way. "Our tables are over there."

"I sure hope business is better for you than it has been here. Pies aren't doing so well today."

Rachel licked her lips as she studied the pies on Nancy's table. "Apple-crumb, shoofly, and lemon sponge are all my favorite."

"Would you like to try a slice?" Nancy asked. "I already have an apple-crumb cut."

"It's real tempting, but I'd better not spoil my appetite, or I won't be able to eat any of the lunch I brought along."

Nancy smiled. "How's your mamm doing these days? The last few times I've seen her, she was in her wheelchair. Doesn't she use her crutches anymore?"

"She does some, though I think it's difficult for her to walk like a stiff-legged doll. Mom says the older she gets, the harder it is, so she uses her wheelchair more often than the braces these days." Rachel fanned her face with her hand. "Well, guess I'll be moving on. It's awful hot and muggy today, so I think I'll see if I can find a bit of shade somewhere."

Nancy nodded. "I know what you mean. If I weren't here alone, I'd be doing the same thing."

"I'd be happy to watch your table awhile," Rachel offered.

"Danki, but my sister Emma will be along soon. I'm sure she'll be willing to let me take a little break."

"All right then. See you later, Nancy." Rachel moved away from the table and found the solace she was looking for under an enormous maple tree growing in the field behind the market. She was about to take a seat on the ground, when she caught sight of Silas Swartley. Her heart slammed into her chest as she realized he was heading her way.

Silas gritted his teeth as he made his way to the backside of the farmers' market. He had just come from the Yutzys' table, and the few minutes he'd spent talking to Reuben's folks had made him feel sick at heart. They'd told Silas that they had a pretty good inkling of what their son was up to. . .or at least they knew some of it. Silas was sure Reuben hadn't told his folks everything he'd been thinking of late, but then, he hadn't really told Silas all that much the last time they'd spoken, either.

Reuben had always had a mind of his own, even when they were children attending the one-room schoolhouse together. Silas remembered one time when Reuben had skipped school and gone to the lake for a day of fishing. When he'd come back to school the following day, Reuben had expressed no repentance. The ornery fellow had bragged about the three fish he'd caught and how he'd gotten out of taking the spelling test they were supposed to have that day. Even though Reuben had to stay after school every day for a week and do double chores at home, he hadn't been tamed in the least.

Silas drew in a deep breath. He figured he'd best forget about Reuben, because it wasn't likely that his stubborn friend would listen to anything he had to say. Might be best for him to concentrate on Anna, since she suddenly seemed discontent with her life. He hoped to change all that, though. If Anna would agree to court him, maybe soon they could talk about marriage and settling down to start a family of their own.

Silas had decided to head out to the field behind the market to think things through, when he noticed Anna's little sister Rachel sitting under a giant maple tree. *Hmm. . .she might be the one I need to talk to.*

He hurried across the grassy area and plunked down beside her. "Hey, Rachel. What's new with you?"

Rachel couldn't believe Silas had taken a seat beside her, but it tickled her pink that he had. "Not much new with me," she said. "How about you?"

"Same old thing, I guess." Silas removed his straw hat and fanned his face with the brim. "So, what are you doing out here by yourself?"

"Trying to get cooled off." For one crazy moment, Rachel had an impulse to lean her head on Silas's shoulder and confess her undying love for him. She didn't, of course, for that would have been far too bold. And it would have only proved to him that she really was quite immature.

"Sure is a warm day we're having. Whew! Even under the shade of this big old tree, it's hot."

She nodded and looked upward.

"What are you lookin' at?"

"Oh, I thought I heard a bluebird whistling."

Silas tipped his head way back. "Really? Where is it?"

"I'm not sure. Maybe I'm just hearing things—hoping a bluebird might show itself."

Silas chuckled. "I thought I was the only one who liked to listen for the bird sounds."

"You're not alone; that's one of my favorite pastimes."

He glanced over at the people crowding around all the market tables. "Say, Rachel, I was wondering if we could talk."

"I thought we *were* talking."

He grinned and dropped his hat to his knees. "I guess we were, at that. What I really meant to say was, can we talk about your sister?"

Rachel frowned. She might have known Silas hadn't planned to talk about her. She shrugged, trying not to let her disappointment show. "What about Anna? She's the sister you were referring to, right?"

Silas lifted his gaze toward the sky. "Of course I meant Anna. It couldn't be Elizabeth I want to talk about. I'm no cradle robber, you know."

Rachel felt as though Silas had slapped her across the face. Even though he was speaking about her twelve-year-old sister, she still got his meaning. She knew Silas wouldn't dream of looking at her because she was five years younger than he. Besides, what chance did she have against the beauty of her older sister?

In a surprise gesture, Silas touched Rachel's chin and turned her head so she was looking directly at him. Her chest fluttered with the sensation of his touch, and it was all she could do to keep from falling over. "Did you hear what I said, Rachel?"

"I—I believe so, but what was it you wanted to say about Anna?"

"You and your sister are pretty close, isn't that right?"

She gulped and tried to regain her composure. "I used to think so."

"Anna probably talks more to you than anyone else, correct?"

Rachel shook her head. "I think she tells her friend Martha Rose more than she does me these days."

Several seconds went by before Silas spoke again. "I suppose I could talk to Martha Rose, but I don't know her all that well. I'd feel more comfortable talking to you about Anna than I would to her best friend."

Rachel supposed she should feel flattered that Silas wanted to speak with her, yet the thought of him using her only to learn more about Anna irked her to no end.

"Okay," she said with a sigh. "What is it you want to know about my sister?"

"Can you tell me how to make her pay me some mind? I've tried everything but stand on my head and wiggle my ears, yet she still treats me like yesterday's dirty laundry. I tell you, Rachel, it's got me plumb worn out trying to get sweet Anna to agree to courting."

Sweet Anna? Rachel thought ruefully. *Silas, you might not think my sister's so sweet if you knew that she has no plans to let you court her.*

Rachel felt sorry for poor Silas, sitting there all woebegone, pining for her sister's attention. If she wasn't so crazy about the fellow herself, she might pitch in and try to set things right between him and Anna. "I think only God can get my sister thinking straight again." She looked away, studying a row of trees on the other side of the field.

"You're kind of pensive today," Silas remarked. "Is it this oppressive heat, or are you just not wanting to help me with Anna?"

Rachel turned to face him again. "I think a man who claims to care for a woman should speak on his own behalf. Even though my sister and I don't talk much anymore, I know her fairly well, and I don't think Anna would like it if she knew you were plotting like this."

Silas's forehead wrinkled. "I'm not plotting. I'm just trying to figure out some way to make Anna commit to courting. I thought maybe you could help, but if you're gonna get all peevish on me, then forget I even brought up the subject."

Now I've gone and done it. Silas will never come to care for me if I keep making him mad. Rachel placed her trembling hand on Silas's bare arm, and the sudden contact with his skin made her hand feel like it was on fire. "I–I suppose it wouldn't hurt if I had a little talk with Anna," she mumbled.

A huge grin spread across Silas's summer-tanned face. "You mean it, Rachel? You'll really go to bat for me?"

She nodded slowly, feeling like she was one of her father's old sows being led away to slaughter. First she'd promised Dad to help Anna and Silas get together, and now she'd agreed to speak to Anna on Silas's behalf. It made no sense, since she didn't really want them to be together. But a promise was a promise, and she would do her best to keep it.

Chapter 4

That Sunday, church was to be held at Eli and Laura Yoder's place. They only lived a few farms from the Beachys, so the buggy ride didn't take long at all.

Many Amish carriages were already lined up near the side of the Yoders' house, but Dad managed to find an empty spot near Eli's folks' home. Joseph helped Mom into her wheelchair, while Dad unhitched the horse and put him in the corral; then everyone climbed out of the buggy and scattered in search of friends and relatives to visit before church got started.

Rachel noticed Silas standing on one end of the Yoders' front porch, and she berated herself for loving him so much. She was almost certain he would never love her in return. She wasn't sure he even liked her. She either needed to put him out of her mind or figure out some way to make him take notice of her.

Silas seemed to be focused on Anna, who was

talking with Martha Rose Zook and Laura Yoder at the other end of the porch. *Guess I'd better speak to Anna soon, before Silas comes asking if I did.* Rachel joined her sister and the other two women, but she made sure she was standing close enough to Anna so she could whisper in her ear. "Look, there's Silas. He seems to be watching you."

"So?"

"Don't you think he's good-looking?"

Anna nudged Rachel in the ribs. "Since you seem so interested, why not go over and talk to him?"

Rachel shook her head. "It's you he's interested in, not me."

"I think we'd better hurry and get inside. Church is about to begin," Anna said, conveniently changing the subject.

Rachel followed her sister into the Yoders' living room, where several rows of backless, wooden benches had been set up. She would have to speak to Anna about Silas later on, even though she knew it would pain her to do it.

The men and boys took their seats on one side of the room, while the women and girls gathered on the other. Rachel sat between her two sisters, and Mom parked her wheelchair alongside a bench where some of the other women sat.

All whispering ceased as one of the deacons passed out the hymnals. In their usual chantlike voices, the congregation recited several traditional German hymns. Next, one of the ministers delivered the opening sermon. This was followed by a time of silent prayer, where everyone knelt. Then Deacon Shemly read some scripture, and Bishop Wagler gave the main sermon.

During the longer message, Rachel glanced over at Anna, who sat twiddling her thumbs as she stared out the window.

What's that sister of mine thinking about? Rachel had a terrible feeling that Anna's interest in worldly things might lead to trouble. What if Anna were to up and leave the faith?

Rachel clenched her teeth. *No, that can't happen. It would break Mom and Dad's hearts, not to mention upsetting the whole family. Why, we'd have to shun our own flesh and blood!* She shuddered just thinking about the seriousness of it. Right then, she vowed to pray more, asking the Lord to change her sister's mind about things. She would even make herself be happy about Anna and Silas courting if it meant Anna would alter her attitude.

Rachel felt a sense of relief when the benediction was given, followed by a few announcements and the closing hymn. It wasn't that she didn't enjoy church, but all those troubling thoughts rolling around in her head made her feel fidgety and anxious to be outside.

Once the benches had been moved and tables set up, the women served a soup-and-sandwich lunch. Rachel and Anna joined several other young women as they brought out the food to the men.

After the men finished eating, the women and children took their places at separate tables.

When the meal was over and everything had been cleared away, men and women of all ages gathered in small groups to visit. The younger children were put down to nap, while the older ones played games on the lawn. Some of the young adults joined in the games, while others were content to just sit and talk.

Rachel didn't feel much like playing games or engaging in idle chitchat, so she decided to take a walk. Walking always seemed to help her relax and think more clearly. She left Anna talking with a group of women and headed in the direction of the small pond near the end of the Yoders' alfalfa field.

The pool of clear water was surrounded by low-hanging willow trees, offering shade and solitude on another hot, sticky day in late July. Feeling the heat bearing down on her, Rachel slipped off her shoes and socks, then waded along the water's edge, relishing the way the cool water tickled her toes. When she felt somewhat cooler, she plunked down on the grass. Closing her eyes, Rachel found herself thinking about the meeting she'd had with Silas the day before. She'd only made one feeble attempt to talk to Anna about him and knew she really should try again. It was the least she could do since she had made a promise.

A snapping twig caused Rachel to jump. She jerked her head in the direction of the sound and was surprised to see Silas standing under one of the willow trees. He smiled and lifted his hand in a wave. It made her heart beat faster and was just enough to rekindle her hope that he might actually forget about Anna and come to love her instead.

"I didn't know anyone else was here," Rachel murmured, as Silas moved over to where she sat.

"I didn't know anyone was here, either." Silas removed his straw hat and plopped down on the grass beside her. They sat in silence for a time, listening to the rhythmic birdsong filtering through the trees and an occasional *ribbet* from a noisy bullfrog.

Rachel thought about all the times Silas had visited their farm over the years. She remembered one day in particular when a baby robin had fallen from its nest in the giant maple. Silas had climbed that old tree like it was nothing, then put the tiny creature back in its home. That day, Rachel gave her heart to Silas Swartley. Too bad he didn't know it.

"I just talked to Reuben Yutzy," Silas said, breaking into Rachel's thoughts. "He's been working for a paint contractor in Lancaster for some time now."

She nodded but made no comment.

"Reuben informed me that he's leaving the Amish faith." Silas slowly shook his head. "Can you believe it, Rachel? Reuben's been my friend since we were kinner, and I never expected he would want to leave." The lines in Silas's forehead deepened. "Since he started working for that English man, Reuben's been doing a lot more worldly things. I tried talking to him the other day, but I guess nothing I said got through. Reuben's made up his mind about leaving, and he seems bent on following that path."

"Many of our men work in town for paint contractors, carpenters, and other tradesmen," Rachel reminded. "Most of them remain in the faith in spite of their jobs."

"I know that's true, but I guess Reuben's not one of 'em." Silas gave his earlobe a quick tug. "Reuben told me that he bought a fancy truck awhile back, but he's been keeping it parked outside his boss's place of business so none of his family would know."

Rachel fidgeted with her hands. She wanted to reach out and touch Silas's disheartened face. It would feel so right to smooth the wrinkles out of his forehead. She released a deep sigh instead. "Things are sure getting *verhuddelt* here of late."

Silas nodded. "You're right about things being mixed-up. I think something else is going on with Reuben, too."

"Like what?"

"I'm not sure. He dropped a few hints, but when I pressed him about it, he closed up like a snail crawling into its shell. Said he didn't want to talk about it right now." Silas grimaced. "I'm thinking maybe a woman is involved."

"An Englisher?"

"Might could be. It wouldn't be the first time an Amish man fell for an English woman." Silas shrugged. "That's what happened to Eli Yoder a few years back, you know."

"But Laura joined the Amish faith."

"That's true, but it's an unusual situation and doesn't happen very often."

Rachel slipped her socks and shoes back on before she stood. "I should be getting back to the house, I expect. If Mom misses me, she'll probably send Joseph out looking, and I'm not in any mood to deal with my cranky brother today."

"Joseph's not happy?"

"Nope. He's got a big crush on Pau–" Rachel covered her mouth with the palm of her hand when she realized she had almost let something slip. "As I was saying, I need to head back."

"Wait!" Silas jumped to his feet. "I was wondering if you've had a chance to speak with Anna yet."

Rachel's face heated up as she turned to face him. "I–I haven't said much to her on the subject, but I still believe it would be best if you spoke with her yourself, and you'd better do it soon, before it's too late."

"How's things at your place?" Rebekah asked her friend Mary Ellen as the two of them sat on the front porch visiting and watching the children play on the lawn.

Mary Ellen smiled. "Never a dull moment with

Eli and Laura's two living right next door. Those little ones keep Laura hopping all the time."

Rebekah sighed and maneuvered her wheelchair closer to the swing where Mary Ellen sat holding Martha Rose's little girl, Amanda. "Sure wish I had a couple of *kinskinner* like this one to love on."

"You'll have grandchildren sooner than you think." Mary Ellen gave her granddaughter's chubby legs a little squeeze. "I heard that Silas Swartley's been courting your Anna, so I wouldn't be surprised if a wedding wasn't in the near future for them."

Rebekah shook her head. "Silas did take Anna home from a singing awhile back, but from what I've been told, there's nothing more to it. Of course, that's not to say that Silas wouldn't like for there to be more. Me either, for that matter."

"Silas seems like a nice enough fellow. I would think Anna would be anxious for him to come calling."

"My eldest daughter's not acting like herself these days." Rebekah lowered her voice some. "Fact is, I'm kind of worried about all three of my oldest kinner."

Mary Ellen's eyebrows lifted high on her forehead. "How come you're worried?"

"Well, Anna's been saying things to rile her daed, like how come he doesn't want to put in a phone at the greenhouse and maybe he should modernize some."

"Maybe she thinks you'd have more customers if you had a phone."

"That could be, but the fact that she won't let Silas court her when they've been friends since they were little makes me wonder if she's got her eye on someone else, or maybe she's just feeling discontent with things."

"Why would she be discontent? She joined the church last fall, so I would think she'd be all settled in by now."

"I can't really say what's going on with her." Rebekah shrugged. "Maybe it's just my imagination, or maybe it's some kind of phase she's going through. I'm hoping it will pass real soon."

"You said all three of your oldest have you worried. What's going on with Joseph and Rachel?"

Rebekah's voice lowered another notch. "Joseph is carrying a torch for Pauline Hostetler, and he hasn't got the courage to tell her that he cares. That's made him kind of moody lately."

"I see. And Rachel? What's her problem?"

"I'm not sure about Rachel. She's been acting strange for some time, kind of like a young woman in love, only she doesn't have a boyfriend, so I know that's not the case."

Mary Ellen bent her head and kissed the top of Amanda's head. "If they could only stay sweet and innocent like this little girl, we grandmothers wouldn't have so much to worry about."

Rebekah chuckled. "Jah, but knowing us, we'd find something else to fret over."

Rachel and her family had begun packing up to leave the Yoders' place, when she noticed Silas had Anna cornered next to his courting buggy. Her sister didn't look any too happy, and Rachel couldn't help but wonder what was being said. She inched a bit closer, hoping to catch a word or two. Eavesdropping had become a habit, it seemed, but she couldn't seem to help herself. Besides, it wasn't like she was doing it on purpose. People just seemed to be in the wrong place at the wrong time.

"I think it would be best if you'd forget about me," she heard Anna say. "You really should find someone better suited to you."

Silas shuffled his feet a few times, turning his hat over and over in his hands. "Don't rightly think there's anyone better suited to me, Anna."

"If you think about it, you'll realize that we don't have much in common. Never have, really." Anna shrugged. "On the other hand, I know who would be just right for you."

Me. . .me. . . Rachel squeezed her eyes shut, waiting to hear Silas's next words.

"Who might that be?"

"Rachel."

"Don't start with that again, Anna."

Rachel's eyes snapped open. She had to give

up this silly game of bouncing back and forth from hope to despair. It only proved her immaturity, which was exactly why Silas saw her as a mere child.

"She likes a lot of the same things you like, Silas. Besides, I think she's crazy about you." Anna nodded toward her family's buggy, where Rachel stood, dumbfounded and unable to move. She would probably never be able to look Silas in the face again.

Silas didn't seem to notice Rachel, for he was looking right at Anna. "As I've said before, Rachel's not much more than a kinner. I need someone who's mature enough for marriage and ready to settle down."

"Rachel is *eighteen*, soon to be *nineteen*," Anna said. "Give her a few more months, and she'll be about the right age for marrying."

"But it's you I love, Anna." Silas's tone was pleading, and if Rachel hadn't been so angry at her sister for embarrassing her that way, she might have felt pity for the man she loved.

"Rachel, are you getting in or not?" Dad's deep voice jerked Rachel around to face him.

"What about Anna? She's still talking to Silas over by his buggy." Rachel pointed in that direction, but Dad merely grabbed up the reins.

"I'm sure Silas will see that Anna gets home," Mom put in. "After all, you did mention that he's sweet on her."

Rachel's throat ached from holding back tears, and she reached up to massage her throbbing temples. Silas thought she was just a child, and he was in love with Anna. At the rate things were going, she might never get to use the things she'd put in her hope chest. She glanced Silas's way one last time, then hopped into the buggy and took her seat at the rear.

Joseph glanced over at her. "Why are you lookin' so down in the mouth?"

"It's none of your business."

"I'll bet she'll tell me. I'm a girl, and girls only share their deepest secrets with another girl. Isn't that right, sister?"

Before Rachel could answer Elizabeth's question, Perry put in his two cents' worth. "Aw, Rachel's probably got a bee in her kapp 'cause she don't have a steady boyfriend yet. She's most likely jealous of Anna gettin' to ride home with Silas." He gave Rachel an impish smile. "That's it, huh? You're green with envy, right?"

"Leave Rachel alone," Mom called from her seat at the front of the buggy. "If she wants to talk about whatever's bothering her, she will. Now, let's see how quiet we can make the rest of this ride home."

As Anna pressed her body against Silas's buggy, she felt like a mouse cornered in the barn by a hungry cat. Couldn't Silas just accept the fact that she didn't love him? Why did he keep going after her like this? If only she felt free to tell him what was on her mind.

If she could just reveal her secret. . .

"So, what do you have to say, Anna? Can I give you a ride home so we can talk some things through?"

Silas's pleading voice pulled Anna's thoughts aside, and she gritted her teeth. "Danki for the offer, but I think I'll just walk home today."

His eyes widened. "On a hot day like this, you want to walk all the way home when I'm offering you a ride in my open buggy?"

She nodded. "There's really nothing more for us to say, so I'd appreciate it if you'd leave me alone."

Silas pulled back as if he'd been slapped, and his face turned bright red.

Anna hated being rude, but Silas obviously didn't want to take no for answer, and speaking so bluntly seemed to be the only way she could get through to him. "I don't mean to hurt your feelings, Silas, but it wouldn't be right for me to lead you along when I know we can't have a future together."

"We could have if you'd give it half a chance."

"Sorry, but I can't do that."

"Why'd you accept a ride home in my buggy after the last singing then?"

Anna swallowed hard. How could she offer an answer to that without revealing her secret? "I probably shouldn't have accepted that ride, and I'm sorry if you got the impression that it meant anything more than just a friendly ride home."

Anna stepped away from Silas's buggy and darted off before he had a chance to respond. She had to get away now before she ended up telling him the truth.

Chapter 5

The following day, Rachel felt more fretful than ever. She'd hardly said more than two words to anyone all morning and was sorely tempted to tell Anna that she had overheard some of her conversation with Silas yesterday. In fact, she was working up her courage and praying for the right words as she hung a batch of laundry on the line.

When Anna came out of the greenhouse and headed in Rachel's direction, she decided this was as good a time as any. Rachel waved and called for her sister to come on over. Anna merely gave a little nod and kept walking toward the barn. A short time later, she emerged with one of the driving horses, then began to hitch the mare to the buggy parked nearby.

Rachel dropped one of Perry's shirts into the wicker basket, but before she could move to intercept Anna, their mother called, "Where are you going?"

"I've got to run some errands in town," Anna

explained. "Then I may stop by and see Martha Rose for a bit."

"You be careful now," Mom called. She sat on the front porch in her wheelchair, shelling peas into a large ceramic bowl sitting in her lap.

"I will," Anna hollered, as she stepped into the buggy.

"And don't be out too late, neither. There was a bad accident last week along the main highway. It was getting dark, and the driver of the car didn't see the Amish carriage in time."

"I'll be careful, Mom." Anna flicked the reins, and the horse and buggy were soon out of sight.

Rachel walked back to the wicker basket, bent down, and snatched a pair of Dad's trousers. "Guess I'll have to catch Anna later on," she mumbled.

"Rachel!"

"Jah, Mom?"

"When you're done with the laundry, I'd like you to go over to the greenhouse and help your daed awhile. I've got several things here at the house needing to be done, so it doesn't look like I'll be able to work out there today."

"What about Anna? She's the one who likes working with flowers."

"She's running some errands in Paradise."

Rachel already knew that. What she didn't know was why. Couldn't *she* have gone to town so Anna could have kept working in the greenhouse? Life wasn't always fair, but she knew there was no point in arguing, so she cupped her hands around her mouth and hollered, "Okay, Mom! I'll go over to the greenhouse as soon as I'm finished here."

Silas's morning chores were done, but he had a few errands to run for his dad. He decided this would be a good time to stop by the Beachys' greenhouse and have a little talk with Anna. Maybe he'd even buy Mom a new indoor plant or something she could plant in her flower garden. That would give him a good excuse for stopping at Grandma's Place, and it might keep Anna from suspecting the real reason for his visit.

Half an hour later, Silas stepped inside the greenhouse and was surprised to see Rachel sitting behind the counter, writing something on a tablet. "Guder mariye," he said, offering her a smile. "Is Anna about?"

"Nope. Just me and my daed are here today." She motioned toward the back room. "He's repotting some African violets that have outgrown their containers."

Silas's smile turned upside down. "I thought Anna usually worked in the greenhouse. She isn't sick, I hope."

Rachel tapped her pencil along the edge of the counter. "She went to Paradise. Had some errands to run."

Silas scratched the back of his head. "Hmm. . .

guess maybe I can try to catch up with her there. I have some errands to run today, too." He turned toward the door, all thoughts of buying a plant forgotten. If he hurried, he might make it to Paradise in time to find Anna. The town wasn't so big, so if she was still running errands, he was bound to spot her. "Have a nice day. See you later, Rachel."

Anna. . .*Anna*. . .*Anna*. . . Rachel gripped her pencil so hard, her knuckles turned white. Was getting Anna to agree to court him all Silas ever thought about? He hadn't bothered to ask how Rachel was doing or even make any small talk about the weather.

"I heard the bell ring above the door," Dad said as he entered the room. "Did we have a customer?"

Rachel was about to answer when she felt a sneeze coming on. She grabbed a tissue from the box under the counter, leaned her head back, and let out a big *ker-choo*!

"*Got segen eich*–God bless you."

"Danki."

"You're not coming down with a summer cold, I hope." Dad's forehead wrinkled, and he looked at Rachel with obvious concern.

She shook her head. "I think I'm allergic to all these flowers. I do okay with the ones growing outside, but being cooped up with 'em in here is a whole different matter."

"Guess working in the greenhouse isn't exactly your idea of fun, huh?"

She turned her head away as she felt another sneeze coming on. "*Ker-choo!*" She held her finger under her nose. "Truth is, I would rather be outside."

"How come the doorbell jingled and we have no customers?" Dad asked, making no mention of her preference.

"It was Silas Swartley. He was looking for Anna, and when I told him she was running errands in Paradise, he hightailed it right out of here."

Dad chuckled. "Love is in the air. There's no doubt about it."

Rachel nibbled on the end of her pencil, remembering the way Silas always looked whenever he spoke of her sister. It made her sick to her stomach, knowing he was so sweet on Anna when she didn't love him in return.

Dad grinned like an old hound dog that had just been given a bone. "Someday your time will come, Rachel. Just be patient and have the hope that God will send the right man your way."

"I'm hoping," she mumbled. "Hoping and praying for a miracle."

By the time Silas had reached the town of Paradise, his horse was breathing heavy, and the poor animal's sides were lathered up pretty good. Silas knew he shouldn't have made the gelding trot all the way there, but he'd been in such a hurry to see if he could find Anna that he hadn't thought about what he was doing to his horse.

He pulled up to the back of the variety store and secured the horse to the hitching rail that had been put there for Amish buggies. "Sorry about making you run so much," he said, as he rubbed the horse's flanks with a rag he'd taken from the back of the buggy. "I'll get you a bucket of water, and then you can rest while I go inside and see if there's any sign of Anna."

Silas took care of his horse first thing. Then he hurried into the store. After checking every aisle and asking both of the women who worked in the store if they'd seen Anna Beachy, he realized that Anna wasn't in the store, nor had she been there any time today.

"Guess I'll have to check somewhere else," he mumbled as he climbed back in his buggy. "She couldn't have left town already."

For the next hour, Silas drove around Paradise, checking inside every store and asking all the clerks if they had seen Anna. Not one person remembered seeing her, and Silas thought it was more than a bit strange. If she had really come to town to run some errands, then surely he would have spotted her by now, or at least someone would have remembered seeing her come into their store. Maybe Anna had changed her mind about going to Paradise and had gone to one of the other small towns in the area to do her shopping.

Silas knew it would take too long for him to travel from town to town looking for Anna, and he'd probably miss her anyway. Finally, with an exasperated groan, he took his seat in the buggy again and gathered up the reins. "There's no hurry getting home," he mumbled. "So I may as well let my horse walk all the way."

It was after nine o'clock, and the sun had nearly set, yet Anna still hadn't returned home. Dad and Mom sat on the front porch, talking about their workday, while Rachel kept Elizabeth entertained with a game of checkers she'd set on the little table at one end of the porch. Joseph and Perry were out in the barn, grooming the horses and cleaning Joseph's courting buggy.

Rachel had just crowned her last king and was about to ask her little sister if she wanted to give up the game and have another piece of funny-cake pie their Mennonite neighbor had given them earlier that day, when a horse and buggy came up the graveled drive. It was Anna, and before she even got the horse reined in, Dad was on his feet.

"Why are you so late, daughter?" He ran toward the buggy, shaking his finger all the way. "You sure couldn't have been running errands all this time."

The porch was bathed in light from several kerosene lamps that had been set out, but the night sky was almost dark. Rachel knew Anna wasn't supposed to be out alone after the sun went down because of the risk of an accident, even with the battery-operated lights on their buggy.

Rachel peered across the yard and strained to hear what Anna and their father were saying. *Sure hope that sister of mine hasn't done anything foolish.* An unsettled feeling slid through Rachel as she watched Anna step down from the buggy.

"Your mamm and I were gettin' worried," Dad's deep voice announced.

Mom coasted down the wheelchair ramp. "Oh, thank the Lord! I'm so glad to see you're safe."

"Sorry. I didn't realize it was getting so late," Anna apologized.

"Well, you're home now, and that's what counts. We can talk about where you've been all this time after I get the horse and buggy put away." Dad quickly unhitched the mare and led her off toward the barn.

"Anna, where's your apron and head covering?" Mom asked, as Anna stepped in front of the wheelchair.

Rachel studied her sister closely. Sure enough, Anna wasn't wearing anything on her head, and the black cape and apron she'd been wearing over her dark blue cotton dress when she'd left home were off, too. No cape. No apron. No head covering. What in the world was that girl thinking?

Anna reached up to touch the top of her head.

"I. . .uh. . . guess I must have left my kapp someplace."

Elizabeth stepped off the porch. "That makes no sense, sister. How could you have left your kapp anywhere when it's supposed to be on your head?"

Anna shot Elizabeth a look that could have stopped the old key-wound clock in the parlor, but she pushed past her little sister and stepped onto the porch without any comeback at all.

"Wait a minute, Anna." Mom propelled herself back up the ramp. "We need to talk about this, don't you think?"

"Can't it wait until tomorrow? I'm kind of tired."

Rachel gulped. If Anna were a few years younger, she would have had a switch taken to her backside for talking to their mother that way. What in the world had come over her?

"It may be getting late, and you might be tired, but this is a serious matter, and it won't wait until tomorrow," Mom said with a shake of her head.

Anna pointed at Rachel, then Elizabeth. "Can't we talk someplace else? No use bringing the whole family into this."

Mom folded her arms and set her lips in a straight line, indicating her intent to hold firm. "Maybe your sisters can learn something from this discussion. I think it would be a good idea if they stay—at least until your daed returns. Then we'll let him decide."

Rachel sucked in a deep breath and held it while she waited to see what Anna's next words would be.

"Guess I don't have much say in this." Anna folded her arms and dropped to the porch swing with a groan.

Elizabeth moved back to the checkerboard. "Are you gonna make your next move, Rachel? I just took one of your kings while you were starin' off into space."

Rachel jerked her thoughts back to the game they'd been playing. "I don't see how you managed that. . .unless you were cheating. I *was* winning this game, you know."

Elizabeth thrust out her chin. "I wasn't cheating!"

Rachel was about to argue the point further, but the sound of her father's heavy footsteps on the stairs drew her attention away from the game again.

"Joseph's tending the horse." Dad looked down at Anna, who was pumping the swing back and forth like there was no tomorrow. "Now, are you ready to tell us where you've been all day?" A muscle in his cheek began to twitch, and Rachel knew it wasn't a good sign. "Why aren't you wearing your apron and kapp, Anna?"

Rachel flinched, right along with her older sister. Their father didn't often get angry, but when he was mad enough to holler like that, everyone knew they had better listen.

"I. . .uh. . ." Anna stared at the floor. "Can't we talk about this later?"

Dad slapped his hands together, and everyone,

including Mom, jumped like a bullfrog. "We'll talk about it now!"

Anna's chin began to quiver. "Couldn't I speak to you and Mom in private?"

He glanced down at Mom, who had wheeled her chair right next to the swing. "What do you think, Rebekah?"

"I guess it might be best." She turned her chair around so she was facing Rachel and Elizabeth. "You two had better clear away the game. It's about time for you to get washed up and ready for bed anyway."

"But, Mom," Elizabeth argued. "I'm almost ready to skunk Rachel and–"

Rachel shook her head. "You'd better do as Mom says. You can skunk me some other time." She grabbed up the checkerboard, let the pieces fall into her apron, folded up the board, then turned toward the front door. As curious as she was about where Anna had been and why she'd come home without her kapp or apron, Rachel knew it was best to obey her parents. She would have a heart-to-heart talk with her rebellious sister tomorrow morning. Until then, she'd be doing a whole lot of praying.

As Anna sat on the porch swing, waiting for her sisters to go inside the house, her mind swirled with confusion. If she told her folks the truth about where she had been all day, it wouldn't just get her in trouble. She would be breaking a promise she'd made not to say anything yet about her plans.

She closed her eyes and clenched her fingers until they dug into the palms of her hands. *If I make up a story to tell Mom and Dad, and they find out later that I lied to them, they'll be crushed, and I'll be in big trouble; that's for certain sure.*

Someone touched Anna's knee, and she opened her eyes. Her mother had pushed her wheelchair even closer to the swing, and her father stood directly behind the chair. "Anna, are you ready to tell us where you've been all day?" Mom asked in a near whisper.

Anna swallowed around the lump in her throat as tears blinded her vision.

"You'd best be tellin' us now." Dad's wrinkled forehead and squinted eyes let Anna know that he was nearly out of patience.

"I. . .uh. . .was with Silas Swartley all day," Anna said in a shaky voice. She sniffed a couple of times and blinked in an attempt to clear away her tears.

Mom's lips turned into a smile. "Why didn't you just say so in the first place? We have nothing against Silas; you know that."

"What about your apron, cape, and kapp?" Dad motioned to the front of Anna's dress, devoid of its cape and apron. "You had all three on when you left home earlier. How come you're not wearing any of 'em now?"

Anna drew in a deep breath and blew it out

quickly. "Well, I. . .uh. . .the thing is–"

"Quit thumpin' around the shrubs and tell us the truth!"

"I'm not wearing my apron and cape because I spilled ice cream all over myself."

"And the head covering?"

Anna's face heated up. She was getting in deeper with each lie she told, but she felt like a fly trapped in a spider's web and didn't know what to do.

"Answer your daed's question, Anna," Mom prompted. "Where's your kapp, and why aren't you wearing it now?"

"Silas. . .well, he wanted to see how I would look with my hair down, so I took the head covering off and removed the pins from my hair for a short time."

Mom gasped, and Dad stomped his foot.

"I know it was wrong, but it felt right at the time, and after I pinned up my hair again, I forgot to put the kapp back in place." Anna glanced toward the buggy shed. "Guess I left the kapp, along with the apron and cape, inside the buggy."

"We're glad you and Silas are courting, but we can't have you running off like that without telling us where you're going," Mom said, reaching out to pat Anna's knee again.

Dad shook his finger in Anna's face. "And I won't stand for you taking off your kapp and letting your hair down in front of Silas. Is that understood?"

"Jah."

"You're a baptized member of the Amish church now, not some *eegesinnisch*—willful—teenager going through her rumschpringe days."

Anna stared down at her hands, folded in her lap. "I know, Dad, and I'm sorry. Don't know what came over me, really."

Mom smiled. "You're in *lieb*, that's what. Young people do all kinds of things they'd not do otherwise when they're in love with someone."

"That doesn't give her the right to be doin' things she knows are wrong and could get her in trouble with the church," Dad put in.

Mom lifted her hand from Anna's knee and clasped her hand. "She knows what she did was wrong, and I'm sure she won't do it again. Right, daughter?"

Anna nodded as tears rolled down her cheeks. She knew what she had really done today wouldn't set well with her folks when they learned the truth, and the lies she'd just told them had only made it worse. But she didn't feel she could undo any of it now. Later, once everything had been said and done, she would tell them both the truth. In the meantime, she had to keep the promise she'd made for a little while longer.

Chapter 6

When Rachel came downstairs the following morning, she found Mom and Anna busy fixing breakfast.

"You're late." Anna stirred the oatmeal so hard Rachel feared it would fly right out of the pot. "How do you think you're going to run a house of your own if you can't be more reliable?"

"Anna Beachy, just because you got up on the wrong side of the bed doesn't give you the right to be *schlecht* with your sister this morning." Mom sat at the kitchen table, buttering a stack of toast, and the look on her face let Rachel know she wouldn't tolerate anyone being crabby this morning.

Rachel hurried to set the table, deciding it was best to keep quiet.

Anna brought the kettle of oatmeal to the table and plopped it on a pot holder, nearly spilling the contents. "Like as not, you'll be getting married someday, Rachel, and I was wondering if you'd care to have my hope chest."

Rachel glanced at her mother, but Mom merely shrugged and continued buttering the toast. Anna was sure acting funny. Of course, she'd been acting strange for several weeks now, but today she seemed even more unsettled. Rachel could hardly wait until breakfast was over and she had a chance to corner Anna for a good talk. She was dying to know where her sister had been last night and what had happened during her discussion with their folks.

"I've already got a start on my own hope chest, but thanks anyway." Rachel gave Anna a brief smile.

"I'd sure like to go to Emma Troyer's today," Mom said, changing the subject. "She's feeling kind of poorly and could probably use some help with laundry and whatnot. Trouble is, I've got too much of my own things needing to be done here and out at the greenhouse, as well."

Anna's eyes brightened some. "I'll go," she said almost too quickly as she went to the refrigerator and took out a pitcher of milk.

Mom nodded. "If you don't dally and come straight home, then I suppose it would be all right. You'll have to wait until this afternoon, though. I need help baking pies this morning."

"This afternoon will be just fine."

Rachel could hardly believe her ears. Wasn't Anna in any kind of trouble for coming home late last night and not wearing her apron, cape, and kapp? What sort of story had she fed the folks so that Mom was allowing her to take the buggy out again today? Worse yet, if Anna went gallivanting off, Rachel would probably be asked to help in the greenhouse for the second day in a row. She'd planned to do some bird-watching this afternoon and maybe, if there was enough time, go fishing at the river. From the way things looked, she'd most likely be working the whole day, so there would be no chance of her having any kind of fun.

"Did I hear someone mention pies?" Elizabeth asked as she skipped into the room. "I sure hope you're plannin' to make a raspberry cream pie, 'cause you know it's my favorite."

Mom reached out and gave the child a little pat on the backside when she sidled up to the table. "If you're willing to help Perry pick raspberries, maybe we could do up a few of your favorite pies." Her forehead wrinkled slightly. "Our raspberry bushes are loaded this summer, and if they're not picked soon, the berries are liable to fall clean off. Now that would surely be a waste, don't you think?"

Elizabeth's lower lip jutted out. "I don't like to pick with Perry. He always throws the green berries at me."

"I'll have a little talk with your brother about that. Now, run outside and call the menfolk in for breakfast."

"Okay, Mom."

Elizabeth scurried out of the room, and Mom clicked her tongue. "That girl has more energy than she knows what to do with."

Rachel smiled, but Anna just took a seat at the table and sat staring across the room as though she were in a daze.

A few minutes later, Dad and the brothers came in along with Elizabeth, whose exuberance continued to show as she rushed over to the table.

"Slow down," Dad admonished. "The food's not going anywhere."

"I know, but I'm hungry," the child said as she pulled out a chair beside Mom's wheelchair.

Dad merely grunted in response, and everyone else took their seats, as well. As soon as the silent prayers had been said, Elizabeth began eating.

"Guess you really were hungry," Mom said with a chuckle.

Rachel glanced over at Anna, who seemed more intent on pushing the spoon around in her bowl than in eating any of the oatmeal she had prepared. If only she could get into Anna's head and figure out what she was thinking.

Conversation at the table was kept to a minimum. Everyone seemed anxious to finish the meal and get on with their day. When breakfast was over and the dishes had been washed, dried, and put away, Anna excused herself to go feed the hogs, and Rachel headed to the henhouse to gather eggs. After she was done, she hoped she might be able to have a little chat with her big sister.

With basket in hand, Rachel started across the yard, wishing she could go for a long walk. The scent of green grass kissed by early morning dew and the soft call of a dove caused a stirring in her heart. There was no time for a walk or even for lingering in the yard, because she had chores to do and knew she had best get them done quickly if she wanted to catch Anna before she left.

A short time later, Rachel reached under one of their fattest hens and retrieved a plump, brown egg. A few more like that, and she'd soon have the whole basket filled. By the time she had finished the job, ten chunky eggs rested in the basket, and several cranky hens pecked and fussed at Rachel for disturbing their nests.

"You critters, hush now. We need these eggs a heap more than you, so shoo!" She waved her hands, and the hens all scattered.

When an orange-and-white barn cat brushed against Rachel's leg and began to purr, she placed the basket on a bale of straw and plopped down next to it. She enjoyed all the barnyard critters. They seemed so content with their lot in life. Not like one person she knew, who suddenly seemed so dissatisfied and couldn't give Silas the time of day.

"What am I going to do, Whiskers?" Rachel whispered. "I'm in love with someone, and he don't even know I'm alive. All he thinks about is my older sister." Her eyes drifted shut as an image of Silas flooded her mind. She saw him standing in the meadow, holding his straw hat in one hand and running his long fingers through his dark chestnut hair. She imagined herself in the scene, walking slowly toward Silas with her arms outstretched. Closer and closer she came to him, until. . .

"Sleepin' on the job, are you?"

Rachel's eyes popped open, and she snapped her head in the direction of the deep voice that had pulled her out of her pleasant reverie. "Joseph, you about scared me to death, sneaking up that way."

He chuckled. "I wasn't really sneaking, but I sure thought you'd gone off to sleep there in your chair of straw." He sat down beside her. "What were you thinking about that put such a satisfied smile on your face?"

Rachel gave Joseph's hat a little yank so it drooped down over his eyes. "I'll never tell."

Joseph righted his hat and jabbed her in the ribs with his elbow. "Like as not, it's probably some fellow you've got on your mind. My guess is maybe you and Anna have been bit by the summer love bug."

Rachel jabbed him right back. "I wouldn't talk if I was you. Anyone with halfway decent eyesight can see how much you care for Pauline."

"Pauline doesn't see me as anything more than a friend. When she came back to Pennsylvania after her time of living in Ohio, I'd thought maybe I might have a chance, but she doesn't seem to know I'm alive." He gave his right earlobe a quick tug. "I wonder if it's our age difference that bothers her, or maybe she just doesn't find me appealing."

Rachel touched his shoulder and gave it a gentle squeeze. "I wouldn't take it personal if I was you. I've got a hunch that Pauline's thinking about the age difference, same as Silas."

Joseph's eyebrows lifted. "That makes no sense, Rachel. Silas and Anna are the same age."

Rachel could have bit her tongue. If she wasn't careful, she would end up telling her big brother that she was crazy in love with Silas and wished like everything that he loved her, too.

"Speaking of Anna, has she ever told you that she's in love with Silas?"

Joseph leaned over to stroke the cat's head, for Whiskers was now rubbing against his leg. "She hasn't said anything to me personally, but she's been acting mighty strange here of late. I hear tell she got in pretty late last night; and some other times, Anna's whereabouts haven't been accounted for, either. What other reason could she have for acting so sneaky, unless she's been seeing Silas in secret?"

Rachel remembered Silas saying he was going to Paradise yesterday and that he hoped to find Anna there. Could she possibly have spent the day with him? She really wanted to know.

Rachel grabbed the basket of eggs and jumped up. "I've got to get these back to the house. See you later, Joseph!" She tore out of the barn and dashed toward the hog pen, where she hoped to find Anna still feeding the sow and her brood of piglets. In her hurry, she tripped over a rock and nearly fell flat on her face. "Ach! The last thing I need this morning is to break all the eggs I've gathered."

She walked a little slower, but disappointment flooded her soul when she saw that Anna wasn't at the pigpen.

Back at the house, Rachel found Mom, Anna, and Elizabeth rolling out pie dough at the kitchen table. Each held a wooden rolling pin, and Rachel noticed that Elizabeth had more flour on her clothes than she did on the heavy piece of muslin they used as a rolling mat.

"You're just in time," Mom said with a nod of her head. "Why don't you add some sugar to the bowl of raspberries on the cupboard over there?"

Rachel put the eggs in the refrigerator, then went to the sink to wash her hands. "Elizabeth, it sure didn't take you and Perry long to pick those berries. How'd you get done so fast?"

"Mom helped." Elizabeth gave Rachel a wide grin. "Her wheelchair fits fine between the rows, and she can pick faster'n anybody I know."

Mom chuckled. "When you've had as many years' practice as me, you'll be plenty fast, too."

Rachel glanced at Anna. She was rolling her piecrust real hard—like she was taking her frustrations out on that clump of sticky dough. Every once in a while, she glanced at the clock on the far wall and grimaced. Rachel figured this probably wasn't a good time to be asking her sister any questions. Besides the fact that Anna seemed a mite testy, Mom and Elizabeth were sitting right there. It didn't take a genius to know Anna wasn't about to bare her soul in front of them.

Rachel reached for a bag of sugar on the top shelf of the cupboard. She'd have to wait awhile yet. . .until she had Anna all to herself.

The pie baking was finished a little before noon, and Anna, who seemed quite anxious to be on her way, asked if she could forgo lunch and head on over to Emma's.

"I suppose that would be okay," Mom said. "I could fix you a sandwich to eat on the way."

Anna waved her hand. "Don't trouble yourself. I'm sure Emma will have something for me to eat."

Mom nodded but sent Anna off with a basket of fresh fruit and a jug of freshly made iced tea. "For Emma," she stated.

Rachel finished wiping down the table, then excused herself to go outside, hoping her sister hadn't left yet. She saw Anna hitching the horse to the buggy, but just when she was about to call out to her, Dad came running across the yard. "Not so late tonight, Anna!"

Anna climbed into the buggy. "I'll do my best to be back before dark."

Dad stepped aside, and the horse moved forward.

Rachel's heart sank. *Not again! Am I ever going*

to get the chance to speak with that sister of mine? With a sigh of resignation, she turned and headed back to the house. Today was not going one bit as she'd planned.

Chapter 7

Rachel gripped the front porch railing, watching as Anna climbed out of the buggy and began to unhitch the horse. It was almost dark. She could hardly believe her sister would be so brazen as to disobey their parents two nights in a row. *What kind of shenanigan is Anna pulling now? Why is she acting so defiant all of a sudden?*

Before Rachel had a chance to say anything to her sister, Dad was at Anna's side, taking the reins from her. "Late again," he grumbled. "You know right well we don't like you out this late. You'd better have a good excuse for this. Something better than what you told us last night."

Rachel wanted to holler, "What did you tell them last night?" Instead, she just stood like a statue, waiting to hear Anna's reply.

Anna hung her head. "I. . .uh. . .need to have a little heart-to-heart talk with you and Mom."

"Fine. I'll do up the horse, then meet you inside." Dad walked away, and Anna stepped onto the porch. She drew Rachel into her arms.

"What was that for?" A feeling of bewilderment mixed with mounting fear crept into Rachel's soul.

Anna's eyes glistened with tears. "No matter what happens, always remember that I love you."

Rachel's forehead wrinkled. "What's going on, Anna? Are you in some kind of trouble?"

Anna's only response was a deep sigh.

"I've been wanting to talk to you all day–to see why you've been acting so strange and to find out how come you were late getting home last night."

Anna drew in a shuddering breath. "Guess you'll learn it soon enough, because I'm about to tell Dad and Mom the truth about where I was then and why I'm late again tonight."

"Weren't you running errands in Paradise yesterday?"

Anna shook her head.

"And today–didn't you spend the day at Emma Troyer's?"

"I went to Lancaster both times," Anna admitted as she sank into one of the wicker chairs sitting on the front porch. "I know you probably won't understand this, but I'm going to have to leave the Amish faith."

Rachel's mouth dropped open. "What? Oh, no. . .that just can't be!"

"It's true."

"But how can you even think of doing such a

thing now that you've been baptized and joined the church? Don't you know what it will mean if you leave now?"

A pathetic groan escaped Anna's lips, and she began to cry.

Rachel knelt in front of the chair and grasped her sister's trembling hand. "I'm guessing the folks don't know," she said, hoping this was some kind of a crazy mistake and that as soon as Anna was thinking straight again, she would say it was only a joke and that everything would be all right.

"I made up some story about why I was late last night."

"What story was that?"

"I said I was with Silas all day, and the reason I wasn't wearing my cape and apron was because I spilled ice cream all over me."

"And the kapp? How come you weren't wearing that last night?"

Anna winced as though she'd been slapped. "I lied about that, too. Said Silas wanted to see me with my hair down, so I took the kapp off and forgot to put it back on before I headed home."

Rachel's mind whirled like Mom's gas-powered washing machine running at full speed. First Anna had said she wasn't interested in Silas; then she'd lied and said she was. It made no sense. And why would her sister do something so bold as to let her hair down in front of Silas—or anyone else, for that matter?

The words Rachel wanted to speak stuck in her throat like a wad of chewing gum.

"You. . .you. . .really lied to the folks about all that?" she finally squeaked.

Anna nodded.

"And they believed you? I mean, you said the other day that you had no interest in Silas."

"I know, but I wanted to throw them off track." Anna swallowed so hard her Adam's apple jiggled up and down. "I've got to tell them the truth now; there's no other way."

Rachel made little circles with her fingers across the bridge of her nose. This wasn't good. Not good at all. Anna had been lying to Mom and Dad and saying things about leaving the Amish faith. How could she be so mixed-up? What in the world was happening to their family?

Rachel had every intention of questioning her sister further, but Dad stepped onto the porch just then. "Let's go into the kitchen, Anna." He pointed at Rachel. "You'd better go on up to bed."

Obediently but regretfully, Rachel stood, offering Anna a feeble smile. At this rate, she would never find out the whole story.

When Rachel entered the kitchen, she discovered her mother working on a quilt. A variety of lush greens lay beside vivid red patches spread out on the table, making it look like a colorful jigsaw puzzle.

"Isn't it nice?" Mom asked as she glanced up at

Rachel. "This is going to be for Anna's hope chest, seeing as to how she's got herself an interested suitor and all. Why, did you know that she snuck off yesterday just to be with Silas Swartley? The little scamp told us she wasn't interested in him, but it seems she's changed her mind."

Before Rachel could comment, Dad and Anna entered the room. "*Gut nacht*, Rachel," Dad said, nodding toward the hallway door.

"Good night," Rachel mumbled as she exited the room, only closing the door partway. She stopped on the stairwell, out of sight from those in the kitchen. She knew it was wrong to eavesdrop, but she simply couldn't go to bed until she found out what was going on with her sister.

"Anna, you said you had something to say," Dad's voice boomed from the kitchen. "Seems as though you ought to start by explaining why you're so late."

"She was probably with Silas again," Mom interjected. "Anna, we don't have a problem with him courting you, but we just can't have you out near dark by yourself. It's much too dangerous."

Rachel knew Anna was taking the time to think before she spoke, because there was a long pause and a shuffling of feet. Suddenly, her sister blurted out, "I lied about me and Silas. He's not courting me, and I–I'm sorry to be telling you this, but I'll be leaving the faith."

Goose bumps erupted on Rachel's arms as she

peered through the crack in the doorway and saw Mom's face blanch.

"You're what?" Dad hollered.

"I–I'm leaving because I got married today."

"You were supposed to be at Emma's," Mom said as though the word *married* had never been mentioned.

"What are you talkin' about, girl?" Dad sputtered. "How can you possibly be married?"

"Reuben Yutzy and I got married today by a justice of the peace in Lancaster." Anna's voice sounded stronger by the minute. "We've been seeing each other secretly for some time now, and yesterday we went to get our marriage license."

Rachel clasped her hand over her mouth as she stifled a gasp. This was worse than she had imagined, and it simply couldn't be true.

"What caused you to do such a thing?" Dad's back was to Rachel, and she could only imagine how red his face must be.

"If it's Reuben you love and wanted to marry, why did you hide it?" Mom's voice quavered like she was close to tears. "Why didn't Reuben speak with one of the deacons about the two of you getting married? We could have had the wedding this fall, and–"

"I'm sure you must know that Reuben hasn't been baptized or joined the church yet, and he doesn't plan to, either." There was a pause, and Anna cleared her throat a couple of times. "So that means I'll have to leave the Amish faith in order to be with him."

"You can't be serious about this!"

"Daniel, you'll wake the whole house." Mom's voice lowered to a near whisper, and Rachel had to strain to hear what was being said.

"I don't care if I do wake everyone! This is most serious business our daughter has brought to us tonight."

"Can't we at least discuss this in a quiet manner?" Mom asked in a pleading tone.

Dad shuffled his feet a few times, the way he always did whenever he was trying to get himself calmed down. A chair scraped across the kitchen floor. "Sit down, daughter, and explain this rebellious act of yours."

Rachel stood twisting the corners of her apron, too afraid to breathe. Nothing like this had ever happened in the Beachy home, and she couldn't imagine how it would all turn out.

"Reuben and I have been in love for some time, and I was hoping he would decide to join the church, but he wants to go English, so if I'm to be with him, then–"

"You could have told him no–that you wouldn't marry him unless he joined our church."

"Dad, please try to understand. I love Reuben so much, and I feel that my place is with him no matter which world we must live in."

"So you just snuck off and got married without

consulting any of us first? Is that the way we do things in this family, Anna?" When Mom stopped speaking, she released a muffled sob.

Dad leaned over so he was looking Anna right in the face. "Why'd you wait so long to tell us this? Why weren't you honest from the beginning?"

"I was afraid if I was up front with you about this that you wouldn't understand and would try to talk me out of marrying Reuben."

He nodded. "That's right. We would have. Any decent parent would try to make their kinner understand the consequences of a choice such as this."

Mom let loose with another sob, and it nearly chilled Rachel to the bone. She leaned against the wall, feeling as if her whole world was caving in around her. How could she have been so blind? Anna had been telling her that she didn't love Silas, yet she'd been leading the poor fellow on. She'd been acting secretive and kind of pensive lately, too. Rachel should have asked her sister what was going on much sooner. If Anna had been straight with her about things, maybe she could have talked some sense into her stubborn head.

"As you probably know, Reuben's got himself a job working for a paint contractor in Lancaster," Anna continued. "That's where we plan to live—in an apartment Reuben found for us. I just came home tonight to explain things and gather up my belongings. Reuben's home telling his folks now, too, and he's coming to get me in the morning."

"I won't hear this kind of talk in my house!" There was a *thud*, and Rachel was pretty sure her father's hand had connected with the kitchen table.

"Oh, Daniel, now look what you've gone and done," Mom said tearfully. "All my squares are verhuddelt."

"Our daughter's just announced that she's gotten married today and plans to leave the faith, and all you can think about is your mixed-up quilting squares? What's wrong with you, *fraa*?"

"But. . .but. . .Anna was raised in the Amish faith," Mom blubbered. "She's been baptized and has already joined the church, so we'll have to shun her now."

"Don't you think I know that already?"

Rachel chanced another peek to see how things were looking. Dad paced back and forth across the faded linoleum. Mom had gathered up the quilting pieces that had been scattered all over the table. Anna just sat with her arms folded.

"I know you don't understand my decision to go English with Reuben, but I love him ever so much."

Dad slapped his hands together, and Rachel jumped back behind the door. "You're our firstborn child, Anna, and it's gonna break our hearts if you run off and leave your faith behind."

"I'm not giving up my faith in God," Anna defended. "We'll find another church where we can worship God."

"Are you sure you can't talk Reuben into staying Amish?"

"No, Mom. Reuben's set on leaving. He likes having a truck to drive, and he enjoys many other modern things."

"Maybe I should have a little talk with that young fellow. Might could be that he'll come to his senses once I set him straight on a few things."

"Please, Dad, don't do that. I'm sure it will only make things worse."

"You'd have to give up your way of dress if you left," Mom said.

"I know."

"Since Reuben's not joined the church, he won't be shunned, but you will be, Anna. Surely you must realize the seriousness of this."

"I know it won't be easy." Anna sighed. "For Reuben's sake, I'll just have to deal with it."

Dad's fist pounded the table again. "You can't do this, Anna. I forbid it!"

Rachel shuddered. Whenever their father forbade anyone in the family to do anything, that was the end of it, plain and simple. No arguments. No discussion. But if Anna was already married to Reuben, then she had to consider what he wanted now, didn't she?

Anna sucked in a huge sob. "I'm sorry, Mom and Dad, but my place is with Reuben, and the two of us will be moving to Lancaster in the morning no matter what anyone says."

Rachel had heard all she could stand, and a raw ache settled in the pit of her stomach. She turned and tiptoed up the stairs as quickly as she could. Her oldest sister was about to be shunned, and there wasn't a thing she could do about it.

Morning came much too quickly as far as Rachel was concerned. To make matters worse, she had awakened feeling as though she hadn't slept at all. Part of her heart went out to her sister, for she seemed so sincere in her proclamation about loving Reuben and needing to leave the Amish faith because of his desire to go English. Another part of her heart felt sorry for poor, lovesick Silas. What was he going to say when he got wind of this terrible news? He'd been friends with Anna a long time and had brought her home from a singing not long ago. He must believe he had a chance with her.

And what about the greenhouse? Who would help Mom and Dad with that? Anna had been working there for several years, and the folks weren't getting any younger. Eventually they would need someone to take the business over completely.

Rachel slipped out of her nightgown and into a dress, feeling like the weight of the world rested on her shoulders. She was sure that she would be asked to fill in for Anna at the greenhouse. Joseph liked flowers well enough, but he was busy working the fields, and Dad often helped in the fields, especially during harvest season. If Rachel were forced into the confines of the stuffy, humid greenhouse, she would hardly have any time for watching birds, hiking, or fishing. She knew it was selfish, but she was more than a little miffed at Anna for sticking her with this added responsibility.

A sudden ray of hope ignited in Rachel's heart. With Anna leaving, Silas might begin to take notice of her.

She poured some water from the pitcher on her dresser into the washing bowl. *Guess I could even tolerate working with flowers all day if I had a chance at love with Silas.*

The idea stuck in Rachel's mind like unbuttered taffy, and she splashed some water on her face, hoping the stinging cold might get her thinking straight. As the cool liquid made contact, she allowed her anxiety to fully surface. Silas wasn't going to turn to her just because Anna was no longer available. Besides, even if by some miracle he did, Rachel would be his second choice. She'd be like yesterday's warmed-over stew.

Her shoulders drooped with anguish and a feeling of hopelessness. She wasn't sure she wanted Silas's love if it had to be that way. But then, she *was* a beggar, and beggars couldn't be choosy.

Rachel hung her nightgown on a wall peg and put her head covering in place. She might look ready to face the day, but in her heart she sure wasn't ready.

She hated the thought of going downstairs. After everything that had gone on between Anna and the folks last night, Rachel had a pretty good notion what things would be like with the start of this new day. As much as she might like a chance with Silas, she didn't want it this way. Anna's leaving would affect them all.

A sudden knock on the door startled her. "Who is it?"

"Rachel, it's me. Are you up?" Anna called through the closed door.

"Just getting dressed. Tell Mom I'll be right down to help with breakfast."

"Could I come in? I need to talk to you."

"Jah, sure."

When Anna opened the door, Rachel saw immediately that she had been crying. Probably most of the night, truth be told. She also noticed that her sister's hope chest was at her feet.

Anna bent down and pushed the cumbersome trunk into Rachel's room. "I can't stay long," she said in a quavering voice. "I'll be leaving soon, but I wanted you to have this before I go."

Rachel's heart slammed into her chest. Should she tell Anna she had been listening in on her private conversation with the folks last night or play dumb? Probably wouldn't be a good idea to let her know she had been eavesdropping.

"You're leaving?" she mumbled.

Anna nodded.

"Where are you going?" Rachel asked, making no mention of what she knew about Reuben or saying anything concerning the hope chest Anna had slid to the end of her bed.

"Last night after you went upstairs, I told Mom and Dad that I've been secretly seeing Reuben Yutzy."

"Really?"

"Jah."

"But Reuben's not a member of the church yet, and from what I hear, he's kind of wild."

Anna frowned. "Reuben's got a hankering for some modern things, but he's really a nice fellow." She took a seat on the edge of Rachel's bed. "The thing is. . .well, Reuben and I got married yesterday."

"You. . .you did?" Rachel hated playing dumb like this, but if Anna had any idea that Rachel already knew about her plans, she'd probably be too miffed to share anything else that was on her mind.

"We went to Lancaster and got married by a justice of the peace. Then a few hours later, Reuben went home to tell his folks, and I came here to tell ours. Last night was the final time for me to sleep in my old room, because this morning, Reuben's coming for me. We'll be leaving."

Rachel sucked in her breath and flopped down beside her sister. "But. . .but where will you go?"

"We'll be living in an apartment in Lancaster."

Anna sighed. "Of course, the folks are pretty upset, but they need to realize that I love Reuben, and my place is with him now."

"What about your hope chest?" Rachel's voice dropped to a near whisper. "Won't you be needing all your things now that you're married and about to set up housekeeping?"

Anna shook her head. "The apartment Reuben rented is fully furnished. Besides, the things in that chest would only be painful reminders of my past." She nodded at Rachel. "Better that you have 'em."

Rachel was sorely tempted to tell her sister that there wasn't much point in her having one hope chest, much less two, since she would probably never marry. She thought better of it, though, because she could see from the dismal look on Anna's face that saying good-bye was hurting her badly.

"If you renounce your faith, you'll be shunned. You've been baptized into membership, Anna. Have you forgotten that?"

Anna blew out her breath. "Of course I haven't forgotten. Leaving my home and family is the sacrifice I have to make. There isn't any other way that I can see."

Rachel jumped up. "Yes, there is! You can talk Reuben into forgetting all this nonsense about going English. You can stay right here and marry Reuben again in the Amish church." Strangely enough,

Rachel found herself wishing Anna had accepted Silas's offer to court her. With him, at least, she knew Anna would be staying in the faith.

What am I thinking? Here I am, so in love with Silas that my heart could burst, and I'm wishing my sister could be making plans to marry him.

Rachel's vision clouded with tears as she thought about how this news would affect the man she loved. "What about Silas? You rode home with him in his courting buggy from a singing not long ago. Didn't that mean anything?"

Anna dropped her gaze to the floor. "I–I didn't mean to lead Silas on, but even if I weren't planning to leave, I wouldn't have married Silas. I don't love him. I never have."

Rachel planted her hands on her hips as she stared hard at her sister. Anna seemed almost a stranger to her now. What had happened to her pleasant childhood playmate? Where had the closeness she'd once felt with Anna gone?

"Silas is a wonderful man, and he loves you. Doesn't that count at all?"

Anna lifted her head to look at Rachel. "I'm sorry for Silas, but I have to go with my heart." She drew in a deep breath. "What do *you* want out of life, Rachel?"

Rachel swallowed hard. "That's easy. I want love. . .marriage. . .and lots of kinner."

"Since you're so worried about Silas, why don't you try to make him happy? Maybe the two of you will marry someday, and he'll give you a whole houseful of children."

Rachel shook her head. "I wish I could make Silas happy, but I can't, because he doesn't love me."

Chapter 8

Not one word was said during breakfast about Anna's plans to leave. It was almost as if nothing had gone on last night. Rachel figured her folks either were hoping they could talk Anna and Reuben out of leaving and into getting married again within the church or had already begun the shunning.

When breakfast was over, Dad went outside. Rachel was at the sink doing dishes, and when she glanced out the window, she saw him hitch up the buggy and head on down the road. She thought it was odd that he hadn't said where he was going.

A short time later, Dad returned with Deacon Byler following in his own closed-in rig. Rachel was out in the garden with Elizabeth when she saw the two men climb down from their buggies.

Rachel straightened and pressed a hand against her lower back to ease out some of the kinks. The deacon stepped close to the garden and nodded at her. "Where's your sister Anna? I'm here to speak with her."

Before Rachel could reply, Anna came out of the house, lugging an old suitcase down the steps. She wasn't wearing her kapp, cape, or apron. At least she wore a dress, and her hair was pinned up in a bun.

Deacon Byler marched right on over to her. "I understand you and Reuben Yutzy are planning to leave the Amish faith."

Anna nodded. "That's right. My husband will be here soon to pick me up."

"Your husband, huh?"

Anna nodded again.

Rachel dropped the beet she had just dug up and held her breath, for she feared the worst was coming. Even though she couldn't do anything about Anna leaving, she knew she must do something to offer a little bit of support. "Keep working," she told Elizabeth. "I'll be right back." She hurried across the yard to stand beside Anna.

Anna gave Rachel a sad smile. Then she turned to face the deacon again. "I don't like disappointing my family, and I feel awful about the lies I told them, but I'm a married woman now, and I've got to be with my husband."

The deacon crossed his arms as his forehead wrinkled. "Deacon Shemly is speaking with Reuben right now, so maybe he can convince him to stay and become a member of our church."

Anna shook her head. "I doubt he'll change his mind."

Deacon Byler turned toward Dad. "I guess we need to wait and see how things go between Deacon Shemly and Reuben."

Dad nodded.

The deacon headed back to his buggy, and Anna looked up at her father with tears shimmering in her eyes. "Sorry, but I don't think Reuben will change his mind, which means I won't, either."

Dad said nothing in return. He stared at Anna for a few seconds as if he were looking right through her. Then he stalked off toward the barn.

Rachel didn't know what she could say, either. She felt sick at heart over the way things were going, and reality settled over her like a dreary fog. If Anna left the faith, nothing would ever be the same at home.

"No one understands the way I feel," Anna moaned. She took a seat on the top porch step and rested her chin in the palms of her hands.

Rachel seated herself beside Anna and reached over to take her hand. "Being in love can make us do things we never expected we'd do."

Anna nodded and sniffed deeply. "I hate the thought of leaving home or being shunned by my family, and I did try to talk Reuben into joining the church, but he's determined to leave."

Rachel squeezed Anna's fingers, though she

didn't think the gesture offered much comfort. "Guess I'd probably do the same thing if the man I loved was determined to leave home and had asked me to marry him and leave my family and friends."

Anna glanced over at her and squinted. "Are you in love with someone?"

Rachel chewed on her lower lip a few seconds. Finally, she nodded.

"Mind if I ask who?"

"I–I'm in love with Silas Swartley."

A smile lifted the corners of Anna's lips. "I thought so."

"You thought so?"

"Jah. I've had a feeling for some time that you had an interest in him."

"Has it been that obvious?"

"To me, at least. I've seen the way you look at Silas with such longing, and the things you've said about him being so good-looking and nice made me realize you must care for him."

Rachel released a sigh. "Silas has been in love with you for a long time, Anna. He doesn't see me as anything more than a child, so it makes no difference how I feel about him."

Anna opened her mouth as if to reply, but Reuben pulled up in his fancy red truck, interrupting their conversation. She stood and glanced back toward the house, then looked at Rachel again. "I spoke with Mom right after breakfast and told her

I'd be leaving as soon as Reuben showed up, but she didn't want to come outside, so we said our good-byes in there."

Rachel stood, too, smoothing the wrinkles in her long, green dress and swallowing against the lump in her throat. "I guess she thought it would be too painful to see you drive away." She grabbed Anna in a hug. "I'm sure gonna miss you. Write soon and let me know how you're doing, okay?"

Anna nodded fiercely as tears welled in her eyes. "I know the brothers are already out in the fields, so would you tell them good-bye for me?"

"Jah, sure."

"And Dad, too."

"Why don't you tell him yourself? I haven't seen him come out of the barn, so I'm guessing he's still in there."

Anna shook her head. "You saw the way Dad looked at me when Deacon Byler was here. He's awful angry about this decision I've made, and I doubt he'd even want to say good-bye."

Reuben tooted the truck's horn, and Anna picked up her suitcase and hurried down the steps. She stopped off at the garden to give Elizabeth a hug, then opened the passenger's door of Reuben's shiny red truck and climbed right in.

Rachel sank onto the porch step with a groan.

Reuben had just started to back the truck up when

Anna's father came running out of the barn, waving his arms.

Hoped welled in Anna's soul. Maybe Dad wanted to tell her good-bye after all. Maybe he didn't want her to leave with this awful dissension between them. "Better wait and see what he wants," she said, looking over at her husband.

"Jah, okay." Reuben put his foot on the brake, and Anna pushed the button to let her window roll down. But Dad went around to Reuben's side of the truck, not hers.

"Guess you'd best roll down your window then," she said to Reuben.

He grunted but did as she asked.

As soon as the window was down, Dad stepped close to the truck and leaned over until his head was nearly inside. "Did Deacon Shemly come by your place this morning?"

Reuben's only reply was a quick nod.

"I guess he didn't talk any sense into you, or you wouldn't be taking my daughter away."

"I'm not trying to cause any trouble for your family, but I've gotten used to so many modern things since I started working for Vern Hanson, and I've become used to having a truck that I don't think I could do without."

Dad's eyebrows drew together as a deep frown crushed his strong features. "Oh, but you think it's okay for me to do without my daughter?"

Reuben reached across the seat and took hold

of Anna's hand, which gave her added courage and made her feel just a bit better. "I love Anna, and she's my wife now, so she belongs with me."

"If you love her so much, then you ought to be willing to join the Amish church and keep her from being shunned."

"This isn't just Reuben's decision," Anna said, leaning across the seat so she could look her father in the eye. "I've been feeling kind of discontent here of late, and–"

"And nothing!" Dad clapped his hands together. "You're only doin' this to please this young man, and apparently neither of you cares about who you're hurting in the process of having what you think you want." He stepped away from the truck and slowly shook his head. "Well, go on then. Go on out into the English world and forget you ever had an Amish family who cared about you!"

Tears clogged the back of Anna's throat and her vision blurred. "I love you, Dad. I love all my family, but my place is with my husband." She looked over at Reuben and managed a weak smile. "Let's go now, shall we?"

Reuben took his foot off the brake and turned the truck around. As they headed down the driveway, Anna turned and saw Rachel standing on the porch, waving at them. Anna waved back as tears coursed down her cheeks. When Reuben pulled onto the main road, she lifted her hand in one final wave, and then they were gone.

As Rebekah sat in front of the window overlooking the back porch, watching her firstborn child drive away, it was all she could do to keep from breaking down. All the expectations she'd had for her daughter had been dashed away in one fell swoop. She wanted to swaddle Anna in a blanket–keep her warm and safe. But it was too late for that now; her baby was gone.

She drew in a deep breath and closed her eyes as her mind took her back to that wonderful day when Anna had been born. . . .

"It's a girl," Rebekah whispered, as Daniel entered the birthing room, wearing an anxious expression. "God has given us a miracle baby."

Daniel bent his head to kiss Rebekah's cheek. Then he reached out his finger and stroked the side of the baby's tiny head. "She's a miracle, all right." He glanced back at Rebekah and smiled. "She's a beautiful child, and she looks just like her mamm."

Tears welled in Rebekah's eyes. "All those months I spent asking God for a miracle, I never expected Him to answer in such a wunderbaar way." She kissed the top of the baby's downy head. "Let's call her Anna *after my dear grandma; is that okay?"*

"That's fine by me." Daniel's smile widened.

"If the next one's a boy, then I get to name him, though. Agreed?"

She smiled and nodded. "Jah, sure. If God chooses to give us another miracle, you can name the boppli *whatever you choose."*

As Rebekah's thoughts drifted slowly back to the present, the pain in her heart lessened a bit. If God could perform so many miracles, allowing her to give birth to five babies after the doctors had said she might never conceive, then He could do anything.

"Dear Lord," she whispered in prayer, "You blessed Daniel and me with our special kinner to raise, so now I'm committing my oldest child into Your hands and asking that You give her a life full of love, joy, and miracles beyond measure." She paused as tears clogged her throat and clouded her vision. "Please let Anna know that we love her despite the shunning she's brought on herself by choosing to marry Reuben and go English."

Chapter 9

Rachel tossed and turned in her bed for most of the night. Knowing Anna wasn't in her room across the hall left a huge empty spot in her heart. Until recently, she and Anna had shared secrets and hopes for their future. For some time, Rachel had known something was going on with Anna, but she'd thought her sister was only going through a phase that would pass. Never in a hundred years would she have suspected that Anna was interested in Reuben or that the two of them had been secretly courting. And the fact that they'd run off and gotten married by an English justice of the peace was the biggest shock of all.

Rachel closed her eyes and tried to picture Anna married to Reuben, making their home in Lancaster, wearing English clothes, and living the fancy, modern life.

"Does Silas know about this yet?" she whispered into the night. Surely Silas's heart would be broken when he heard the news, for he'd lost Anna not only to the modern world, but to one of his childhood friends, no less. Thinking about Silas helped Rachel feel a little less sorry for herself, and it was a reminder for her to pray for him.

Ping! Ping! Rachel rolled over in bed. What was that strange noise? *Ping! Ping!* There it was again. She sat up and swung her legs over the side of the bed. It sounded like something was hitting her bedroom window, but she couldn't imagine what it might be.

She hurried across the room and lifted the window's dark shade. In the glow of the moonlight, she could see someone standing on the ground below. It was a man, and he appeared to be tossing pebbles at her window, of all things.

"Who's wanting to get my attention at this time of night?" Rachel muttered as she grabbed her robe off the end of the bed.

Quietly, so she wouldn't wake any of the family, she tiptoed in her bare feet down the stairs, being careful not to step on the ones that creaked. When she reached the back door, she opened it cautiously and peered out. She could see now that it was Silas Swartley standing on the grass, bathed in the moonlight.

Rachel slipped out the door, closing it quietly behind her, and dashed across the lawn. "Silas, what are you doing out here in the dark, throwing pebbles at my window?"

He whirled around to face her. "Rachel?"

She nodded. "What's up, anyhow?"

Looking more than a bit befuddled, Silas shifted his long legs and gave his suspenders a quick snap. "I. . .uh. . . thought it was Anna's window I was throwing stones at. I've been wanting to speak with her for several days but never seem to get the chance."

Rachel's heartbeat quickened. So Silas didn't know. He couldn't have heard the news yet, or else he would have realized Anna wasn't here. She took a few steps closer and reached out to touch his arm. "Anna's not in her room, Silas."

"She's not? Where is she, then?"

Rachel's lower lip quivered, and she pressed her lips tightly together, trying to compose herself. This was going to be a lot harder than she'd thought. "I hate to be the one telling you this, but Anna ran off and got married last night. She left home this morning."

Silas's mouth dropped open like a window with a broken hinge. "Married? Left home?" He stared off into space as though he were in a daze, and Rachel's heart went out to him. She had to tell him the rest. He had the right to know. Besides, if he didn't hear it from her, he was bound to find out sooner or later. News like this traveled fast, especially when an Amish church member left the faith to become English.

"Anna married Reuben. They're leaving the church, and—"

"Reuben Yutzy and my Anna?"

Rachel nodded. The motion was all she could

manage given the circumstances. Even in the darkness, she could see the pained expression on Silas's face.

"This can't be. It just can't be," he muttered.

They stood staring at each other as crickets creaked and the cornstalks in the field beside her house rustled in the night air. Rachel's shoulders rose and fell, as she struggled not to cry. If only she had the power to turn back the hands of time and make everything right. If she could just think of a way to make her sister come home. But what good would that do? Anna was already married to Reuben, and nothing Rachel could say or do would change that fact.

Silas began to pace. "I knew Reuben was dissatisfied with our way of life. I also knew he was hanging around some English fellows who seemed intent on leading him astray." He stopped, turned, and slowly shook his head. "But I had no idea Anna was in on it, too. I thought I knew her better than that."

Rachel trembled. She didn't know if her shivering was from the cool grass tickling her bare feet or if it stemmed from the anger she felt rising in her soul. There was only one thing she was certain of–Silas was trying to lay the blame on her sister's shoulders.

"Anna wasn't *in* on this. She became *part* of it because she loves Reuben and wanted to be with him."

"Did she tell you that?"

"Not in so many words, but she did say she and Reuben have been secretly seeing each other and that they're in love. She made it clear that her place is with him."

Silas grunted. "She probably influenced him to make the break. Anna always has been a bit of a rebel."

Rachel's heart thumped so hard she feared it might burst wide open. How dare Silas speak of her sister that way! She gasped for breath, grateful for the cool night air to help clear her head. "Anna might have a mind of her own, but she's not the kind of person who would try to sway someone else to leave the church. I know for a fact that it was Reuben who wanted to go English, and I believe Anna loves him so much that she couldn't say no."

Silas drew in a deep breath, trying to get control of his emotions. It seemed his whole world was falling apart, but he knew he had no right to blame Anna for it. He'd just talked to Reuben a few days ago, and his friend had made it clear that he wanted many of the things the world had to offer. He was working for an English man, had bought a fancy red truck, and had even told Silas that he wasn't happy being Amish anymore. Truth be told, Silas had halfway expected Reuben to leave the faith. What he hadn't expected was that Anna would be leaving, too—especially not as Reuben's wife.

"If I had it in my power to make things turn out differently, I surely would," Rachel said, breaking into Silas's troubling thoughts.

When he looked down at her, he noticed that her chin quivered like a leaf caught in a breeze. For one brief moment, Silas was tempted to take Rachel into his arms and offer comforting words. Trouble was, he had no words of comfort. . .for Rachel or himself. All he felt was anger and betrayal. His friend had taken his girl away, and Anna had led him on all these years. How could he come to grips with that knowledge and not feel bitter?

Silas dipped his head in apology. "I'm sorry for snapping at you, Rachel. I know none of this is your fault. It's just such a shock to find out you've lost not one, but two special friends in the same day." He sniffed. "This had to be going on between Reuben and Anna for some time, and I was just too blind to see it. What a *dummkopp* I've been, thinking Anna and I had a future together. Why, I chased after her like a horse running toward a bucket of fresh oats, even though she kept pushing me away. She must have thought I was *ab im kopp*."

Rachel grabbed hold of his arm and gave it a shake. "Stop talking that way! You're not a dunce, and you're not off in the head for loving someone. Reuben had you fooled, and Anna had our whole family fooled." She shook her head. "No one's to blame but Anna and Reuben. They should have been honest with everyone involved. They shouldn't have waited so long to tell us their plans, and they should never have lied to cover up what they were doing."

Silas nodded. "You're right, Rachel. They deserve to be shunned."

"That's the part I dislike the most. It's hard enough to have Anna leave home, but to realize we're gonna have to shun our own kin is the worst part of all." Rachel grimaced. "Since Reuben hasn't joined the church, he won't be shunned at all, but my poor sister will be paying the price for his selfishness."

"That was her choice, so she ought to be prepared for the consequences." Silas blew out his breath and took a few steps back. "Guess I should be gettin' on home. My mission here is over. As much as it pains me to say it, Anna's out of my life for good."

Rachel rubbed her hands briskly over her arms like she might be getting cold, and for the second time, Silas was tempted to embrace her. He caught himself in time, though, remembering Anna's words the other day when she'd said she thought Rachel might be interested in him. If he hugged her, even in condolence, she might get the wrong idea. No, it would be better if he didn't say or do anything that might lead Rachel on. Things were messed up enough. No sense making one more mistake.

"See you at the next preaching service," Silas

said before he turned and sprinted up the driveway where his horse and buggy stood waiting. Rachel would have to find comfort from her family, and he would find solace through his work on the farm.

Anna glanced over at her husband sleeping as soundly on his side of the bed as a newborn babe. A lump formed in her throat as tears gathered in her eyes. She loved Reuben so much and wanted to be with him at all costs, but it pained her to know how much she'd hurt her family by leaving the Amish faith to join Reuben in the modern, English world. During their secret courtship, she had tried several times to convince him to stay Amish, but he'd flatly refused. That meant she either had to break up with him or agree to go English, too.

It's so strange, she thought, as she slipped out of bed and padded across the room to stand in front of the window, *but there were times when we were courting that I actually thought I would be happier living the English way of life. Now I'm not so sure.*

She glanced around their small, sparsely furnished bedroom, devoid of many decorative items. It wasn't that Reuben didn't want fancy things; they just didn't have enough money to buy much yet, and since they hadn't had a traditional Amish wedding, they'd received no wedding gifts, either.

Anna pulled the curtain aside and stared at the

moonlit sky. *Guess I'll need to look for a job soon so we'll have enough money to pay the rent on this apartment, make Reuben's truck payment, and be able to buy a few fancy electronic gadgets Reuben's been wanting to have.*

Tears slipped from her eyes and rolled down her cheeks. *Dear Lord, help me to be content with the life Reuben wants us to have, and help my folks understand the decision I made to go English.*

Chapter 10

On the first day of August, an unreal stillness hung in the hot, sticky air. The inside of the house felt like an oven, so Rachel had wandered outside after lunch, hoping to find a cool breeze. She found, instead, her younger brother and sister engaged in an all-out water skirmish.

Squeals of laughter permeated the air as the twins ran back and forth to the freshly filled water trough, filling their buckets and flinging water on one another until they were both drenched from head to toe.

Rachel chuckled at their antics and stepped off the porch, thinking she might join them. The flash of a colorful wing caught her attention instead. Her gaze followed the goldfinch as it sailed from tree to tree, finally stopping at one of the feeders in the flower garden. When it had eaten its fill, it flew over to the birdbath on the other side of the yard. Dipping its tiny black head up and down, the finch drank of the fresh water Rachel had put there early that morning.

Rachel loved watching the birds that came into their yard. Loved hearing their melodic songs. Loved everything about nature.

"*Per-chick-o-ree,*" the finch called.

"*Per-chick-o-ree,*" Rachel echoed.

She watched until the bird flew out of sight; then she moved across the yard toward the clothesline. In this heat, the clothes she had washed and hung this morning were probably dry.

Rachel had only taken a few clothes off the line, when she heard a small voice nearby. Apparently Elizabeth had given up her water battle with Perry, for she was crouched next to the wicker basket, staring up at Rachel with an expectant look on her face. The child's hair, which was supposed to be secured at the back of her head in a bun, hung down the back of her wet dress like a limp rag.

"Elizabeth, did you say something to me?" Rachel asked.

The child nodded.

"What was it?"

"Dad says Anna and Reuben won't make it in the English world and that they'll come to their senses and return home again. I was wondering what you thought about that."

Rachel knelt next to her sister and wrapped her arms around the little girl's shoulders. "We're all hoping Anna and Reuben will return to our way of life, but we need to face the fact that it might not happen."

"How come?"

"Reuben has it in his mind that he wants to live as the English do, and the last letter I got from Anna said she's working as a waitress at some restaurant in Lancaster. She and Reuben are married now, and they've settled into an apartment there."

"Why can't they live here with us?" Elizabeth asked, her blue eyes looking ever so serious.

Rachel drew in a deep breath and blew it out in a rush. How could she explain something to her little sister that she didn't fully understand herself? "Well, it's like this, Elizabeth—"

"That'll be enough, Rachel!" Dad's deep voice cut through the air like a knife. He grabbed hold of Elizabeth's arm and pulled her to her feet. "Get on up to the house and change out of those wet clothes. Your mamm's been looking for you, and I'm sure she's got something useful you can be doing."

"But Dad, Rachel was trying to tell me some things about Anna and Reuben."

"We've had enough talk about Anna and her wayward husband."

Elizabeth tipped her head as she stared up at their father with questioning eyes. "We hardly talk about my older sister anymore."

"And it's for the best." Dad gave Elizabeth a little push as he turned her toward the house. "I said your mamm could use your help with some things, so be off with you now."

With head down and shoulders slumped,

Elizabeth trudged off. Dad watched until she disappeared into the house; then he turned to face Rachel. "You ought to discourage Elizabeth from talking about Anna. The child's still young and doesn't understand all the things of the world yet. She might think what Anna's done is perfectly okay with us."

"Elizabeth meant no harm in asking, and I didn't think it would hurt to try to explain things a bit." Rachel's eyes filled with tears, and she blinked a couple of times, hoping to keep them at bay. Things were bad enough around here; she didn't want any hard feelings between her and Dad.

"Jah, well, be careful what you say from now on." Dad's voice softened some. "We've lost one daughter to the world, and I don't want my other kinner getting any such thoughts." He turned toward the greenhouse, calling over his shoulder, "When you're done with the laundry, I could use your help. We're likely to have a lot more customers still today."

Rachel grabbed a towel from the line and gave it a good snap. "Always trouble somewhere," she mumbled.

When the back door opened and slammed shut, Rebekah looked up from where she sat at the table, rolling out the dough for an apple-crumb pie. Elizabeth rushed into the room, her clothes soaking wet, her long hair streaming down her back, and wearing such a scowl on her face.

"What's with the long face, daughter? Did Perry get the best of you again?"

Elizabeth nodded, and her chin trembled slightly.

"Was it so bad that he made you cry?"

"No, Mom. It's what Dad said to me, not anything Perry did this time."

Rebekah swiveled her wheelchair so she was facing Elizabeth. "What'd your daed say that has you so upset?"

"He says there's been enough talk about Anna, and he called Reuben *wayward*." Elizabeth wrinkled her forehead. "What's that mean, Mom?"

Rebekah motioned her daughter over to the table, then turned her wheelchair back around. "Have a seat, and I'll try to explain things a bit."

"Jah, okay." Elizabeth pulled out a chair and plunked down, letting her elbows rest on the table. "So what's *wayward* mean?"

"*Wayward* means that someone's kind of lost their way."

"Reuben's lost?"

"Sort of."

"Does that mean Anna's lost, too?"

Tears sprang to Rebekah's eyes as she thought about the choice her firstborn child had made when she'd agreed to marry Reuben and leave the faith. She drew in a deep breath and released it with a huff that lifted the ties of her kapp. "Anna's lost to us in many ways, because her decision to leave our church means we'll have to shun her now."

Elizabeth nodded soberly.

"But she's still part of our family, and it will always be so." Rebekah touched Elizabeth's shoulder and gave it a gentle squeeze. "No matter what happens in the days ahead, we'll love her and accept her decision to go English the best way we can."

"Dad, too?"

Rebekah swallowed around the burning lump pushing against the back of her throat. "Someday I hope he'll come to grips with all this, but in the meantime, I think it's best if we keep quiet about Anna whenever your daed's around."

"What's gonna happen when Anna comes for a visit? Can we still talk to her like she's our sister?"

"Jah, of course. She can't share a meal at the same table with us, and we're not supposed to have any business dealings with her, but there's no rule that says we can't talk to her."

Elizabeth nodded. "Want me to help with the pie makin' now?"

"As soon as you've changed out of those wet clothes and we get your hair put back in place."

Elizabeth pushed away from the table and scurried out of the room. Rebekah resumed rolling out the mound of dough she'd left waiting on the cloth-covered table. Things would go better soon. At least she hoped they would.

"Ah-ha! So this is where you've been all morning." Joseph squinted and shook his finger at his little brother, who stood in front of the horses' watering trough, drenched with water from head to toe. "When I sent you back to the barn with one tired horse and asked you to bring another, I didn't think you'd be gone for nearly an hour."

Perry hung his head as he dragged the toe of his boot through the mud. "Sorry. I was hot, and Elizabeth came along, soon after I put Tom away—"

"The two of you decided to have a water battle, right?"

Perry lifted his head and gave Joseph a sheepish-looking grin. "You should have seen her, Joseph. She was so wet she looked like a drowned little *hundel*."

Joseph bit back a smile. He could only imagine how much water must have been thrown at his little sister's expense. She probably did look like a drowned pup.

"I didn't just play in the water 'cause I was hot, neither."

"Oh? What other reason might you have had?"

"When I came back from the fields with Tom, I spotted Elizabeth sitting on the back porch looking kind of sad." Perry blinked a couple of times and lifted his chin. "She's been awful gloomy since Anna left home, so I thought it might be good if I came up with something that would take her mind off Anna and make her laugh."

"That's admirable of you, Perry, but I didn't send you out of the fields to get cooled off or to try to make Elizabeth feel better about missing Anna," Joseph scolded. "I expected you to bring back a fresh horse, and you cost me nearly an hour's worth of work waiting on you, so now we'll have to stay in the fields that much longer."

Perry frowned. "Ah, it's summertime, Joseph. I oughta be able to have some fun, don't ya think?"

"You can have all the fun you want when your work's done for the day."

"By that time, I'm too tired to do much of anything but sleep."

Joseph ruffled his little brother's hair. "Summer's nearly over, and you'll be back in school soon. Then you won't have to work half as hard."

"Jah, right. Besides all my chores to do at home, I have to work my tired brain takin' all the tests Teacher Nancy gives us scholars." Perry grunted. "It's enough to make my head explode."

Joseph chuckled. How his little brother liked to exaggerate. He pointed to the barn. "Time's a-wasting, so let's get that horse you came after and make our way back to the fields."

"Jah, okay."

As they headed for the barn, Perry glanced toward the greenhouse near the front of their property, and frowned. "Sure doesn't seem right with Anna not helpin' the folks in the greenhouse anymore, does it?"

Joseph gritted his teeth. Nothing seemed right at their place these days, and Dad seemed to be affected by Anna's decision to go English most of all. Maybe it was because he was supposed to be the head of the family, and he felt as if he'd failed to live up to the job. Could be that Dad was more angry at himself than Anna. It might even be that he thought if he'd been a better father, Anna wouldn't have been led astray by Reuben.

"Did ya hear what I said about Anna?" Perry gave Joseph's shirtsleeve a tug.

"I heard. Just thought it best not to comment."

Perry raised his eyebrows but said nothing.

As they stepped into the barn, Joseph sent up a silent prayer on Anna's behalf and another for them all to feel less tension.

Chapter 11

It was another warm day, and Rachel, accompanied by Elizabeth, had gone to the town of Intercourse to buy some things their mother needed. Since Dad paid Rachel for working in the greenhouse, she bought a few new things for her hope chest—just in case.

"How about some lunch?" Rachel asked her little sister when they'd finished their shopping. "Are you hungry?"

Elizabeth giggled and scrambled into the buggy. "You know me, Rachel; I'm always hungry."

"Where would you like to go?" Rachel asked, tucking her packages behind the seat, then taking up the reins.

"I don't care. Why don't you choose?"

Rachel nodded and steered the horse in the direction of the Good 'n Plenty restaurant. The girls soon discovered that the place was crowded with summer tourists and that the wait would be about half an hour.

Elizabeth said she needed to use the restroom, so Rachel stood in the hallway outside the door, waiting for her. She grimaced when a man walked by wearing a baseball cap with an inscription on the front that read Born to Fish. Forced to Work.

That's just like me. I'd love to go fishing every day and never have to work in the greenhouse again, but that's not likely to happen, I guess.

As the fisherman disappeared, Rachel caught a glimpse of a young Amish man coming from the door that led to the restaurant's kitchen. She thought nothing of it until she got a good look at him. It was Silas Swartley, and he was heading her way.

"It's nice to see you, Rachel. How are things?"

Rachel slid her tongue across her lips and swallowed hard. Why did Silas have to be so cute? Why had she allowed herself to fall in love with him? Except for biweekly preaching services, she hadn't seen much of Silas since that night he'd come to the house, looking for Anna. The fact that Rachel had been the one to give him the shocking news about her sister running off with his friend still stuck in her craw. It should have been Reuben or Anna doing the telling, not her. But no, they left without thinking of anyone but themselves. Seeing Silas standing here now, looking so handsome yet unapproachable, left Rachel speechless.

Silas held a wooden crate in his hands, and he

shifted it slightly as he took a step closer to her. "Has the cat got your tongue, or are you gonna answer my question?"

"W-what question was that?"

"I asked how things are."

She swallowed again. "Oh, about the same as usual. How's it at your place?"

"Everything's about the same with us, too. I brought in a crate of fresh potatoes from our farm. This restaurant buys a lot of produce from us." Silas nodded his head toward Rachel. "How come you're here?"

"Elizabeth and I came to town for a few things. We're here for lunch." She suppressed a giggle. "Why else would we be at the Good 'n Plenty?"

Silas's summer-tanned face turned red like a cherry, and he stared down at his boots. "I. . .uh. . . don't suppose you've heard anything from Anna."

Rachel swallowed once more, only this time it was in an attempt to dislodge the nodule that had formed in her throat. It wasn't so surprising that Silas would ask about Anna. He was obviously still pining for her. Truth be told, Silas was probably hoping Anna would change her mind about being English and come home again. But even if she did, what good would that do him? Anna was a married woman now–out-of-bounds for Silas Swartley.

"Anna wrote me a letter the other day," Rachel said. "She's written to her friend Martha Rose a couple of times, too–and of course, to our mamm."

"What'd she say in her letter to you? Or would you rather not share that information?"

"It was nothing special." Rachel shrugged. "Just that she and Reuben are pretty well settled in now. She got herself a job as a waitress, and Reuben's still painting houses and all."

A lady wearing some strong-smelling perfume walked out of the women's restroom, and Rachel's nose twitched as she fought the urge to sneeze. "Guess they've got to have lots of money, since they're living in the modern world and will probably be buying all sorts of fancy gadgets."

Silas's dark eyebrows furrowed. "Sure wish Anna would've waited awhile to marry Reuben and not run off like that. Maybe if she'd thought it through and given me more time to win her heart, things might have turned out differently for all of us."

From the things her sister had said about Silas, Rachel doubted he could have ever won Anna completely over, but she wasn't about to tell him that. No point hurting his feelings more than they'd already been. "Anna's gone now, and I'm pretty sure she's never coming back," she mumbled.

"How can you be so sure?"

"I just know, that's all. My sister and her husband are walking a different path now, and Anna made it clear in her letter that it was her choice to join Reuben in the English world, and she hopes we'll accept her decision."

Silas shook his head. "I've known Anna since

we were kinner, and I always thought we were good friends. It's hard to accept the idea that there's no future for me and her now."

Rachel's heart ached for Silas, but more than that, it ached for herself. She was sure he would always love Anna, even if they couldn't be together. So much for hoping he might ever be interested in plain little Rachel. Hopeless, useless daydreams would get her nowhere, yet no matter how hard she tried to push it aside, the dream remained. "The future rests in God's hands," she mumbled as Elizabeth came out of the restroom.

"Jah." Silas turned and headed out the door.

Silas left the Good 'n Plenty feeling like someone had punched him in the stomach. Anna and Reuben weren't coming home. Old memories tugged at his heart. He had trusted Anna, and she'd betrayed that trust by sneaking off with his friend, the whole time letting Silas think she cared for him. Could he ever trust another woman not to hurt him that way? Even if Anna changed her mind and came back, he knew she would never be his. She was a married woman now. . .married to his friend Reuben.

Deep in his heart, Silas knew he had to accept things as they were and get on with his life, but no matter how hard he tried, he couldn't imagine any kind of life without Anna Beachy.

Poor Rachel. She had looked so sad. He figured

Anna's leaving must have hurt Rachel as much as it had him, only in a different sort of way. He would have to remember to pray for her often. . .and all the Beachys, for that matter. No Amish family ever really got over one of their own running off to become English, and from the look he'd seen on Rachel's face today, he figured she had a long ways to go in overcoming her grief.

Silas climbed into his buggy and gathered up the reins. "Giddap there, boy," he said to his horse. "I've got some work waiting for me to do at home, so let's get going."

"Was that Silas Swartley you were talkin' to?" Elizabeth asked when she stepped up to Rachel.

"It was him all right."

Elizabeth stared up at Rachel. "Well, what'd he have to say?"

Rachel wrinkled her nose. "If you must know, little *naasich* one, he was asking about Anna."

"I'm not nosey. I just wondered what he had to say, that's all."

"Jah, okay." Rachel knew that just because she felt frustrated over the conversation she'd had with Silas, it wasn't right to be snippy with Elizabeth.

"I think he used to be real sweet on our big sister. I heard Mom say somethin' about it to Dad once."

Rachel grimaced. "Jah, he was. I'm afraid he's

still pretty broken up over her and Reuben leaving."

Elizabeth grabbed Rachel's hand and squeezed her fingers. "Anna's never comin' back, is she?"

"Probably not, unless it's just for a visit."

"Can we hire a driver and go to Lancaster sometime? I'd surely like to see my big sister again."

"That probably isn't such a good idea," Rachel said, pulling her sister along as they made their way down the hall. "At least, not right now."

"How come?" the child persisted.

"Because Dad won't like it. Maybe later, down the road, he'll be willing to let us go there."

"I miss Anna a lot."

"Me, too." Rachel felt sick at heart because she couldn't visit her sister. How could she explain all this to Elizabeth when she couldn't make sense of it herself? She knew if they went to Lancaster to see Anna without telling Dad and he found out about it, he'd be furious. Besides, that would be a sneaky thing to do, and there'd already been enough sneaking going on in their family lately, which she knew wasn't right. And what if Elizabeth took a liking to the modern way Anna was living and decided to seek after worldly things herself? It might be better for everyone if they visited with Anna at their own place, not hers. Of course, Dad might have some things to say about Anna coming to visit them right now, too.

In all of Rachel's eighteen years, she couldn't remember ever seeing her father so angry and determined to make one of his children pay for a decision that went against his will. *Of course,* she reasoned, *Dad might be acting so perturbed because he's upset that Anna's leaving has put us all in a position where we have to shun our own flesh and blood.*

"Your table is ready now," a young Mennonite waitress said as they returned to the restaurant's waiting area.

Rachel smiled, glad for the diversion. Maybe after they were seated, Elizabeth's mind would be on filling her empty stomach and not on Anna. Might could be that the discussion would be dropped altogether, and they could eat a quiet, peaceful lunch.

Much to Rachel's chagrin, no sooner had they taken a seat at the table and placed their orders, than the questions began again.

"Are Mom and Dad really mad at Anna?" Elizabeth blinked several times. "They never talk about her anymore."

Rachel drew in a deep breath and offered up a silent prayer. She needed God's wisdom just now, for sure as anything she didn't want to make things worse by telling her sensitive, young sister something that might upset her even more.

"It's like this," she began, carefully choosing her words. "I'm sure the folks still love Anna very much, but they also love being Amish. They believe in the Ordnung and want to abide by the rules of our church."

Elizabeth nodded soberly. "I've tried talking about Anna several times, but Dad always says it would be best if I'd forget I ever had her as an older sister. How can I do that, Rachel? Anna's still my big sister, ain't it so?"

Rachel was tempted to correct the girl's English but decided it would be best not to make an issue of it right now. She reached across the table and gently touched Elizabeth's hand. "Of course she's still your sister, and nothing will ever change that. As I've told you before, Anna's moved away now, and she wants to live like the English."

Elizabeth's lower lip trembled. "She really don't want to be Amish no more?"

"I'm afraid not. But we can surely pray that someday she and Reuben will change their minds and be willing to reconcile with the church." Hot tears stung the backs of Rachel's eyes. Today had started off well enough, but after seeing Silas, talking about Anna with him, and now trying to make Elizabeth understand how things were, she felt all done in. She had no answers. Not for Silas, not for Elizabeth, and not for herself. As far as Rachel was concerned, her life would never be the same.

She lifted her water glass and took a sip. If only she could get Silas to take notice of her now that Anna was out of his life. She was here; Anna wasn't. If only God would make Silas love her and not her older sister, who was now out of his reach.

As she set the glass back down, a little voice in

Rachel's head reminded her that God never forced a person to love anyone–not even Him. If Silas was ever going to get over losing Anna, it would have to be because *he* chose to do so, not because of anything Rachel might say or do.

I can still hope, though. Rachel was reminded of what the Bible said in Psalm 71:14: "*But I will hope continually, and will yet praise thee more and more.*" She would definitely continue to hope.

Chapter 12

One evening, Rachel's family went out the front porch to sit awhile because it was still too hot inside the house to go to bed. Mom was in her wheelchair, mending one of Joseph's shirts. Dad sat beside her in the rocker, reading the Amish newspaper, *The Budget*. Joseph and Perry sat on the steps, playing a game, and Rachel shared the porch swing with Elizabeth. It was a quiet, peaceful night, in spite of the sweltering August heat.

Rachel mechanically pumped her legs as she gazed out at the fireflies rising from the grass like a host of twinkling lights. An owl hooted from a nearby tree, the gas lantern hanging nearby purred, and the sun dipped slowly below the horizon, transforming the sky into a hazy pink. If not for the fact that Rachel still missed Anna so much and had been forced to take her place in the greenhouse several hours a day, she would have felt a sense of contentment as she soaked up God's handiwork.

Of course, I've lost Silas, too, she reminded herself.

Ever since Anna and Reuben had left, Rachel sensed that Silas was mourning his loss. She'd seen him at preaching services several times, and no matter how hard she tried to be friendly, he remained aloof. Maybe she should give up the hope of him ever seeing her as a woman he could love. "It's just a silly dream," she murmured.

"What'd you say?" Elizabeth nudged Rachel with her elbow.

Rachel's face heated up. "Nothing. I was only thinking out loud."

"Daydreaming is probably more like it," Joseph said with a chuckle. "I've never known anyone who could stare off into space the way you do and see nothing at all. A daydreaming little tomboy, that's what you are."

Rachel grimaced. Was Joseph looking for an argument tonight? Maybe he'd had a rough day out in the fields. Could be that Perry had been goofing around and hadn't helped enough. Or the hot weather might be all that was making her big brother a bit cross.

"If you ever plan on any man marrying you, then you'd better turn in your fishing pole for a broom." Joseph shook his head. "A grown woman isn't supposed to climb trees, splash around in the river like a fish, and stand around for hours gawking at dumb birds."

Rachel folded her arms and squinted at Joseph. "I refuse to let you ruffle my feathers."

He snickered. "Aw, I wasn't trying to upset you. I was just funnin' with you, that's all. We need some fun around here, wouldn't you say?"

Rachel shrugged. "I thought maybe you were *gridlich* because you'd had a rough day."

"I think we're all a bit cranky," Dad spoke up. "A few more sweltering days like this, and everything in the garden will dry up, like as not."

Mom nodded. "I've had to water things in the greenhouse a lot more than usual, too."

"Everyone has their share of troubles," Perry put in. "Did ya hear about Herman's Katie breakin' her arm?"

Rachel's ears perked right up. "Silas's mamm?"

Perry nodded. "Jah. Heard it from her son Sam this morning when we went fishin' at the pond near Swartley's place."

"When did this happen?" Mom questioned. "And how?"

"Sometime yesterday. Sam said she fell down the cellar stairs."

Mom clicked her tongue. "Ach, poor Katie. How's she going to manage all her chores with only one good arm?"

"Guess her boys will have to chip in and help out more," Dad commented. "It's a downright shame she doesn't have any girls."

"I could give her a hand," Rachel volunteered, trying to keep the excitement she felt over the idea out of her voice. She did feel bad about Katie's arm, and she really did want to help, but the main reason she'd suggested it was because she thought if she went over there every day, it would give her a chance to see Silas.

"You helping Katie out is a nice thought," Dad said, "but you're needed here, especially in the greenhouse. August is a busy time, what with so many tourists coming by and all. I'm helping Joseph and Perry in the fields part of each day now, and we sure can't expect your mamm to handle things in the greenhouse all by herself."

"I used to manage pretty well when I was a young woman," Mom said with a wistful sigh. "Guess those days are well behind me now, because I get all done in if I try to do too much on my own anymore."

"How 'bout me?" Elizabeth chimed in. "I like flowers. Can't I help in the greenhouse?"

Mom looked over at Elizabeth and smiled. "I appreciate the offer, but I need someone at the house to keep things running and get the noon meal fixed for the menfolk."

Joseph turned to face his mother. "Say, I've got an idea."

"What might that be?"

"Why don't you ask Pauline Hostetler to help out with the greenhouse? I know for a fact that she loves flowers."

"And how would you be knowin' that?" Dad gave Joseph a quick wink.

His face turned beet red, and he started squirming a bit but gave no reply.

"Joseph's sweet on Pauline." Perry chuckled. "I saw him talkin' to her at the last preaching service."

Rachel couldn't believe her bashful brother had finally taken the initiative with Pauline. She thought this bit of news might be beneficial to her, as well. She jumped off the swing and raced over to her mother's wheelchair. "I really would like to help out at the Swartleys'. If Pauline agrees to work at the greenhouse, I'd even be willing to pay her with some of the money I've made this summer."

Mom's eyebrows drew together. "Now why would you do something like that? It's your daed and I who should pay any hired help, not you, Rachel."

Rachel shifted from one foot to the other. If she weren't careful, she would end up giving away her plans to win Silas. "I–I just thought, since you'd have to pay someone to take my place, I'd be obliged to help with their wages."

Mom smiled. "That's very generous of you, Rachel, but it won't be necessary."

"I can help Katie Swartley then?"

"If it's okay with your daed, then it's fine by me," Mom said with a nod.

"Won't bother me none, as long as Pauline agrees to the terms." Dad looked over at Joseph, who seemed to be studying the checkerboard hard. "Son, since this was your idea, I think you should drive over to the Hostetlers' place tomorrow morning and ask Pauline if she'd like to work in the greenhouse for a few weeks."

Joseph's face turned a deep shade of red, but he nodded, and his lips turned up slightly. "Sure, I guess I can do that."

Rachel smiled, too. If things went well, by tomorrow afternoon she might be on her way to winning Silas's heart.

Anna released a sigh as she flipped off the air-conditioning unit in their apartment and took a seat on the sofa. It was too hot without it but too cold whenever it was left on for more than an hour. Oh, how she wished they had a big porch to sit on during the warm, humid days of summer, or even a few shade trees would help. But no, they were stuck in this dinky apartment with only a couple of windows, and nothing but the sidewalk and the street next to it to look at. She longed for a view of the river, like the one not far from her folks' house. She missed the cows grazing in their pasture, the beautiful flowers growing in her mother's garden, the fresh produce she could pick at will, and she missed her family most of all.

The sharp ringing of the telephone caused Anna to jump. She hurried across the room to the small table where it sat and picked up the receiver. "Hello."

"Hi, Anna, it's me. Just wanted you to know that I'll be working later than I thought."

She glanced at the small clock sitting beside the phone. It was already seven, and Reuben should have been home an hour ago. "How come you have to work longer?"

"My boss got the job of painting a couple of rooms at his dentist's office. Dr. Carmen would like to have it done right away, but the only time we can work on the place is when he doesn't have patients. So we'll be starting it this evening and will work through the night if need be."

Anna grimaced, and a trickle of sweat rolled down her forehead. How was she going to endure this long, hot night without Reuben? How could she tell him that it was okay if he worked late again without letting the disappointment in her voice show?

"You still there, Anna?"

She shifted the phone to her other ear. "I'm here."

"Well, don't wait up for me, because like I said before, I could be pretty late."

"Okay. See you in the morning, then."

Anna hung up the phone and shuffled over to the window, feeling as if she bore the weight of the world on her shoulders. During the time she and Reuben had been secretly courting, she'd felt such a sense of excitement and looked forward to the future with him. Now, every day seemed monotonous and dreary—especially those days when Reuben worked late or didn't feel like visiting with her. All he seemed to care about when he came home from work was watching the television he'd recently purchased or sleeping in his lounge chair.

Oh, how she wished they could return to their old way of life, but whenever she mentioned the idea, Reuben got angry. She knew it would only drive a wedge between them if she continued to pressure him to go back home and join the Amish church. The best thing to do was quit pining for her old life and try to focus on her new life with Reuben in the English world.

Chapter 13

As Joseph guided his horse and buggy up the Hostetlers' driveway the following morning, his stomach did a little flip-flop. He'd talked to Pauline a couple of times since she had returned to Pennsylvania, but every time he got close to her, he felt like his tongue was tied in knots.

"Maybe I'll do better this morning," he said as he pulled on the reins to get his horse slowed down. "I sure hope Pauline's willing to work at the greenhouse."

Joseph halted the horse in front of the hitching rail near the barn and climbed down from the buggy. After he'd secured the horse, he sprinted around the back of the house and took the porch steps two at a time. He rapped on the door and was surprised when Pauline answered on the second knock.

"Guder mariye, Joseph," she said, offering him a pleasant smile and pushing back a tendril of pale blond hair that had escaped her kapp. "What brings you by our place so early this morning?"

He shifted from one foot to the other as he stared into her pretty blue eyes. "Well, I. . .that is—"

"Is something wrong? You're acting kind of nervous."

He took a deep breath and forced himself to stand still. "Guess I'd better start over."

She waited patiently for him to continue.

"The thing is, Silas Swartley's mamm broke her arm, so Rachel's offered to go over there and help out for a while during the daytime hours."

"That's too bad about Katie."

He nodded. "So if Rachel's over at the Swartleys' and Dad's helping me and Perry out in the fields, that means Mom will have to be alone in the greenhouse."

Pauline's eyebrows drew together. "Your mamm's not as young as she used to be, and I'm sure it must be hard for her to handle things in the greenhouse by herself."

"You're right, and that's why I'm here."

She tipped her head and looked at him in a strange kind of way. Then a light seemed to dawn. "Are you wanting me to come work in the greenhouse until Rachel's done helping the Swartleys?"

"Jah, if you're free to do so."

Pauline nodded enthusiastically. "I'd be happy to help, and I think I'd rather enjoy working around flowers every day."

Joseph released a sigh of relief. "That's good to hear. Jah, real good." He turned to go but pivoted back around. "I'll let the folks know you'll be over soon then, okay?"

She nodded. "I'll be there as quick as I can."

As Joseph climbed back into his buggy, a sense of hope welled in his soul. If Pauline came over to help in the greenhouse for a few days, he might get the opportunity to see her more. If he could work up the nerve, he might even be so bold as to ask if he could come calling on Pauline sometime.

Silas and his younger brothers, Jake and Sam, had just returned from the fields. Silas spotted a horse and buggy parked in the driveway, but before he could say anything, Jake hollered out, "Looks like we've got ourselves some company!"

Silas shrugged. "Probably one of Mom's friends come to see if she needs any help."

"I hope they brought something good to eat," Sam put in. "Now that Mom's arm is busted, she won't be doing much baking."

Silas flicked his twelve-year-old brother's straw hat off his head. "It's the same old story with you. Always hungry, aren't ya?"

Sam flashed him a freckle-faced grin and bounded up the porch steps. "Last one to the table is a *fett kuh*!"

"You'll be the fat cow." Silas raced his brothers into the kitchen, each of them laughing and grabbing at one another's shirts as they turned this way and that.

Jake and Sam made it to the sink first, because Silas had stopped short inside the door, his gaze fixed on Rachel Beachy, who seemed to be busy setting the table. She glanced over at him and smiled, and his heart felt as though it had stopped beating for a few seconds. He'd never noticed it before, but Rachel had two little dimples—one in each cheek. Had she never smiled at him before, or had he just been too blind to notice? Today Rachel almost looked like a mature woman. Could she have changed that much since he'd last seen her?

"Guess that's your buggy outside," Silas said, feeling as if his tongue had been glued to the roof of his mouth.

"It's mine, all right," she answered. "I'm here to help your mamm until her arm gets better."

Silas's mouth dropped open. "You're going to stay with us?"

"No, silly. Rachel will be coming over every morning and staying until after supper," Mom said.

Silas really felt stupid now. Here his mother stood at the stove, stirring a pot of soup with her one good arm, and he hadn't even noticed her until she'd spoken.

He removed his hat and hung it on a wall peg. "That's real nice of you, Rachel. Nice of your folks to let you come, too."

Rachel placed a loaf of bread on the table. "If Pauline Hostetler hadn't been willing to take my place at the greenhouse, I probably couldn't have come."

"Did ya bring anything good to eat?" This question came from Sam, who had already taken his place at the table.

"Samuel Swartley, where are your manners? Sometimes I don't know what gets into my boys." Mom shook her head and clucked her tongue. "Rachel came to help, not furnish the likes of you with all kinds of fattening goodies."

"Actually, I did bring some chocolate chip cookies." Rachel motioned toward a basket in the cupboard.

Sam started to get up, but Silas placed a restraining hand on his shoulder. "You'd better eat your lunch first, don't you think?"

"What's for lunch, and where's Pap?" Jake asked as he joined his brothers at the table.

"Vegetable soup and ham sandwiches, and your daed's not back from town yet," Mom answered.

Silas and his brothers waited until Rachel and Mom took their seats, and then all heads bowed in silent prayer.

Later, after everyone had eaten their fill, Rachel offered the cookies as dessert.

Silas smacked his lips after the first bite. "Umm... these are real tasty. You didn't bake 'em yourself, did you, Rachel?"

"Of course," she replied a bit stiffly. "I may be just a little tomboy in some folks' eyes, but I can cook, bake, sew, clean, and do most everything else around the house."

Silas didn't have a clue what he'd said to make Rachel go all peevish on him, but she seemed kind of miffed. He shrugged and reached for another cookie.

As Rachel cleared away the lunchtime dishes, her mind focused on Silas, who had gone back out to the fields with his brothers. She wished she could figure him out. One minute he smiled and said how nice it was for her to help out, and the next minute he made fun of her, the way Joseph often did.

Was Silas really making fun of me? a little voice niggled at the back of her mind. *He did say my cookies were good, and he only asked if I had baked them.* Maybe she was being overly sensitive where Silas was concerned. Maybe she'd tried too hard to make him take notice of her by smiling sweetly and bringing those cookies. Maybe she should play hard to get, like some other young women often did when they were trying to get a man's attention.

"That wouldn't be right," Rachel mumbled, as she placed the dirty dishes in the sink. Besides, she wasn't Anna, so if Silas was ever going to take notice of her, it wouldn't be because she was playing hard to get.

"Did you say something?" Katie asked, stepping up to Rachel.

Rachel's face heated up. "Guess I was talking to myself."

Katie grinned. Her chubby cheeks always seemed to be wearing a smile.

"If you ever need someone to talk to, I've got a good pair of ears for listening."

"Danki. I'll keep that in mind." Rachel moved over to the stove to retrieve the pot of water she'd heated to wash the dishes. "I can finish up in here. I'm sure you're probably feeling tired by now. Why don't you go and rest awhile?"

Katie handed Rachel the dishrag. "I think I'll take you up on that offer. My arm's hurting a bit, so some aspirin and a good nap might do me some good."

"What else are you needing to have done today?"

"Let's see now. . . . It's too hot to do any baking, but if you feel like it, maybe you could mix up a ribbon salad. That's Silas's favorite kind." Katie nodded toward the pantry. "I think there are a few packages of Jell-O and some other ingredients you'll need in there. Last time I checked the refrigerator, we had plenty of whipping cream, milk, and cream cheese, so you should be able to put it together in time for supper."

A short time later, Rachel had prepared the ribbon salad and was just placing it inside the refrigerator when the back door swung open. Thinking it was probably Herman Swartley returning from town, Rachel turned toward the door and smiled. Her smile was quickly replaced with a frown when she saw Silas standing there, holding his hand and grimacing in obvious pain.

She hurried to his side, feeling as if her breath had been snatched away. "What is it? Are you hurt?"

"I got a big old splinter in my thumb, and it's all your fault."

Rachel's hands went straight to her hips. "My fault? How can you getting a splinter be my fault?"

Silas lowered his head sheepishly. "I took a handful of your cookies out to the fields, and after I ate a few, I forgot to put my gloves back on. Next thing I knew, I was grabbin' hold of the wagon, and here's what I've got to show for it." He held up his thumb for her inspection.

Rachel bit back a smile, even though her stomach did a little flip-flop as she thought about how much the sliver must hurt. "So, it's my fault you weren't wearing your gloves, huh?"

He nodded and looked her right in the eye, which made her stomach take another big nosedive. "If you weren't so good at making cookies, I wouldn't have grabbed a handful. And if I'd had my gloves on, I sure wouldn't have all this pain right now."

Silas's voice had a soft quality about it, yet he spoke with assurance. Rachel thought she could sit and listen to him talk for hours. "Take a seat at the table, and I'll have a look-see," she instructed. "Do you know where your mamm keeps her needles and such?"

Silas's eyes were wide, and his mouth hung slightly open. "You're not planning to go pokin' around on my thumb, are you?"

She tipped her head to one side. "How else did you expect me to remove that old splinter?"

Silas swallowed so hard she saw his Adam's apple bob up and down. "Guess you've got a point." He nodded toward the treadle sewing machine positioned along the wall nearest the fireplace. "I think you'll find all your doctoring tools over there."

Rachel went to the sewing machine and opened the top drawer of the wooden cabinet. She found plenty of needles, a pair of tweezers, and even a magnifying glass. She figured Silas's mother must have had some experience taking out slivers, since she had three boys and a husband.

"It might be best if you close your eyes," Rachel said, as she leaned close to Silas and took his hand in hers. This was the closest she'd ever been to him, and it took all her concentration to focus on that nasty sliver and not his masculine scent or the feel of his warm breath blowing softly against her face.

"I ain't no boppli." Silas clamped his teeth together. "So I'll keep my eyes open, thank you very much."

"As you like." Rachel jabbed the needle underneath the sliver and pushed upward.

"Yow! That hurts like crazy!" Silas's face turned white as a sheet of paper, and Rachel feared he might be about to pass out.

She clenched her own teeth in order to keep from laughing out loud. So Silas didn't think he was a baby, huh? "Maybe you'd better hang your head between your knees and take some deep breaths."

Once Silas had his head down, Rachel grabbed his hand again and set right to work. It was hard to ignore his groans and yowls, but in short order she had the splinter dug out. "Let me pour some peroxide over it and give you a bandage. Do you know where those are kept?"

Silas sat up straight and took several deep breaths before he answered. "In the cupboard. Just above the sink."

Soon she'd cleansed the wound and put a bandage in place. When Silas smiled at Rachel, she thought her heart had quit beating. *How could Anna have turned this special man away in exchange for Reuben Yutzy? I don't understand what she thought was so special about her want-to-be-English husband.*

"Danki, Rachel. That splinter was a nasty one, and I don't think I could have taken it out myself."

"*Gern gschehne*–you're welcome."

Silas stood and started for the door but pivoted back around. "Say, I was wondering. . .that is. . ."

"What were you wondering?"

For several seconds, he stood with a faraway look in his eyes. Finally, with a shake of his head, he turned toward the door. "Never mind. It was nothing important."

The door clicked shut behind him, and Rachel sank into a chair. Was there any hope for her and Silas, or had she just imagined that he had looked at her with some interest?

With every step Silas took as he headed back out to the fields, he thought about Rachel and how motherly she had looked while she'd worked to remove the splinter from his thumb. Her pale blue eyes, framed by lush, dark lashes, and those cute little dimples made her look irresistible. Her voice, sweeter than a bluebird calling to its mate, had almost mesmerized him.

I'll bet she'll make some lucky fellow a good wife someday. She'll probably be a great mother, too, since she can bake such tasty cookies. He smiled. *And she's even an expert at removing slivers.*

He kicked at a stone with the toe of his boot. *What am I doin' letting myself think such thoughts? If I'm not careful, I'll end up thinkin' I've got feelings for that girl.*

"Girl," Silas mumbled as he bounced another rock across the dry ground. "That's all Rachel is. . . just a girl."

Silas didn't know why, but here lately, he'd begun to feel strangely attracted to little Rachel, and that bothered him more than he cared to admit. Maybe the best way for him to handle these strange feelings was to keep a safe distance from Rachel.

Jah, that's just what I'll have to do.

As Joseph headed home in his horse and buggy

after running some errands in town, he was surprised to see Pauline walking along the edge of the road. He pulled on the reins and guided the horse over to the shoulder. "Where you heading?" he called to her.

"One of my buggy wheels broke, so I'm walking home to get some help."

"Climb in, and I'll give you a lift."

"Danki." Pauline stepped into the buggy. "Whew! Sure is a hot day. I didn't relish the idea of walking the next couple of miles to my place, so this ride is much appreciated."

"I'm more than happy to do it." Joseph smiled. "I'd offer to fix your wheel, but like a dummkopp, I forgot to put the toolbox in the buggy when I left home this morning."

"That's okay. My daed can do it." She tipped her head and smiled. "And you're not a dunce, Joseph Beachy."

His face heated up, and he gathered up the reins in order to get the horse moving again. He wished he could think of something else to say, but being this close to Pauline made him feel so nervous it was all he could do to keep his mind focused on his driving. If only he could think of some way to make her take notice of him. If he just weren't three years younger than her. Now that Eli Yoder was married and out of the picture, Joseph thought he might have a chance with Pauline, and if she could get to know him better, she might decide their age difference didn't matter so much.

"Have you been real busy this summer working in the fields?" Pauline asked, breaking the silence.

He nodded. "Mom says things have been busy at the greenhouse, too."

"Jah. We've had plenty of customers, all right." She sighed. "I've enjoyed working around the flowers and wouldn't mind doing it all the time."

He grunted. "My sister Rachel would argue with you on that."

"She doesn't like flowers?"

"Not the indoor kind. Says they make her sneeze."

"Maybe she's allergic to some of them."

"That's what she says, but I think it's just her excuse to get out of working in the greenhouse."

"Why doesn't she like working there?"

"She'd rather be outside climbing trees so she can get a better look at some dumb bird she wants to watch." Joseph glanced over at Pauline, and when she smiled, he found himself beginning to relax. He loosened his grip on the reins a bit and smiled in return.

"I guess Rachel's kind of a tomboy, huh?"

"Jah."

"I've never tried climbing a tree, and I think if I did, I'd probably fall out and break something."

"Rachel's taken a tumble or two over the years, but so far she's never broken any bones." He wrinkled his forehead. "If you want my opinion, she's way too old to be climbing up in trees."

"Next to working in my mamm's flower garden, my favorite thing to do is bake."

"What kinds of things do you like to bake?"

"Cookies. . .pies. . .cakes. . ."

The mention of food made Joseph's stomach rumble, and he hoped Pauline couldn't hear it. He coughed a couple of times, trying to cover up his embarrassment, and kept his eyes looking straight ahead.

They pulled into the Hostetlers' driveway a few minutes later, and he felt a keen sense of disappointment.

"Danki for the ride," she said, offering him another pleasant smile that set his heart to racing.

"Gern gschehne."

Pauline stepped down from the buggy, and just before Joseph got the horse and buggy moving again, she looked up and asked him a question. "What kind of pie do you like, Joseph?"

"I like 'em all, but I guess shoofly's really my favorite."

"I'll bake you one soon as a thank-you gift for giving me a ride home."

"There's no need for that. I was glad to do it."

"You're a nice man, Joseph Beachy." Before Joseph could think of anything sensible to say, Pauline hurried off toward the barn.

Joseph clucked to the horse and headed back down the driveway, whistling a silly tune and smiling so hard his cheeks began to ache. Pauline had said he was a nice man, not a boy. Maybe there was some hope that she might take an interest in him—at least as a friend.

Chapter 14

Over the next few weeks, Rachel helped Katie every day she could. She got up an hour early in order to get her own chores done at home; then right after breakfast, she headed over to the Swartleys' place. Katie's arm seemed to be hurting less, but she would have to wear the cast for another three weeks, which meant she still had the use of only one arm.

Things weren't going as well with Silas as Rachel had hoped. Ever since the day she'd removed his splinter, he had seemed kind of distant. She had to wonder if he was trying to avoid her, although she couldn't think why, since she'd made every effort to be pleasant. It might be that Silas's aloofness was because he was so busy in the fields. On most days, she saw him only during lunch and supper, and even then, he appeared tired and withdrawn.

Today was Saturday, and Katie had enlisted the help of another Amish woman so Rachel could work in the greenhouse with Pauline. Dad had taken

Mom, Elizabeth, and Perry to Bird-in-Hand, where they would be selling some of their plants and fresh-cut flowers at the indoor farmers' market. Since Saturday was always a big day at the greenhouse, they didn't want to leave Pauline alone, and that meant Rachel was expected to stay and help out. Joseph also stayed behind, saying he had some chores to do.

As Rachel began watering plants, the musty scent of wet soil assaulted her senses, causing her to sneeze and making her wish she could be outside instead of cooped up in a much-too-warm greenhouse. She glanced over at Pauline, who was busy waiting on some English customers. The tall, blond-haired woman certainly had changed since she'd returned from Ohio. Instead of being distant and sometimes cross, Pauline had become outgoing and cheerful. Rachel could remember a few years ago when Pauline had been jilted by Eli Yoder. She hadn't tried to hide her bitter feelings.

Rachel couldn't be sure what had brought about such a dramatic change in Pauline, but she suspected it had something to do with the time Pauline had spent in Ohio. She was certain of one thing—Joseph was glad Pauline had returned to Pennsylvania. He seemed to have set his reservations aside about his and Pauline's age difference, because Rachel had noticed that for the last couple of weeks he'd been hanging around Pauline every chance he got. It made her wonder if she could do something to help Pauline and her big brother get together.

When the customers left the greenhouse, Rachel moved over to the counter where Pauline stood. "You can take your lunch break now if you want. I'll wait on anyone who might come in during the next hour."

Pauline nodded and grabbed the small cooler she used as a lunch bucket from underneath the counter. "I think I'll eat outside. Might as well enjoy the good weather while it lasts. Fall's almost upon us. Can you tell?"

"Jah. Mornings and evenings seem much cooler now. Won't be any time at all until the leaves start to change."

Pauline was about to open the door, when Rachel called out to her. "I think Joseph's still in the barn. Would you mind going there and letting him know that the sandwich I made for him is in the refrigerator?"

Pauline smiled. "I think I can do better than that. I'll go on up to the house, fetch the sandwich and something cold to drink, then take it out to Joe myself, along with the pie I brought him."

Ah, so it's Joe *now, is it?* Rachel hid her smile behind the writing tablet she'd just picked up. Maybe she wouldn't have to play matchmaker after all. "What's this about a pie?"

"He gave me a ride home a few weeks ago after my buggy lost a wheel." Pauline's cheeks turned a light shade of pink. "When he mentioned that he liked shoofly pie really well, I said I would bake him one."

"That big brother of mine does like his pies. It's a good thing he works so hard in the fields, or he might be packing on some extra weight due to his hearty eating habits."

"There's not a speck of fat on Joe from what I can see. Lots of muscle, but no fat." The color in Pauline's cheeks deepened, and she dropped her gaze to the floor. "Well, guess I'd best be getting up to your house to get his lunch."

"See you later, Pauline. Oh, and tell *Joe* I said hello and that I hope he enjoys his lunch."

Joseph had just set out another bale of straw for the horse's stall he was cleaning when he heard the barn door open and click shut. He turned and saw Pauline heading toward him, and his stomach did its usual flip-flop. He hoped he would be able to speak to her without his tongue getting tied in knots again.

"I brought you some lunch, Joe," Pauline said, lifting the small cooler she held in her hands as she stepped up to him.

Joe? Since when had she started calling him *Joe*? Not that he minded the nickname. Truth be told, Joseph saw the familiarity as a good sign. Maybe Pauline was starting to have feelings for him—or at least see him as a good friend, which he hoped could be the beginning of something more.

He reached under his straw hat and wiped the

sweat from his brow. "What did you make for me?"

"Actually, it was Rachel who made your sandwich and filled a jug with milk. I just offered to go up to the house and get it from the refrigerator and then bring it out to you." Her face turned kind of pink, and she dropped her gaze to the floor.

"Even so, it was nice of you." He studied her further, trying to get a feel for what she might be thinking.

The color in her cheeks deepened, and she giggled, kind of nervous-like.

"I. . .uh. . .also brought you that shoofly pie I promised to make for you a few weeks ago."

Joseph took the cooler and flipped open the lid. "There's a whole pie in here, Pauline."

She nodded. "You said it was your favorite kind, and I didn't think a slice or two would do."

"Danki. That was sure nice of you." He licked his lips, and his stomach rumbled despite his best efforts to keep it quiet. "Would you care to join me? We could pull up a bale of straw and have ourselves a little picnic."

Pauline glanced over her shoulder, like she was worried someone might come through the door. Then in a voice barely above a whisper, she said, "I need to be honest with you about something, Joe."

He tipped his head in question.

"The cooler you're holding has my sandwich in it, too."

"It does?"

"Jah. When I volunteered to bring your sandwich out to you, I kind of had it in mind that we could eat our lunches together."

Joseph's lips curved into a smile as a sense of joy spread over him like a warm bath on a cold day. "I'd like that, Pauline. Jah, I'd like that a lot."

Silas wasn't sure it was such a good idea to be going to the Beachys' greenhouse today, but his buggy was already pulling into the graveled parking lot, so he figured he may as well carry out his plan.

When he entered the greenhouse, Rachel greeted him from behind the front counter, where she sat reading a book.

"I thought you'd be swamped with customers," he said, removing his straw hat and offering her a smile.

Rachel jumped off her stool and moved swiftly to the other side of the counter. "We were busy earlier, but since it's almost noon, I think everyone must be eating their lunch about now." She took a few steps toward him. "I'm surprised to see you here today."

He shuffled his feet a few times and glanced around the room. "Uh, where's Pauline? I thought she was working here now."

Rachel nodded, and her eyebrows drew together. *Have I said something wrong?*

"Pauline does work here, but she's on her lunch

break right now. Want me to see if I can find her?" As Rachel moved toward the door, her shoulders slumped.

Silas stopped her by placing his hand on her arm. "I didn't come by to see Pauline."

"You didn't?"

He shook his head.

"What did you come for?"

He rocked back and forth on his heels, with one hand balled into a fist and the other hanging on to his hat tightly. "I'm wondering. . .that is. . ."

"Are you needing a plant or some cut flowers? Mom and Dad took quite a few to the market this morning, but I think we still have a good supply in the back room."

Silas cleared his throat a few times, trying to decide the best way to broach the subject that had brought him here. He fanned his face with his hat, hoping the action might give him something to do with his hands, as well as get him cooled down some.

"You okay, Silas? You're looking kind of poorly. Want to sit awhile?"

"Maybe that would be a good idea." He pulled up an empty crate and plunked down with a groan. "Whew! Don't know what came over me, but I was feelin' a little woozy for a minute there."

"Maybe you're coming down with the flu or something." Rachel placed her hand against his forehead. Her fingers felt cool and soft, making it even more difficult for Silas to think straight.

"I'm not sick," he asserted. "It's just warm in here, that's all."

Rachel nodded and took a few steps back. "It's always a bit stuffy in the greenhouse, which is one of the reasons I don't like working here."

"What would you rather be doing?"

She gave him another one of her dimpled smiles. "Fishing. . .bird-watching. . .almost anything outdoors."

Their gazes met, and the moment seemed awkward. Silas swallowed hard. If he was ever going to ask her, he'd better do it quick, because right now he felt like racing for the door and heading straight home.

"The reason I stopped by was to see if you might want to go to the lake with me tomorrow. Your brother Joseph and me were talking the other day, and he mentioned that you like to fish. So I thought maybe we could do a bit of fishing, and if we're lucky, get in some bird-watching, too."

Rachel stood staring at him like she was in some kind of a daze. For a minute, he wondered if he would need to repeat himself.

"Since tomorrow is an off Sunday and there won't be any preaching service, I guess it would be a good time for some outdoor fun." Her voice came out in a squeak, and she blinked a couple of times.

He jumped up. "You mean you'll meet me there?"

She nodded. "How about I fix us a picnic lunch to take along? Fishing always makes me hungry, and later tonight I was planning to bake some more of those chocolate chip cookies you like so well."

"Sounds good. How about making some of that wunderbaar ribbon salad you fixed for our supper awhile back? That was awful tasty, too," he said with a wink.

Rachel smiled as her face turned a deep shade of red. "I think that can be arranged."

Silas licked his lips in anticipation of what was to come. He was glad he'd finally gotten up the nerve to ask Rachel to go fishing. "Let's meet at the lake around nine o'clock. How's that sound?"

"Sounds good to me," she said, walking him to the door.

"Say, Anna, wait up a minute, would you?"

Anna halted before she stepped out the back door of the restaurant where she worked. She was tired after a long day, and her feet ached something awful. The last thing she wanted to do was chit-chat with her coworker Kathryn Clemmons. She drew in a deep breath and turned around. "What's up?"

"The last time we talked, you said you hadn't found a church since you'd moved to Lancaster, so I was wondering if you and your husband would like to go church this Sunday with me and Walt."

Anna's heartbeat picked up speed at the mention

of church. She'd been wanting to go, but whenever she mentioned the idea to Reuben, he always said he was too tired from working so much overtime. It seemed that all he wanted to do on Sundays was sleep or watch TV.

She swallowed hard, then chose her words carefully. "I appreciate the offer, Kathryn, but my husband's been working a lot of overtime lately, and Sundays are the only days he has to sleep in."

"That's too bad." Kathryn's dark eyes held a note of sympathy. "Maybe you could come this Sunday without him—so you can see if you would enjoy our church."

Anna swallowed again, trying to dislodge the persistent lump crowding her throat. Did Kathryn know how miserable she felt these days? Her life was nothing like she had envisioned it when she'd agreed to marry Reuben and go English. Instead of taking long walks together or enjoying a ride in Reuben's truck the way they used to when they'd been secretly courting, now they barely saw each other. And when they were together, Reuben was tired and cross, which only made Anna more lonely and depressed. She needed something that might help pull her out of this slump.

"I guess maybe I could go alone. Maybe in time, Reuben will feel up to joining me."

"You won't have to go alone." Kathryn placed her hand on Anna's shoulder and gave it a gentle squeeze. "Walt and I will be happy to come by and get you on Sunday morning. Can you be ready by ten thirty?"

Anna nodded. "I'm sure I can."

As soon as Silas returned home, he went straight to the barn to get out his fishing gear. Besides the fishing pole, several fat worms, extra tackle, and line, he'd decided to take along his binoculars and the new book he'd recently bought on bird-watching.

He grinned as he grabbed his pole off the wall. It amazed him that Rachel liked to fish and study birds, but he was glad they had that in common. Neither one of his brothers showed the least bit of interest in watching birds or fishing with him, and now that Reuben was gone, he'd been forced to fish alone.

Silas frowned. He hadn't thought about Reuben for several weeks, and he wished he wasn't thinking of him now. Reminders of Reuben always made him think about Anna, and he wasn't sure he was completely over her yet. He'd loved her a lot, and she'd hurt him badly. A fellow didn't get over being kicked in the gut like that overnight. Matters of the heart took time to heal, and until a moment ago, Silas had begun to think his heart might be on the way to mending.

"I'll feel better once I'm seated on the dock at the lake with my fishing pole in the water and the warm sun against my back," he muttered.

"Who ya talkin' to, Silas?"

Silas whirled around. His brother Sam stood looking up at him like he was some sort of a bug on the wall. "I wasn't talking to anyone but myself, and you shouldn't go around sneaking up on others."

Sam scrunched up his freckled nose. "I wasn't sneaking. Just came out to the barn to feed the cats, and I heard you talking about going fishing."

Silas nodded. "That's right. I'll be headed to the lake in the morning."

"Can I go along?"

"Naw, I'd rather go alone. Besides, you don't even like to fish."

"I know, but it might be better than hangin' around here all day. Ever since Mom got that cast on her arm, she's been askin' me to do more chores."

"Things will go better soon. Mom won't always be wearing her arm in a sling. Besides, there won't be a bunch of chores for you to do on Sunday."

"I guess you're right about that." Sam turned to go, calling over his shoulder, "If it's a girl you're meeting tomorrow, could ya save me a piece of cake from the picnic?"

Silas pulled his fingers through the back of his hair. That little brother of his was sure no dumb bunny. Only thing was, it wouldn't be cake he'd be bringing home tomorrow, because Rachel had said she was going to bake his favorite kind of cookie.

Chapter 15

As Anna combed her hair in front of her dresser mirror, her mind was plagued with doubts. Did she really want to go to church this morning? If Reuben were going along, then she might be more in the mood. But to go alone didn't seem right. Of course, she wouldn't really be alone. Kathryn and her husband, Walt, would be with her. Still, it might be difficult to be with Kathryn, whose husband eagerly attended church every week, and not feel sorry for herself because Reuben showed no interest in anything spiritual these days.

Had he ever? Anna wondered as she turned to look at him sleeping in the bed across the room. Oh, sure, Reuben had attended church with his family throughout his growing-up years, but he hadn't been baptized or joined the church, which was a good indication that he hadn't taken anything of a spiritual nature too seriously yet. If she could only get him to go to church with her, that would be a step in the right direction.

Anna turned from the dresser and moved over to the bed. "Reuben, are you awake?" She nudged him gently with her hand.

"Am now," he responded with a muffled grunt.

She leaned over and kissed his forehead. "I'll be leaving for church soon. Are you sure you won't come with me?"

He pulled the covers around his ears and groaned. "Too tired. Need to sleep."

She released a sigh. Would there ever be a time when Reuben wasn't too tired? Would he ever come to realize that spending time with God—and with her—was more important than working so much or lounging around on Sundays?

"I'll see you shortly after noon." Anna whispered a silent prayer on her husband's behalf, then tiptoed out of the room.

❧

As Rachel stood in front of the kitchen sink, doing up the breakfast dishes, she felt like hugging herself. The thought of going on a fishing date with Silas was enough to take her breath away. She couldn't help but wonder and, yes, even hope that Silas's sudden invitation was a sign that he was beginning to care for her.

Maybe she should start filling her hope chest with a few more things. If Silas enjoyed her company today, he might even offer to take her home from the next singing or young people's function. *Now that would mean we were officially courting.* Rachel smiled to herself. She would have to remember to thank Joseph for letting Silas know how much she liked to fish.

As Rachel's thoughts continued to swirl, she wondered how she could get away without telling her family that she planned to meet Silas at the lake.

She was alone in the kitchen at the moment, so as soon as she finished the dishes, she began packing the picnic lunch she'd promised Silas she would bring, hoping no one would come inside and see how much she'd stashed inside the wicker basket and small cooler she planned to take along.

Rachel had no more than shut the lid on the cooler, when Elizabeth and Perry bounded into the room.

"What's with the picnic stuff?" Perry asked. "Are ya goin' someplace, Rachel?"

She nodded. "I'll be leaving for the lake soon. I plan to do a bit of fishing."

Elizabeth stepped up to the table, where Rachel had placed the cooler and wicker basket. "Can we go along?"

"I don't think that's such a good idea."

"How come?" Perry questioned.

"You two like to throw rocks into the water, holler, and run around." Rachel pursed her lips. "That scares away the fish."

Elizabeth's lower lip jutted out, and Perry squinted at her as he wrinkled his nose.

A sense of guilt came over Rachel. She hated to tell the children they couldn't go along, but if she and Silas were going to get better acquainted, the last thing she needed was her rowdy brother and nosy sister tagging along.

"You meetin' someone at the lake?" Perry asked as he started to open the lid on the cooler.

She held the lid down with one hand and drew in a quick breath. "You two can go to the lake with me some other time, but today I'm going by myself."

Perry grunted and stomped out of the room.

"Guess I'll go with Mom and Dad when they call on some of their friends," Elizabeth said with a shrug.

Rachel leaned down and gave her sister a hug; then, grabbing up the cooler and picnic basket, she hurried out the back door.

The morning sun slid from behind a cloud as Rachel hitched the horse to the buggy a short time later. It was a bit chilly out, but the day held the promise of sunshine and blue skies. She was glad her folks hadn't insisted she go calling with them and was even more relieved that neither of them had asked any questions when she'd told them a few minutes ago that she planned to go fishing at the lake.

Rachel was about to climb into the driver's seat when Dad called out to her. "I'm not so sure I like the idea of you going to the lake by yourself."

"I've been fishing there since I was a kinner, and

I've never had a problem. Besides, plenty of people are usually around, so I probably won't be alone."

Dad left Mom sitting on the porch in her wheelchair and hurried over to Rachel. "That may be, but it isn't good for a young woman to be running around by herself. I think you should take your sister or one of your brothers along."

Rachel placed the picnic basket under the front seat and turned to face her father. "I'm meeting someone."

He gave his beard a couple of yanks. "Ah, so my daughter has a beau now, does she?"

Rachel's face heated up. "He's not a boyfriend, Dad."

He chuckled. "So it is a fellow you're meeting, then?"

She nodded.

"Mind if I ask who?"

"It's Silas Swartley."

He winked at Rachel. "Should I be askin' your mamm to start makin' a wedding quilt?"

Rachel grimaced. "I knew I shouldn't have said anything. Like I stated before, Silas and I are just friends."

"Then why the big secret about meeting him?"

"I–I didn't want anyone jumping to conclusions."

Dad gave her arm a gentle pat. "Your secret's safe with me. Now run along and catch plenty of fish. Some nice, tasty trout would look mighty good on the supper table."

Rachel grinned and climbed into the buggy. Maybe Dad thought there might be some hope for her and Silas, too.

As Silas sat on the dock with his fishing line dangling in the water, he noticed several small boats on the lake, but no one else was on the dock or shoreline. Maybe he and Rachel would be alone all day. Did he really want to be alone with her? He'd thought he did yesterday when he asked her to meet him here. Now that he'd had ample time to think about it, he worried that he might have been a bit hasty making the invitation. What if Rachel thought he was interested in her as more than a friend? What if she thought this was a real date?

Silas stared across the lake, his gaze settling on a crop of trees where several crows sat, making their distinctive call of *caw, caw, caw*. Truth be told, he really did enjoy Rachel's company. The fact that she liked birds and fishing was a benefit, but it was her sweet spirit and appreciation for the simple things in life that had really captured his attention.

She isn't too bad-looking, either. Silas closed his eyes, and Rachel's pleasant face flashed into his mind. Her pale blue eyes and soft, straw-colored hair made her appear almost angelic. Whenever she smiled, those cute little dimples made him want to reach right out and touch her cheeks.

What am I thinking? Rachel is Anna's little sister.

She's five years younger than me and isn't much more than a kinner. He shook his head. *Of course, I do know of some married couples where one is older than the other. Guess five years isn't really so much.*

Silas was driven from his inner conflict when he heard a horse and buggy coming. He turned and waved as Rachel directed her horse onto the grassy spot near the dock.

Rachel smiled and waved at Silas, who sat on the edge of the dock, holding a fishing pole and wearing an eager expression. Was it possible that he was as happy to see her as she was to see him? She prayed it was so.

"Catch anything yet?" she asked, as she stepped down from the buggy.

He shook his head. "Not yet, but then I haven't been here very long."

Rachel grabbed her pole from the back of the buggy, along with the can of night crawlers she'd caught last evening. When she walked onto the dock, Silas slid over, making room for her to sit beside him. "Sure is a nice day. Should have our share of trout in no time." He winked at Rachel, and her heart skipped a beat.

Does he have some feelings for me? She would cling to this glimmer of hope.

The sun shone brightly, the sky was a clear aquamarine, and the lake looked smooth as glass.

Rachel felt a sense of peace settle over her as she cast out her line. It felt so right being here with Silas. If only. . .

No, I mustn't allow myself to start daydreaming. Today, I'm just going to relax and enjoy the company of the man I could surely spend the rest of my life with, if he was willing.

By noon, Silas had caught six trout and four bass, and Rachel had five of each. They both cleaned their own catch, then put the fish inside the small coolers they had brought along.

Silas eyed the picnic basket Rachel had taken from the buggy and placed upon the quilt she'd spread on the ground. "I don't know about you, but I'm starving," he said, as a dark flicker came into his eyes.

"I made plenty, so I'm glad you're hungry."

He dropped to the quilt. "What'd you bring?"

Rachel knelt next to the cooler and opened the lid. "Let's see now. . .ham-and-cheese sandwiches, dill pickle slices, ribbon salad, pickled beet eggs, iced tea to drink, and for dessert. . .chocolate chip cookies."

Silas licked his lips. "Yum. Let's pray; then we'll eat ourselves full!"

As Rachel and Silas ate their lunch, they shared stories, told jokes, and got to know each other better. By the time they'd finished eating, Rachel felt as though she had known Silas all her life. Actually, she had, but not on such a personal level.

TG cass. celery

✓make yogurt cheese

pot. salad celery

Roast

mac. salad

gr. onions

Silas, being five years her senior, had always hung around her older sister, so she'd never had the chance to learn what many of his likes and dislikes were. Today he'd shared his aversion to liver and onions, a dish his mother seemed intent on fixing at least once a month. He'd also talked about his love for God and how he had been praying for the Lord to have His will in his life.

"I believe strongly in prayer," Silas said with obvious conviction. "It's the key to each new day and the lock for every night."

"You're right about that." Even as Rachel said the words, she wondered if she was being sincere. Oh, she believed in prayer, all right. The problem was, she didn't pray as often as she should anymore. Since she'd been keeping so busy helping Silas's mother and trying to keep up with her chores at home, Rachel had let her personal devotions and prayer time slip. It was something she needed to work on, and right then she promised herself that she would spend more time with God.

Silas chewed on a blade of grass as he talked about Reuben and how he had persuaded Anna to go English with him. "If I ever have any kinner, I'm gonna hold a tight rein on 'em so they don't decide to leave the faith."

Rachel leaned back on her elbows and let his words digest fully before she answered. "Holding a tight rein could turn someone's head in the opposite direction. Take a baby robin, for example.

If its mamm never taught it to fly and always kept it protected inside the nest, do you think that bird would ever learn to soar in the air?"

Silas scratched the back of his head and squinted. "Guess you've got a point. You're pretty bright for someone so young."

Rachel felt as though Silas had slapped her on the face with a wet rag. Why did he have to bring up her age? And just when they were beginning to have such a good time. "For your information, I'll be nineteen next Saturday. My mamm was married by the time she was my age, and–"

Silas held up one hand. "Don't get your feathers all ruffled. I sure didn't mean to offend you."

Rachel grabbed their empty paper plates and the plastic containers the food had been in and began slinging them into the picnic basket. Her face felt hot, her hands shook, and tears stung the backs of her eyes. She had wanted this day to be perfect. Maybe it would be better if they ended it now.

She stood and proceeded to move toward her buggy. "Guess I'll head for home."

Silas jumped up and ran after her. "You can't go now, Rachel. We haven't spent any time looking at birds."

She shrugged. "Maybe some other time. I'm not much in the mood anymore."

Silas placed a restraining hand on Rachel's arm. "Please, don't go. I'm sorry if I made you mad."

She swallowed hard, struggling to keep her tears at bay. Silas stood looking at her with those big brown eyes, and he really did look sorry. "I'm not exactly mad. I just get tired of everyone thinking I'm still a kinner." Her arms made a wide arc as she motioned toward the lake. "Could a child catch as many fish as I did today? Could a child have fixed such a tasty picnic lunch or baked a batch of cookies you kept on eating?"

Silas continued to stare at her a few more seconds, then in an unexpected gesture, he pulled her to his chest. "No, Rachel, only a feisty young woman could have done all those things."

Rachel held her breath as Silas moved his fingers in gentle, soothing circles across her back. Was he about to kiss her? She wrapped her arms around his neck and nestled her head against his shoulder.

Then as quickly as Silas had embraced her, he pulled away. "Now that we've got that all cleared up, how's about I get my binoculars and bird-identification book, and the two of us can spend the next hour or so lookin' for some unusual feathered creatures?"

Rachel nodded as a sense of embarrassment rattled through her. Silas's sudden shift in mood hit her like a blow to the stomach, and she wondered what he must have thought about her brazen actions. Even though it was Silas who initiated the hug, she had taken it one step further. Truth be told, Silas had never led her to believe he had any romantic feelings for her. The embrace was probably just a friendly gesture.

"You get your gear, and I'll put away the picnic stuff," she said, scooting away quickly before he could see how red her face must be.

A short time later, Silas and Rachel were seated on the grass, taking turns looking through his binoculars as though their physical encounter had never taken place. In no time at all, they had spotted several gray catbirds, a brown thrasher, a few mourning doves, and several species of ducks on the lake. Silas looked each one up in his bird-identification book, and they discussed the various traits and habitats of those they'd seen.

"Do you have a bird book or binoculars of your own?" he asked.

Rachel shook her head. "Whenever I save up enough money, some other need always comes along, so I just jot notes on a paper about all the interesting birds I see." She was tempted to tell Silas that here lately, she'd spent most of her money buying more things for her hope chest, but she thought better of bringing up that subject. He might think she was hinting at marriage, and she wasn't about to say or do anything that would spoil the rest of the day. Except for that one misunderstanding, their time together had been almost perfect. Even if she never got to be alone with Silas again, she would always cherish the memory of this day.

❧

Rebekah sniffed as she sat at the table reading the letter she'd received from Anna the day before. She'd been so busy when the letter arrived that she'd set it aside and had forgotten about it until she'd spotted it a few minutes ago, lying on the desk under a stack of bills that had also been in the mail.

Anna was doing well and wanted to come home for a visit—maybe for Rachel's birthday. That thought put a smile on Rebekah's lips. Wouldn't it be nice to have the whole family together to help celebrate Rachel's special day? Rebekah would fix a special dinner and bake a cake. Maybe she could talk Daniel into making a batch of homemade ice cream. How wonderful it would be to see Anna again.

"I've got the horse and buggy hitched. You about ready to head out to your brother's place?" Daniel asked, stepping into the room.

Tears gathered in Rebekah's eyes as she lifted the letter she'd been reading. "I heard from Anna again yesterday. She wants to come home for Rachel's birthday."

The corners of Daniel's mouth drew down, and he leaned against the counter with his arms folded. "I don't think so."

"Why not?"

"She's under the ban."

Rebekah released a frustrated sigh. "It's not as if we can't speak to her, for goodness' sake. I think it would be good for her to be here to help celebrate her sister's birthday. I think–"

"No. Absolutely not!" Daniel's lips were set in a thin line, and his eyebrows furrowed, nearly meeting each other at the top of his nose.

"Won't you at least consider this?"

He shook his head.

Rebekah nearly choked on a sob. "She's our daughter, Daniel. Can't you find it in your heart to forgive her for leaving us?"

No comment.

"She's married now, whether we like it or not, and her responsibility is to her husband."

"She can stay with her husband, then. We don't need her around here filling our other kinner's heads with fancy ideas about her new way of life."

"I'm sure she wouldn't do that."

"We were both sure she was being courted by Silas." Daniel grunted. "Yet she lied so we wouldn't know what she was up to with Reuben. Does that sound like someone we can trust?"

Rebekah opened her mouth to respond, but Daniel turned on his heels and headed for the back door. "The kinner are waiting in the buggy, so whenever you're ready to go, we can be on our way." He stepped onto the porch and closed the door.

Rebekah released a shuddering sob. How could she write Anna back and tell her she couldn't come to Rachel's party? What would it take to get through to her stubborn husband?

Chapter 16

After their enjoyable day at the lake, Rachel had expected Silas to be friendlier the following week. He wasn't. In fact, she saw very little of him, and when he did come to the house for meals, he seemed aloof and kind of cranky whenever someone spoke to him. Something wasn't right. She felt it in every fiber of her being. She wanted to ask him what was wrong, but there never seemed to be a good time, what with his family always around.

By Saturday, Rachel was fit to be tied. She had been forced to stay home from the Swartleys' again because Mom and Dad went to town for more supplies. That meant she was needed at the greenhouse, and even worse, it appeared as though her family had forgotten about her birthday. Not one person had said, "Happy birthday" during breakfast, and there was no sign of any gifts. It was such a disappointment not to be remembered on her special day.

Elizabeth and Perry had been left home this

time, and they were still up at the house when Rachel walked out to the greenhouse. She put the OPEN sign in the window, lit all the gas lamps, and made a small fire in the wood-burning stove to take the autumn chill out of the room.

Rachel studied her surroundings, letting her gaze travel from the plants hanging by the rafters on long chains to the small wooden pots and lawn figurines sitting on shelves. Dad had made most of those things, and his expertise with wood was quite evident. Rachel knew her folks loved this greenhouse, and she was also aware that it had been one of the things that had brought them together. Even so, she had no desire to spend so much time helping out here. Today, of all days, she would rather be outside in the fresh air.

"It's my birthday. I should at least be allowed the pleasure of taking a walk to the creek." She plunked down on the stool, placed her elbows on the counter, and rested her chin in the palms of her hands.

Pauline showed up a few minutes later, and Joseph was with her.

"I thought you were out in the barn," Rachel said, nodding at her brother.

He shrugged, and his face turned a deep shade of red. "I was until I saw Pauline's buggy come down the lane."

"Are you planning to help out here today?" Rachel asked, a sense of hope welling in her chest.

"If so, maybe I won't be needed."

"I wish I could, but Perry and I have got to get back out to the fields soon." Joseph cast a quick glance in Pauline's direction, then looked back at Rachel with a silly grin on his face.

"What are you doing here then, if it's not to work?"

"Came to see Pauline. That is, if you have no objections."

Pauline chuckled and elbowed Joseph in the ribs. He laughed and jabbed her right back.

At least somebody's happy today, Rachel thought ruefully. "I think I'll go in the back room and see if any of the plants need watering."

"Okay, sure," Joseph said, never taking his eyes off Pauline.

"Sickening. Downright sickening," Rachel muttered under her breath, as she headed for the middle section of the greenhouse. This day couldn't be over soon enough to suit her.

As Anna put the last of the clean dishes away in the cupboard, she glanced at the calendar on the kitchen wall. A pang of regret shot through her, and she groaned. Today was Rachel's nineteenth birthday, and Anna wouldn't be there to help her sister celebrate. She had received a letter from Mom the other day, saying that it wasn't a good idea for her to come visit just yet. While Mom hadn't actually said it was because of Dad's refusal to forgive her, Anna knew the truth. Dad didn't want her there for Rachel's birthday. Truth be told, he was probably afraid she might influence the younger children to do as she'd done and leave the Amish faith when they were old enough to make that decision.

At least Anna had mailed Rachel a card, and she hoped her sister had gotten it by now. Even so, a card and note weren't the same as being there and sharing the joy of the day with someone she loved.

She knew from Rachel's last letter that she'd been helping out the Swartleys, and she'd even asked Reuben if he'd be willing to drive her over to see Rachel at their place. But no, he'd told her this morning during breakfast that he would be working overtime again tonight and probably wouldn't be home until well after dark. Truth was, Anna didn't think Reuben had any desire to go home for a visit at all.

"Maybe it's for the best that I don't go home so soon, either," she muttered as she closed the cupboard door. After the way her father had acted the morning she'd left home, she wondered if she would ever be welcomed there again. Maybe someday she could talk Reuben into paying a visit to his folks, and then, if she could find Rachel or Mom alone at the greenhouse, she might be able to drop by and say hello. But how would she know if they were alone or if Dad was helping there, too?

Anna released a weary sigh, grabbed her lunch

box, and turned toward the door. It was time to catch the bus for work, and she didn't want to be late.

Silas paced back and forth in front of his open courting buggy. Should he or shouldn't he make this trip? Would his intentions be misrepresented? What exactly were his intentions, anyway? He'd spent the last week trying to sort out his feelings for Rachel, yet he felt more confused now than ever.

Guess what I should have been doing was praying about all this, not trying to think it through by myself. Silas knew he'd been negligent in reading the Bible lately, and his only prayers had been the silent ones said before each meal.

I won't allow myself to move away from You, Lord. He thought about Reuben and Anna and wondered if they went to church anywhere or if they had fallen away from God when they'd left home. He was reminded that up until six months ago, he and Reuben had been friends. He knew from what Reuben's folks had told him that it had been a real disappointment when they'd discovered that Reuben had gone "fancy."

Then there was Anna. Beautiful, spirited, stubborn Anna. Silas had been in love with her since the first grade, when they'd started attending school at the one-room schoolhouse down the road. In his mind's eye, he could still see the back of her cute little head. He'd sat at the desk behind her for all of the eight years they'd gone to school. Anna, with her dazzling green eyes and hair the color of ripe peaches. She'd stolen his heart when he was six years old, and she'd broken it in two soon after he'd turned twenty-three. Would he ever be free of the pain? Would the image of her lovely face be forever etched in his mind? Could he learn to trust another woman?

"It does no good to pine for what you can't have," a voice in his head seemed to say. *"Get on with your life and follow Me."*

Silas moved to the front of the buggy, where his faithful horse patiently waited. He leaned against the gelding's side and stroked his silky ears. "What do you say, old boy? Do we take a little ride, or do we stay home?"

The horse whinnied loudly, and Silas smiled. "All right then. Let's be on our way."

Rachel had just put the CLOSED sign in the window and was about to turn down the lights, when she heard a horse and buggy pull up in front of the greenhouse. Pauline had gone home fifteen minutes ago, and Rachel was anxious to head home herself. She released a sigh. "Guess I can handle one more customer yet."

She opened the front door, and her mouth dropped open when she saw Silas standing on the porch, holding a paper bag in one hand and a bouquet of orange and yellow chrysanthemums in the other.

"Well, well," she said with a giggle. "It isn't every day that someone shows up at the greenhouse carrying a bunch of flowers."

Silas chuckled. "Guess that's true enough. Most folks leave here with flowers, but it isn't likely they'd be bringing 'em in."

Rachel stepped aside to allow Silas entrance. "So what brings you here at closing time?"

He cleared his throat loudly, then handed her the flowers and paper sack. "Just wanted to give you these. Happy birthday, Rachel."

Rachel felt as though all the breath had been squeezed clean out of her lungs. This was such a surprise. Never in a million years had she expected a gift from Silas, especially since he'd been so distant all week. "Danki," she murmured. "How did you know that today was my birthday?"

"You said something about it when we went fishing last Sunday."

Rachel placed the flowers on the counter and opened the paper sack. When she looked inside, she let out a little squeal. "Binoculars and a bird-watching book! Oh, Silas, this is my best birthday present!" The truth was, it was her only present, but she wasn't about to tell him that. It was bad enough that her whole family had forgotten her special day; she sure didn't want to talk about it.

"I was hoping you might like it." Silas took a few steps closer to Rachel. "Now, whenever you see some unusual bird, you can look it up in the book and find out all about its habits and whatnot."

Rachel withdrew the binoculars. "These will sure come in handy."

Silas nodded. "I often put my binoculars to good use."

Rachel swallowed hard. Why was Silas looking at her so funny? Did that gentle expression in his dark eyes and the agreeable smile on his clean-shaven face mean anything more than just friendship? She couldn't come right out and ask, but she needed to know if she dared to hope.

As if he sensed her dilemma, Silas reached out and took Rachel's hand. "I enjoyed our time of fishing and looking at birds the other day. If the weather holds out, maybe we can find the time to do it again."

Rachel flicked her tongue back and forth across her lower lip. The sensation of Silas's touch did funny things to her insides. "I–I'd like that. I had a good time last week, too."

Silas let go of her hand, then turned and moved back across the room. "Guess I should be getting on home. Mom's probably got supper ready."

Rachel followed him to the door. "I need to go up to the house and see about fixing our supper, as well. My folks went to town this morning, and they still aren't back yet, so I'd better be sure there's something ready to eat when they do get home."

When Silas got to the door, he turned and said, "I hear tell there's gonna be a young people's get-together over at Harold Landis's place two weeks from tomorrow. Do you think you might go?"

"Maybe." Rachel shrugged. "If I can get Joseph to take me."

He grinned. "From what I hear, your big brother's got a pretty good reason to bring his courting buggy these days. My guess is he'll be there early."

Rachel nodded. "You're probably right."

Silas opened the door. "Well, see you at preaching tomorrow." He bounded off the porch and climbed into his buggy before Rachel could say anything more.

She smiled to herself. "Guess this wasn't such a bad birthday after all."

A short time later as Rachel stepped out the greenhouse door, holding the bouquet of flowers and paper sack with the birthday presents from Silas, she decided to walk up the driveway and check the mailbox before she headed to the house to start supper. Since the folks had left early this morning and obviously weren't back yet, she figured any mail they may have gotten would still be in the box.

Maybe I'll get a card or two. It would be nice to know that someone else had remembered today's my birthday.

When Rachel reached into the mailbox a few minutes later, she was pleased to discover a card from Anna, along with a note. She placed the flowers on top of the mailbox and set the sack on the ground as she hurriedly read the note, anxious for any word from her sister.

Dear Rachel,

I hope this card reaches you in time for your birthday, and I hope your day is a special one. Reuben and I are doing fine, and we both keep busy with our jobs. Last week Reuben bought a CD player, and we have a TV now, too. I've spent most of the money I'd saved while working at the greenhouse on new clothes, as I needed something other than my plain dresses to wear now that I'm not Amish anymore.

It still feels strange not to wear my head covering, but I do wear my hair pinned up at the back of my head when I'm waiting on tables at the restaurant where I work. Reuben wants me to get my hair cut short, but I'm not sure I'm ready for that. Guess that's kind of silly, seeing as to how I used to say I'd like to have short hair.

I had wanted to be there for your birthday, but Mom's last letter said it would be best if I didn't come for a visit just yet. Besides, Reuben's been working lots of overtime lately, and even some Saturdays, so we probably couldn't have made it there on time anyhow.

I've started attending church with my friend Kathryn from work, but some Sundays, Reuben's so tired all he does is sleep, so he hasn't gone to church with me yet.

Write back when you can, and give my love to all the family.

As always,
Anna

Tears flooded Rachel's eyes, obscuring her vision. She missed Anna so much that it hurt. If only she hadn't fallen in love with Reuben and run off and gotten married. But then, if Anna hadn't fallen for Reuben, she might have ended up marrying Silas, and Rachel would have never had a chance with him.

Rachel cringed as she realized how selfish she was being. Wouldn't it be better to have her sister still living at home and being courted by Silas, than to have her living in the English world and being shunned by her family and friends? If Rachel could bring Anna home and make everything right again at home, she surely would—even if it meant giving up whatever was happening between her and Silas.

Rachel thought about Anna's comment concerning Reuben working long hours and not going to church. She hoped that didn't mean he'd fallen away from God. At least Anna was attending church. She would have to remember to pray for Anna, Reuben, and their marriage.

Rachel bent down and picked up the paper sack, then grabbed hold of the flowers. It was time to head up to the house and get busy with supper. It was time to set her pain of losing Anna aside and get on with life.

She stepped into the darkened kitchen several minutes later and had barely closed the door, when a gas lamp ignited, and a chorus of voices yelled, "Happy birthday, Rachel!"

"What in all the world?" Rachel's mouth fell open as she studied her surroundings. Mom, Dad, Joseph, Perry, and Elizabeth sat at the table, which was fully set for supper. On one end of the cupboard was a chocolate cake, and beside it sat several wrapped gifts. "Elizabeth, did you do all this?"

Elizabeth smiled. "I helped, but Mom did most of the work."

Rachel's eyebrows drew together. "How could that be? Mom and Dad have been gone all day."

Mom grinned like a cat that had chased down a fat little field mouse. "Came back early so we could surprise you."

"But I never heard your buggy come down the lane. I don't see how—"

Dad chuckled. "We used the old road coming into the back of our property."

Tears stung the backs of Rachel's eyes, and she blinked to keep them from spilling over. Her folks really did care. They hadn't forgotten it was her birthday after all.

"What's that you've got in your hands?" The question came from Perry.

"Oh, just the mail." She placed the envelopes on the counter—everything except for Anna's card, which she had stuck under the band of the backside of her apron, not wanting the folks to see it. Dad might be upset by what Anna had said about buying a TV and Reuben not going to church. Besides, since the card was Rachel's, she saw no need to share it with anyone.

"I'm not talkin' about the mail." Perry pointed to the flowers and then to the sack she held.

Rachel's face heated with embarrassment. "It's... uh... a birthday present."

"Who's it from?" Joseph questioned.

"Silas Swartley," she said, trying to keep her voice from quivering.

"Rachel's got a boyfriend! Rachel's got a boyfriend!" Elizabeth taunted.

"No, I don't. Silas is just a good friend. That ought to be clear as anything."

Joseph snickered. "Oh, sure—about as clear as mud. He's a good friend, all right. One who gives you a birthday present and takes you fishing."

Rachel turned to face her father, and her forehead wrinkled in accusation.

He shook his head. "He didn't hear it from me."

Mom shook her finger at Dad. "You knew our daughter had gone fishing with Silas and you never said a word?"

"Rachel asked me not to say anything."

Rachel looked back at Joseph. "If Dad didn't mention it, then how'd you know?"

He shrugged. "Some other folks were out at the lake, you know."

"We never talked to anyone else." Rachel shook her head. "In fact, we were the only ones on the dock."

"That may be true, but there were some boats out on the water," Joseph reminded.

"Spies, don't you mean? I think some folks need to keep their mouths shut where others are concerned."

"Now, don't go getting into a snit about this," Mom said in a soothing tone. "There was no harm done, so come sit yourself down and eat your favorite supper."

Rachel had to admit the fried chicken and mashed potatoes did look tasty. She was plenty hungry, too, so she may as well eat this special supper Mom and Elizabeth had worked so hard to prepare. She would have a serious talk with Joseph later on. Then she'd find out who the informer had been.

Rachel sat on the edge of her bed, looking over the presents she'd received earlier that day. It had been a good birthday, even if Joseph had let the cat out of the bag about her and Silas going fishing together.

Joseph had told her later that it was Amon Zook who'd spilled the beans. Apparently, he'd been fishing on the lake with his son, Ben.

She chuckled softly. "Guess you can't keep anything secret these days."

Focusing on her gifts again, Rachel studied the set of handmade pillowcases Mom had given her and insisted must go into Rachel's hope chest. Dad's gift was a new oil lamp—also a hope chest item, since she already had two perfectly good lamps in her bedroom. Joseph and Perry had gone together on a box of cream-filled chocolates, which Rachel had generously shared with the family after supper. Elizabeth had made several nice handkerchiefs, and Rachel had put those in one of her drawers.

Then there was Rachel's favorite gift of all—the binoculars and bird-identification book Silas had given her. The candy was almost gone. The handkerchiefs would be useful in the days to come. The oil lamp and pillowcases might never be used if Rachel didn't get married. Silas's gift, on the other hand, was something she would use whenever she studied birds in their yard and the surrounding area.

Rachel scooted off the bed and stepped around the cedar chest at the end of her bed, opened the lid, and slipped the pillowcases and lamp inside. She hadn't given her hope chest much thought until recently. Now that Silas was being so friendly, there might be a ray of hope for her future.

" 'But I will hope continually, and will yet praise thee more and more,' " she murmured. "Thank You, Lord, for such a wunderbaar day."

As Rachel closed the lid of the chest, she caught sight of Anna's hope chest sitting in one corner of her room. She was tempted to open it and look through its contents, but she thought better of it. It belonged to her sister, and she still didn't feel right about snooping through Anna's personal things.

She did give the hope chest to me, her inner voice reminded.

Someday if Rachel ever married, she could find a use for the things in both hers and Anna's hope chests. She would wait awhile to see what was inside. In the meantime, she planned to start adding more things to her own hope chest.

Chapter 17

Silas felt a keen sense of excitement as he prepared to go to the young people's gathering that was to be held in Harold Landis's barn. A big bonfire would be blazing, and enough eats would be set out to fill the hungriest man's stomach. Neither the singing, bonfire, nor even the food was the reason he was looking forward to going, however. Simply put, Silas had discovered that he enjoyed spending time with Rachel, and he had a hankering to see her again.

He climbed into his freshly cleaned courting buggy, and his heartbeat quickened as he picked up the reins. The more time he spent with Rachel, the more he was drawn to her. Was it merely because they had so much in common, or was something else going on? Could he possibly be falling for little Rachel Beachy, in spite of their age difference or the fact that she was the sister of his first love? Would she be willing to accept a ride home with him tonight if he asked?

He clucked to the horse to get him moving. "I'd better take my time with Rachel, hadn't I, old boy? Elsewise, there might be no exit for me."

Fifty young people milled about the Landis's barn, eating, playing games, and visiting.

Rachel and Joseph went their separate ways as soon as they arrived, she with some other woman her age, and Joseph with Pauline Hostetler. That really wasn't such a big surprise, since he'd been hanging around her so much lately.

Rachel had just finished eating a sandwich and had taken a seat on a bale of straw, planning to relax and watch the couples around her who had paired off. She was pretty sure her brother would be asking to take Pauline home tonight, and it had her kind of worried. What if he wanted to be alone with his date? What if he expected Rachel to find another way home? It would be rather embarrassing if she had to beg someone for a ride.

She scanned the many faces inside the barn, trying to decide who might be the best choice to ask, should it become necessary. Her gaze fell on Silas, talking with a group of young men near the food table. It would be too bold of her to ask him for a ride, even if they had become friends over the past few months. It was a fellow's place to invite a girl to ride home in his courting buggy, not the other way around. Besides, she hadn't seen much of Silas lately. Every day last week when she'd been at his place helping his mother, Silas had been busy with the fall harvest. They hadn't had a real conversation since a week ago Saturday, when Silas dropped by the greenhouse to give her a birthday present.

Rachel noticed Abe Landis sitting by himself, eating a huge piece of chocolate cake. Abe was the same age as Rachel, and they'd known each other a long time. She could ask him for a lift home, but there was one problem. Abe lived right here. He wouldn't be driving his horse and buggy anywhere tonight.

"Seen any interesting birds lately?"

The question took Rachel by surprise. She'd been in such a dilemma over whom to ask for a ride, she hadn't noticed that Silas stood right beside her. She glanced up and smiled. "Jah, I have."

Silas pushed another bale of straw closer to her and sat down. "You like my birthday present?"

She nodded. "A whole lot."

"Mom's getting her cast off soon. Guess you won't be coming around so much anymore." He stared down at his hands, resting on his knees.

Rachel studied him a moment before she answered. Did she detect a note of sadness in his voice when he mentioned her not coming over anymore, or was it only wishful thinking? If Silas knew how much she loved him yet didn't have feelings for her in return, the humiliation would be too great to bear. "I–I'm glad I could help out," she murmured, "but things will soon be back to normal at your house, so–"

"Rachel, would you like some hot chocolate?" Abe asked as he plunked down on the same bale of straw where Rachel sat. "I'd be glad to get some for you."

Silas's jaw clenched, and he shot Abe a look that could have stopped a runaway horse in its tracks. "Rachel and I were having a little talk, Abe. If she wants anything, I'll be happy to fetch it for her."

Rachel stirred uneasily. What was going on here? If she hadn't known better, she might have believed Silas was actually jealous of Abe. But that was ridiculous. Abe and Rachel were just friends, the same as she and Silas. Abe was only being nice by asking if she wanted some hot chocolate. Surely he wasn't interested in her in a romantic kind of way.

Abe touched Rachel's shoulder. "What do you say? Would you like me to get you something to drink or not?"

Silas jumped up quickly, nearly tripping over the bale of straw where Rachel sat. "Didn't you hear what I said? If Rachel wants anything, I'll get it for her!"

Rachel's heart thumped so hard she feared it might burst open. Why was Silas acting so upset? It made no sense at all. Unless. . .

Abe stood, too. "Don't you think that ought to be Rachel's decision?"

Silas pivoted toward Rachel. "Well? Who's gonna get the hot chocolate?"

Rachel gulped. Were they really going to force her to choose? She cleared her throat, then offered them both a smile. "Me. I'll get my own drink, danki very much." With that said, she hopped up and sprinted off toward the refreshment table.

Silas looked over at Abe and shrugged. "Looks like we two have been outsmarted."

"I think you're right about that." Abe started to move away but stopped after he'd taken a few steps. "Look, Silas, if Rachel and you are courtin', I'll back off. If not, then she's fair game, and I plan on making my move."

Silas's eyes widened. "Your move?" Heat boiled up his spine as unexpected jealousy seared through him like hot coals on the fire.

Abe nodded. "I thought I might ask her to go fishing with me sometime."

"Fishing?"

"Jah. I hear tell that Rachel likes to fish."

"Where'd you hear that?"

"Someone saw her at the lake a few weeks ago. Said she was sittin' on the dock with her fishing pole."

Silas squinted as he leveled Abe with a look he hoped would end this conversation. "That was me she was fishing with there."

"So, you two *are* courting then."

Silas clenched his fists. It wasn't in his nature to

want to hit someone, and everything about fighting went against the Amish way, but right now he struggled with the impulse to punch Abe right in the nose. What was the fellow trying to do—goad him into an argument? He'd always considered Abe to be nice enough, but up until a few moments ago, he hadn't realized Abe was interested in Rachel.

Silas was still trying to decide how best to deal with Abe when Rachel returned, carrying a mug of steaming hot chocolate and a piece of shoofly pie. She smiled sweetly at both of them, then seated herself on the bale of straw.

Silas leaned over so his face was just inches from Rachel's. Her pale blue eyes seemed to probe his innermost being, and his heart begin to hammer. With no further thought, he blurted out, "I'd like to take you home in my courting buggy tonight, Rachel. Would you be willing to go?"

She took a little sip of her drink, glanced over at Abe for a second, then back at Silas. "Jah, I'd be willing."

Now that Rachel had accepted his invitation, Silas wasn't sure how he felt about things. Had he asked merely to get under Abe's skin, or because he really wanted to escort Rachel home?

He looked over at her, sitting so sweet and innocent, and knew the answer to his troubling question. He really did want to take her home. He enjoyed her company, maybe a bit more than he cared to admit. But the truth was, Anna had hurt him badly, and part of him was afraid Rachel might do the same thing.

Silas's disconcerting thoughts were jolted away when Abe slapped him on the back. "All right, I'm satisfied then." With that, Abe walked away, leaving Silas and Rachel alone again.

"What time were you planning to head for home?" Rachel asked as Silas took a seat on the other bale of straw.

He shrugged. "Whenever you're done eating your pie and drinking your hot chocolate."

"Aren't you going to have some?"

He chuckled. "I've already had enough food tonight for three fellows my size."

Rachel finished the rest of her dessert and stood. "Guess I'd better go find Joseph and tell him I won't be riding home in his buggy."

Silas reached for her empty plate and mug. "I'll put this away while you look for him."

"Danki." She offered him a heart-melting smile. He sure hoped he hadn't made a mistake by asking to take her home. What if she jumped to the wrong conclusion and thought one buggy ride meant they were officially courting?

I didn't have to ask her, Silas's inner voice reminded. *I could have conceded to Abe.* He gritted his teeth. *Never!*

Rachel turned and walked away, but her presence stayed with him like the smell of new-mown hay. He really was looking forward to taking her home.

Joseph had been sitting on a log by the bonfire, talking with Pauline for several minutes, when Rachel showed up. He had planned to seek his sister out as soon as he'd asked Pauline if he could escort her home tonight, but she'd beat him to it. There was only one problem—he hadn't spoken to Pauline yet.

"Silas just asked if he could give me a ride home," Rachel said, bending close to Joseph's ear.

He smiled. That was a relief to hear. At least now if Pauline said yes to his invitation, he would be free to escort her home without his little sister sitting in the buggy, listening to everything they said. "No problem. No problem at all. Have a good time, and I'll see you at home."

"Are you taking anyone home tonight?" she whispered.

His face warmed, and he knew it wasn't from the heat of the fire. "Don't know yet. Maybe so."

She smiled and nudged his arm. "Okay. See you at home then."

As soon as Rachel walked away, Joseph turned to Pauline. "Say, I was wondering if. . ."

"What were you wondering, Joe?"

He moistened his lips and swallowed a couple of times. "Would you be willing to let me escort you home tonight?"

Pauline smiled at Joseph so sweetly that he

thought he might turn into butter. "Jah, Joe, I'd be glad to ride home in your courting buggy."

He grinned. "Great. That's just real great."

Chapter 18

A sense of exhilaration shot through Rachel as she sat in Silas's open buggy with the crisp wind whipping against her face. She chanced a peek at her escort, hoping that he, too, was enjoying the ride.

Silas grinned back at her. "I think I smell winter in the air. Won't be too awfully long and we can take out the sleigh."

We? Does he mean me and him going for a sleigh ride? Rachel closed her eyes and tried to picture herself snuggled beneath a warm quilt, snow falling in huge, white flakes, and the sound of sleigh bells jingling in the chilly air.

"What are you thinking about?" Silas asked, breaking into her musings.

Rachel's eyes snapped open. "Oh, winter. . .sleigh bells. . . snow."

He chuckled. "Don't forget hot apple cider and pumpkin bread. Nothin' tastes better after a sleigh ride than a big mug of cider and several thick hunks of my mamm's spicy pumpkin bread."

"My favorite winter snack is popcorn, apple slices, and hot chocolate with plenty of marshmallows."

"I like those things, too. Guess there isn't much in the way of food I don't like." Reaching into his jacket pocket, Silas withdrew a chunk of black licorice. "Want some?"

"No thanks." Rachel studied him as he chewed the candy. In spite of Silas's hearty appetite, there wasn't an ounce of fat on him that she could see. He appeared to be all muscle—no doubt from doing so many farm chores. *I would love him no matter how he looked.* It wasn't hard to picture herself and Silas sitting on the front porch of their own home, looking through binoculars and talking about all the birds nesting in their backyard trees.

She shook her head, hoping to bring some sense of reason into her thinking. Silas was only a friend, and he'd offered her a ride home from the gathering. That didn't mean he had thoughts of romance or marriage on his mind. She couldn't allow herself to fantasize about it, even if she did want more than friendship. She loved Silas so much, and each moment they spent together only made her more sure of it. She didn't want to feel this way; it wasn't safe for her heart. But no matter how hard Rachel tried, she couldn't stop herself from hoping that Silas might someday declare his love for her.

As they pulled into Rachel's yard, she released a

sigh, wishing the ride didn't have to end so soon. If only they could keep on going. If only Silas would ask if he could court her.

He stopped the horse near the barn and turned in his seat to face Rachel. "Danki for letting me bring you home tonight. I enjoyed the ride a whole lot more than if I'd been alone."

"Me, too," she freely admitted.

"You're a special girl, Rachel. I can see why Abe would be interested in you."

"Really?" Rachel's breath caught in her throat, and her cheeks burned with embarrassment. The admiration in Silas's voice had sounded so genuine.

"Jah, I mean it." His gaze dropped to her lips.

For one heart-stopping moment, Rachel had the crazy idea of throwing herself into his arms and begging him to love her. She knew better than to let her emotions run wild, and she had too much pride to throw herself at him.

"Sure you don't want some licorice?" Silas asked, giving her a crooked grin.

All she could do was shake her head, her thoughts were so lost in the darkness of his ebony eyes, where the moonlight reflected like a pool of water.

Rachel's heart pulsated when Silas slipped his arms around her waist and pulled her close to his chest. She tipped her head back and savored the sweet smell of licorice as his lips met hers in a kiss so pleasing it almost lifted her right off the buggy seat.

This was her first real kiss, and she could only hope her inexperience wasn't evident as she kissed him back with all the emotion welling within her soul.

Suddenly, Silas pulled away, looking shaken and confused. "Rachel, I'm so sorry. Don't know what came over me. I sure didn't mean to—"

Rachel held up her hand, feeling as though a glass of cold water had been dashed in her face. "Please, don't say anything more." She hopped down from the buggy and sprinted toward the house as the ache of humiliation bore down on her like a heavy blanket of snow. She wasn't sure why Silas had kissed her, but one thing was certain—he was sorry he had.

All the way home Silas berated himself. Why had he kissed Rachel like that? She must think he was off in the head to be doing something so brazen on their first buggy ride.

As Silas thought more about it, he realized as much as he'd enjoyed the kiss, it hadn't been fair to lead Rachel on like that. She might think because he took her home, then went so far as to kiss her, it meant they were a couple and would be courting from now on.

Was that what it had meant? Did he want to court Rachel? Was he feeling more than friendship for her, or did he only want to be with her because she reminded him of Anna?

Silas slapped the side of his head. "What am I thinking? Rachel's nothing like her older sister. Nothing at all. Guess I'd better commit the whole thing to prayer, because I sure enough wasn't expecting this to happen tonight, and I definitely don't have any answers of my own."

"Sure is a nice night," Pauline said, as Joseph directed his horse and open buggy down the road toward her home.

He nodded. "Jah, sure is." *Especially since you're sitting here beside me–that makes it an extra-special night.*

She looked over at him and smiled, and his heart skipped a beat. "You have a nice buggy, Joe." Her hand slid over the leather seat. "It's obvious that you take real good care of it."

"Danki. I try to keep it up to snuff."

They rode in silence for a time, with the only sounds being the steady *clippity-clop* of the horse's hooves and an occasional nicker. But Joseph didn't mind the quiet. It felt nice to ride along with his *aldi* beside him. At least he hoped Pauline was his girlfriend now.

"What's your family hear from Anna these days?" she asked, breaking into his thoughts. "Is she getting along okay out there in the English world?"

Joseph jerked his head at the mention of Anna's name.

"Did you hear what I said, Joe?"

"Jah, I heard. Just thinkin' is all."

"About Anna?"

He gave a quick nod in reply. He didn't want to spoil the evening by talking about his willful sister. He just wanted to concentrate on having a good time with Pauline. Was that too much to ask?

"Is Anna doing all right?"

He shrugged. "Mom and Rachel have both had letters from her, and from what they said, I guess she's doing okay."

"Mind if I ask how you feel about her leaving?"

"Guess what I feel is a mixture of sadness and anger at her for bringing a shunning on herself, not to mention the hurt she's caused our folks." He grimaced. "Mom doesn't talk about it much, but you can see the look of sadness on her face whenever Anna's name is mentioned."

"That's understandable."

"And Dad–well, he's just plain angry with Anna for running off the way she did, and if he weren't Amish and not given to violence, I'll bet he'd seek Reuben out and punch him right in the *naas*." Joseph's grip tightened on the reins, and a muscle in his cheek quivered.

"Are you angry with Anna and Reuben, too?" Pauline spoke quietly, but her pointed question cut Joseph to the quick.

He nodded. "Jah."

Pauline touched his arm again, only this time her fingers moved up and down in a soothing gesture. "You might not agree with Anna's reasons for leaving the Amish faith, but it was her choice, and the Bible says we must learn to forgive."

"It's not always so easy to forgive when so many people have been hurt."

She nodded. "I know that better than anyone. I was terribly hurt when Eli jilted me and married Laura. I felt that she was an Englisher who didn't belong with our people."

Joseph made no comment, waiting to see if she would say anything more.

"While I was living with my aunt and uncle in Ohio, I came to realize I had to forgive both Laura and Eli. Carrying around all that anger and bitterness was keeping me separated from God." Pauline smiled. "When I released the anger and confessed to God that I'd sinned, I was finally able to forgive those I thought had trespassed against me."

"I know you're right about me needing to forgive Anna, but seeing how Mom, Rachel, and the rest of the family have been affected by all this makes it that much harder."

"Maybe you need to ask yourself how you'd feel if you were in Anna's place."

"What do you mean?"

"If you'd fallen in love with someone the way Anna did Reuben, and then that someone had decided to leave the faith, what would you have done?"

Joseph stared straight ahead as he kept the

horse going steady and contemplated her question. If Pauline had proclaimed her love for him and then said she wanted to leave the Amish faith for the modern, English life, he guessed he probably would go with her. He loved her that much.

He released one hand from the reins and reached over to take hold of Pauline's hand. "Well– if it was someone I truly loved, then I guess I would have gone English, too."

She smiled and squeezed his fingers. Did she know what he was thinking? Did she know how much he cared?

Chapter 19

For the next two weeks, Rachel continued to help out at the Swartleys' as often as she could, and for the next two weeks, she did everything possible to avoid Silas. It made her sick to her stomach to think that he had actually kissed her and then felt sorry about it. She really must be a fool if she thought she had any chance of winning his heart. After that embarrassing episode, she was sure he would never ask her to go fishing again, and he certainly wouldn't invite her to take another ride in his courting buggy.

Silas had tried talking with Rachel on several occasions, but she kept putting him off, saying she was too busy helping his mother. Rachel knew her time of avoidance was almost over, for today's preaching service was being held at their home and was about to begin. She was sure Silas and his family would be here soon.

The three-hour service seemed to last longer than usual, and Rachel squirmed on her bench, trying to focus on the songs, sermons, and prayers. Maybe her discomfort was because she had a view of the bench where Silas sat across the room. Beyond the flicker of a smile, she had no idea what he was thinking. Was it the kiss they had shared two weeks ago? Was he waiting for church to be over so he could corner Rachel and tell her he didn't want to see her anymore? If she kept busy in the kitchen, maybe she could avoid him again today. That's what she planned to do. . .stay busy and away from Silas.

Things went well for a while, but tables had been set up out in the barn for eating, and shortly after the noon meal was served, Rachel went back to the house. She planned to get another pot of coffee for the menfolk and carry out one of the pies she and Mom had baked the day before.

Much to Rachel's surprise, she discovered Silas in the kitchen, leaning against the counter with his arms folded. "I was hoping you'd come in here," he said, taking a few steps in her direction.

She moved quickly toward the stove and grabbed the pot of coffee.

"How about going for a walk with me, so we can talk?" he asked, following her across the room.

Rachel averted his gaze and headed for the door, forgetting about the apple pie she had planned to take back to the barn. "As you can probably see, I'm kind of busy right now."

"You won't be helping serve all day. How about after you're done?"

"I don't think we have anything to talk about, Silas."

He stepped in front of her, blocking the door. "Please, Rachel. . .just for a few minutes. I've wanted to talk to you for the last two weeks, but there never seemed to be a good time." He smiled. "Besides, I had some stuff to pray about."

Rachel nodded slowly. "Jah, me, too."

"So can we meet out by the willow tree, say, in one hour?"

She shrugged. "Okay."

At the appointed time, Rachel donned a heavy sweater and stepped onto the front porch. The afternoon air had cooled considerably, and a chill shivered through her. She caught sight of Silas out in the yard, talking to his cousin Rudy. She started across the lawn but stopped just before she reached the weeping willow tree. Silas was saying something to Rudy, and her ears perked up. Rachel was sure he had mentioned her sister's name, but she wondered why Silas would be talking to his cousin about Anna.

A group of children ran past, laughing and hollering so loud she couldn't make out what either Silas or Rudy was saying.

David Yoder, a little boy with Down syndrome, waved to Rachel, and she waved back, hoping he wouldn't call out her name. The last thing she needed was for Silas to catch her listening in on his conversation.

The children finally wandered off, and Rachel breathed a sigh of relief. She leaned heavily against the trunk of a tree and turned her attention back to Silas and his cousin.

"So you're really in love with her, huh?" she heard Rudy ask.

"Afraid so," Silas answered. "Don't rightly think I'll ever find anyone else I could love as much, and it's tearing me apart."

Rachel's heart slammed into her chest. Even after all these months, Silas still wasn't over Anna. *That's probably why he said he was sorry for kissing me. Most likely, he was wishing it had been Anna and not me in his courting buggy.*

Tears burned the backs of Rachel's eyes. She should have known better than to allow her emotions to get carried away. Silas cared nothing about her, and apparently he never had. He still loved Anna and probably always would, even though she was married and had left the Amish faith. She knew many people carried a torch for lost loves, and because of their pain, they never found love again. Mom had told her once that it almost happened to Rachel's great-aunt Mim. She was jilted by her first love, and for many years she carried a torch for him. Finally, she set her feelings aside and learned to love again. But that was only because she had allowed the Lord to work on her bitter spirit. Rachel wasn't so sure Silas wanted to find love again—especially not with her.

Tired of trying to analyze things, Rachel spun around. She was about to head back to the house, when she felt someone's hand touch her shoulder. "Where are you heading? I thought we were going for a walk."

Rachel shrugged Silas's hand away. "I heard you talking to Rudy. If you're still pining for Anna, then why bother taking a walk with a little kinner like me?"

Rudy, who was walking next to Silas, raised his eyebrows and moved away, but Silas kept pace beside Rachel. When she didn't slow down, he grabbed hold of her hand and pulled her to his side. "We need to talk."

Like a tightly coiled spring, Rachel released her fury on him. "Let go of me!" Her eyes burned like fire, and she almost choked on the huge knot that had lodged in her throat.

"Was is letz do?"

"Nothing's wrong here. I guess everything's just as it should be—or at least the way I figured it was."

Silas opened his mouth as if to say something more, but Rachel darted away without a backward glance. She had been a fool to think she could make Silas forget about Anna and fall in love with her. She'd been stupid to get caught up in a dumb thing like this. . .letting herself hope for the impossible. The one thing she had enjoyed most about her friendship with Silas was how comfortable they seemed with each other. Not anymore, though. That had ended when she'd heard him tell Rudy that he was still in love with Anna. If Silas wanted to pine his life away for a love he would never have, then that was *his* problem. Rachel planned to get on with her life, one way or another.

Silas groaned as he watched Rachel race up the steps and disappear into her house. One of the Beachys' dogs howled, and the mournful sound echoed in his soul. Rachel had heard something he'd told Rudy, but she'd refused to let him explain. Now everything was ruined between them, and it was a bitter pill to swallow. He was sure there was no chance of a relationship with Rachel, because she obviously didn't trust him. Maybe with good reason, too.

Truth of the matter, Silas hadn't been so good at trusting lately, either. He'd said he never wanted to move away from God, but he felt himself slipping away and knew if he didn't do something soon, he might sink into despair.

He moved slowly toward his horse and buggy, kicking at every stone in his path. No point in hanging around here anymore. Maybe he should accept things as they were and just get on with his life.

"Jah, that's what I'll do," he mumbled as he gave

one more rock a hefty kick with the toe of his boot. "I'll forget I had ever considered courting Rachel Beachy!"

"Are you about ready for bed?"

Rebekah turned her wheelchair away from the fireplace and smiled at Daniel. "Soon. Just thought I'd stay up awhile longer and try to get some more mending done."

He moved across the room to stand by her chair. "Are you sure you're not looking for some excuse to wait up for our two oldest kinner?"

"Anna's the oldest," she reminded.

Daniel grunted. "I think it's better if we don't mention her name."

Tears gathered in Rebekah's eyes, and she was powerless to keep them from spilling over. "Why must you be so unforgiving?"

"I'm only thinking of what's best for everyone concerned."

"Everyone concerned?" Her voice rose a notch. "How can you say it's best that we don't talk about our own flesh-and-blood daughter—that we won't welcome her home for a visit?"

Daniel crouched on his haunches and extended his hands toward the fire. "It's gettin' awful chilly at night now. Won't be long until the snow flies."

Rebekah released an exasperated groan. "Changing the subject won't alter the fact that I don't agree with you on something, husband."

He shrugged.

"Neither will giving me the silent treatment."

"I'm not doing that, Rebekah. I just don't want to talk about our wayward daughter tonight."

"When can we talk about her?"

He shrugged again.

"Anna may have gone English, and she may be under the ban, but she's still our daughter, Daniel."

"Don't ya think I know that?" He sat a moment longer, then stood and reached for her hand. "Sorry for snapping. It just upsets me to think that she would join the church and make us think she and Silas had been courting and then sneak off and get married to Reuben Yutzy by a justice of the peace. Reuben's the one with the hankering for modern things; I'm sure of it."

"That may be, but Anna did marry him and agree to go English."

"That's what troubles me so." He rose to his feet. "Guess I must have failed as her daed somehow."

Rebekah shook her head. "You didn't fail, Daniel, and neither did I. We've raised our kinner the best we can, so we mustn't cast any blame on ourselves for the decisions they choose to make." She paused a moment to gauge his reaction, but Daniel just stood shifting his weight from one foot to the other.

"It's not our place to judge," she added. "Only God has that right, you know."

He bent to kiss her forehead. "I'm heading to bed now. Don't be too long, okay?"

She nodded and released a sigh. If Daniel didn't want to talk about this, there wasn't much she could do except pray. She had been doing a lot of that since Anna left home, and she would continue to do so until her prayers were answered.

Chapter 20

Rachel felt a sense of relief when Katie Swartley's cast finally came off and she was able to stay home, even if it did mean spending more time helping Pauline in the greenhouse. Anything would be better than facing Silas every day. Knowing he was still in love with Anna and unable to quit loving him herself, Rachel felt a sense of hopelessness like never before. Everything looked different–the trees weren't as green, the birdsong wasn't as bright. She had nothing to praise God for anymore, and her times of prayer and Bible study happened less often.

That night, the young people were gathering at the Hostetlers' place. Joseph had already made it clear that he was going, and it was obvious that he and Pauline were officially courting. Even though Rachel was happy for them, she couldn't help feeling sorry for herself.

"Are you going to the singing?" her brother asked, as they met in the barn that morning before church.

She shook her head. "I don't think so."

"Why not? It could be the last one for a while, what with the weather turning colder."

She shrugged. "I'd planned to work on my hope chest tonight."

Joseph took hold of her arm as she started to walk away. "It's Silas Swartley, isn't it? You haven't been acting right for the last few weeks, and I have a hunch it's got something to do with your feelings for him."

Rachel felt a familiar burning at the backs of her eyes, and she blinked rapidly, hoping to keep the tears from falling. "I'd rather not talk about Silas, if you don't mind." She shrugged Joseph's hand away. "I need to feed the kittens, and if I'm not mistaken, you've got a few things to do before we leave for church."

Joseph moved into the horse's stall without another word, and Rachel released a sigh of relief. She and Joseph might not always see eye-to-eye, but at least he cared enough about her feelings to drop the subject of Silas.

As Rachel rounded the corner of the barn, she noticed Dad down on his knees beside the woodpile. His face was screwed up in obvious pain, and the deep moan he emitted confirmed that fact. Rachel rushed to his side and squatted beside him. "What's wrong? You look like you're hurting real bad."

"I strained my back trying to lift a hunk of wood for your mamm's cooking stove. Must have bent over wrong." He groaned. "Don't think I can get up on my own, Rachel. Can you go get Joseph?"

Rachel patted her father's shoulder. "Jah, sure. Just hang on a few more minutes and try to relax." She jumped up and bolted for the barn.

Joseph was busy getting one of their buggy horses ready, when Rachel rushed back into the barn with a worried expression. "You'd better come, Joseph. *Schnell*–quickly. Dad's in need of your help."

His eyebrows lifted in question. "I'm busy with the horse, Rachel. Can't Dad get Perry to do whatever needs to be done?"

Rachel clutched his arm as he was about to lead the horse out of its stall. "Dad's hurt his back and can't even stand up. Perry isn't strong enough to get him on his feet, much less help him into the house."

Realizing the seriousness of the situation, Joseph closed the stall door, leaving the horse inside. "Where is he?"

"Out by the woodpile."

Rachel raced from the barn, and Joseph was right behind her. They found Dad down on his knees, his forehead dripping with sweat.

Joseph grabbed Dad under one arm, and Rachel took hold of the other. "On the count of three," Joseph instructed. "One. . .two. . .three!"

Dad moaned loudly when they pulled him to his feet. Walking slightly bent over, he allowed them to support most of his weight as they made their way slowly to the house.

They found Mom sitting in her wheelchair at the kitchen table, drinking a cup of tea. Elizabeth and Perry sat across from her, finishing their bowls of oatmeal.

"Ach, my!" Mom cried. "What's wrong, Daniel? It appears you can barely walk."

Dad grunted and placed his hands on the edge of the counter for support. "My fool back went out on me, Rebekah. Happened when I was getting more wood." He swallowed hard, like he was having a difficult time talking. "Guess I'll have to make a trip to town tomorrow and see Doc Landers for some poppin' and crackin'. He'll have me back on my feet in no time."

Joseph glanced over at Rachel, and she gave him a knowing look. The last time Dad's back went out, it took more than a few days' rest or a couple of treatments with the chiropractor to get him back on his feet. There was no doubt about it: Dad wouldn't be going to church this morning, and more than likely, he'd be flat on his back in bed for the next couple of weeks. That meant more work for Joseph and probably less time for him to spend courting Pauline.

That evening when Silas arrived at the singing, he looked around, hoping to see Rachel. She'd seemed so distant lately—nothing like the fun-loving Rachel he'd gone fishing with a few weeks ago. Maybe he'd have a chance to clear things up with her. Even if he had no possible chance at a future with Rachel, he would still like to be her friend. He remembered how much fun they'd had fishing and studying birds, and his heart skipped a beat at the thought of their kiss.

Silas caught sight of Joseph sitting on one side of the Hostetlers' barn, sharing a bale of straw with Pauline. He hurried over and squatted down beside them. "Did Rachel come with you tonight? I haven't seen any sign of her."

Joseph shook his head. "She stayed home. Said something about working on her hope chest."

"Hmm. . ."

"Besides, our daed hurt his back this morning, and Rachel figured Mom would be needing her help to wait on him."

Silas's forehead wrinkled. "Sorry to hear that. No wonder I didn't see him at church today."

"Jah, and he had to go straight to bed after it happened."

"Will he be able to help you finish the harvest or do any chores at all?"

"I doubt it; he's in a lot of pain—could barely get into bed." Joseph frowned. "Guess that means Perry might have to miss a few days of school so he can give me a hand with some of the chores. I'll be busy helping our Amish neighbors who come to help with the harvesting, and I sure can't do that plus all the other jobs needing to be done."

"No, I guess not." Silas thought he should say more, but Joseph had turned his attention to Pauline, so Silas let his thoughts shift back to Rachel.

Wonder why she would be working on her hope chest? After the way she acted the other night, it was fairly obvious she was done with me. Sure as anything, Rachel isn't stocking her hope chest with the idea of marrying me.

Suddenly, a light seemed to dawn. Maybe Rachel and Abe Landis were more serious about each other than he'd realized. Silas released a groan as he stood. Maybe it was for the best. Rachel might be better off with Abe. They were closer in age, and Abe probably hadn't said or done anything to make Rachel mistrust him.

After Rachel had finished helping Mom and Elizabeth clear the table and wash the supper dishes, she excused herself to go to her room.

"You're not sleepy already, are you?" Mom rolled her wheelchair across the kitchen to where Rachel stood by the hallway door. "Since your daed's in bed and Perry's in his room reading to him, I thought maybe we three women could work on a puzzle or play a game."

Elizabeth jumped up and down. "That sounds like fun. Let's make a big batch of popcorn, too!"

Rachel felt bad about throwing cold water on their plans, but she had work to do upstairs. Besides, she wasn't fit company for anyone right now. "Maybe some other time. I'd planned to work on my hope chest tonight."

Mom's eyes seemed to brighten. "I'm glad to hear that, Rachel. I was beginning to wonder if you were ever going to take an interest in marriage or that hope chest your daed made for your sixteenth birthday."

I've got an interest, all right. Trouble is, the man I want is in love with my married sister. Rachel sure couldn't tell Mom what she was thinking. She knew that even though her mother rarely spoke of Anna anymore, she still missed her and was terribly hurt by Anna's decision to go "fancy." There was no point in bringing up a sore subject, so Rachel smiled and said, "See you two in the morning."

As soon as Rachel got to her room, she knelt on the floor in front of her hope chest. The last time she had opened it, she'd been filled with such high hopes. Back then, she and Silas seemed to be getting closer, and she'd even allowed herself to believe he might be falling in love with her. For a brief time, she'd been praising God and remaining hopeful. But her hopeful dream had been dented when Silas said he was sorry for kissing her, and it had been smashed to smithereens when she'd overheard him telling his cousin that he still loved Anna. "What's the use in having a hope chest if you aren't planning to get married?" she mumbled. "I could never marry anyone but Silas, because he's the only man I'll ever love."

Rachel lifted the lid and studied the contents of her hope chest. There was the lamp Dad had given her, along with the pillowcases Mom had made. She had purchased a few new items, as well—a set of dishes, some towels, and a tablecloth. She'd also made a braided throw rug, some pot holders, and had even been thinking about starting a quilt with the double-ring pattern. There was no point in making one now. The best thing to do was either sell off or give away most of the things in her hope chest. She pulled out the set of pillowcases and the braided throw rug, knowing she could use them in her room. The other things she put in a cardboard box, planning to take them to the greenhouse the following day.

Since Christmas wasn't far off, she was fairly certain she could sell some things to their customers. Anything that didn't sell she would take to Thomas Benner, the owner of the variety store in Paradise, and see if he might put them out on consignment. Maybe she would use the money she made to buy a concrete birdbath for Mom's flower garden. If she got enough from the sales, she might also buy several bird feeders from Eli Yoder, which would bring even more birds into their yard. At least she could still take some pleasure in bird-watching—even though it would have to be without Silas.

Rachel's only concern was what her mother would think when she saw all the things for sale in the greenhouse. Mom had seemed so hopeful about Rachel adding items to her hope chest. If she knew what was really going on, she would probably get all nervous, thinking she'd have to wait until Elizabeth grew up before she could plan a wedding. Of course, if things kept on the way they were with Joseph and Pauline, Mom could be in on their wedding plans.

Rachel closed the empty chest, and in so doing, she spotted Anna's hope chest. All these months it had been sitting in the corner of her room, and never once had she opened it. It was all she had left of her sister. If she opened it now, memories of Anna and reminders of how much she missed her older sister would probably make her cry.

Rachel moved over to Anna's hope chest and knelt beside it. She ran her fingers along the top of the chest as tears slipped from her eyes and rolled down her cheeks. "Oh, Anna, wasn't it bad enough that you broke Silas's heart by marrying Reuben? Did you have to move away and go English on us?" Rachel nearly choked on a sob as she turned away from Anna's hope chest, feeling as if a heavy weight rested on her shoulders. Would she ever see Anna again?

As Anna prepared for bed, her thoughts went to home. Several weeks had passed since she'd received a letter from Mom or Rachel, and it made her wonder if something might be wrong. Could Dad have found out they'd been writing to her? Maybe they'd been too busy working in the greenhouse to write anything lately.

She sighed as she stared at her reflection in the mirror. She not only wore different clothes, but she'd cut her hair a few weeks ago, and that made her look so much different. "I wonder if anyone in my family would recognize me now," she murmured.

"I recognize you," Reuben said, as he stepped up behind her and wrapped his arms around her waist.

She leaned her head against his broad chest and smiled. "I would hope so."

He nuzzled her neck with his cold nose.

"Do you ever miss your folks?" Anna asked.

"Jah, sure, but now I've got you, and you're my family."

"How come you don't go home and visit them?"

"I will when I feel the time is right."

She turned to face him. "You're not being faced with a shunning the way I am, so you can go back anytime you want, and nothing much will have changed."

He shook his head. "That's not so."

"What do you mean?"

"I haven't said anything about this before because I didn't want to upset you, but I ran into my brother Mose the other day, and he said Mom and Dad are still pretty peeved at me for leavin' the way I did. They think it's a sin and a shame that I didn't join the church, and Mom told Mose that I deserve to be shunned, regardless of whether I'd joined the church or not."

"Maybe in time your folks will come to understand." Anna swallowed past the lump in her throat. "I'd like to visit my folks soon, but I'm waiting to hear from Mom again so I know when's a good time to go and whether Dad will allow me to come or not."

Reuben frowned. "A shunning in our district doesn't mean your family can't speak to you. They just aren't supposed–"

She put her fingers against his lips. "Can we talk about something else? This conversation is making me feel depressed."

He leaned over and kissed the tip of her nose. "How about we don't talk at all and just go to sleep? I'm pretty tired, and tomorrow my boss has scheduled us to begin a paint job on a big grocery store, so I really should try to get a good night's sleep."

"You're right; I need to be up early for my job, too." Anna flicked the light switch on the wall and crawled into bed. Maybe in the morning before she left for work, she would write Rachel and Mom both a letter and see what was up.

Chapter 21

Silas tossed and turned most of the night, punching his pillow, thinking about Rachel, and asking God to pave the way for them to be together. He had to see Rachel again and try to explain things. Even if she never wanted him to court her, he needed to clear the air and make her understand the way he felt. If only they could spend more time together. As he finally drifted off to sleep, visions of Rachel's sweet face and her two little dimples filled his senses. If only they could be together. If only. . .

When Silas awoke the next morning, he'd come up with a plan. Rachel had been kind enough to help out at their place when his mother had broken her arm, so now he could return the favor. If he helped Joseph in the fields most of the day, mealtimes would be spent in the Beachys' kitchen. It would be a good opportunity to see Rachel and maybe get in a word with her. Since Rachel's dad was laid up right now, he was sure his help would be most welcome. He would speak to his dad about the idea, and if Pap had no objections, then Silas would head on over to the Beachys' place right after breakfast and volunteer his services.

Rachel had just finished washing and drying the breakfast dishes when she heard a horse and buggy pull into the yard. She peeked out the kitchen window and gulped when she saw who it was. Silas had climbed out of his buggy and was heading toward the house.

Joseph and Perry were in the fields, Elizabeth was at school, and Dad and Mom had gone into town to see Doc Landers. That left Rachel alone at the house. Silas had obviously seen her through the window, because he waved. Rachel sighed. She had no choice but to open the door.

"Guder mariye," Silas said when Rachel answered his knock. "I missed you at the singing last night."

"I had other things to do."

"So I heard." Silas's forehead wrinkled. "I also heard your daed hurt his back."

Rachel nodded. "It goes out on him now and then. He's at the chiropractor's right now." She had no plans to invite Silas inside, so she stepped through the doorway and joined him on the porch, hoping he would take the hint and be on his way.

"I came to help Joseph in the fields. He said your daed won't be up to it now, and since we're all done harvesting over at our place, I figured I'd offer my services here."

Rachel breathed deeply and noticed the stinging sensation of the freshly mown hay hovering over their farm. She flicked an imaginary piece of lint off the sleeve of her dress and tried to avoid his steady gaze. "It's nice of you to offer," she murmured. "Perry stayed home from school to help Joseph today, but it won't be good if he misses too many days."

"That's what I thought." Silas shifted from one foot to the other. "I. . .uh. . .was kind of hoping you and I could have a little talk before I head out to the fields."

"I've got to get to the greenhouse and open up."

"I thought Pauline worked there now. Or did she find herself some other job?"

"She still helps us some because Mom's not up to working full time anymore. But Pauline has chores at her house to do every morning, so she usually doesn't get here until ten or after."

Silas cleared his throat. "Okay, I'll let you get to it then." He pivoted and started down the steps, but when he got to the bottom, he halted and turned back around. "Maybe later we can talk?"

She raised her gaze to meet his and slowly nodded. "Jah, maybe."

Silas noticed tears clinging like dewdrops to Rachel's long, pale lashes, and it was all he could do to keep from pulling her into his arms. Before their misunderstanding, he'd been drawing closer to Rachel, and some of his old fears had been sliding into a locked trunk of unwanted memories. Now he wondered why they had drifted apart and if he could do anything to bring them close again. Maybe the real issue was trust. Did she trust him? Did he trust her? Were either of them trusting God as they should?

A deep sense of longing inched its way into Silas's soul as he continued to stare at Rachel. He had missed seeing her every day, and if the look on her sweet face was any indication of the way she felt, then he was fairly certain she had been missing him, too. Still, she seemed bent on keeping her distance, and he thought it best if he didn't push. At least not now.

"See you later, then." Silas offered Rachel what he hoped was a pleasant smile, then waved and headed off in the direction of the fields.

Rachel entered the greenhouse a short time later, carrying her box of hope-chest items as confusion swirled around in her brain like a windmill flapping against a strong breeze. It was kind of Silas to offer his help, but how would she handle him coming over every day? She had tried so hard to get Silas out of her mind, and him wanting to talk had her concerned. Was he planning to tell her again how sorry he was for that unexpected kiss he gave her a few weeks ago? Did he want to explain why he still loved Anna, even though they could never be together?

Rachel already knew that much, and she sure didn't need to hear it again. She'd made up her mind. She was not going to say anything more to Silas other than a polite word or two no matter how many days he came to help out. Somehow she must keep her feelings under control.

Rachel shivered as goose bumps erupted on her arms, and she knew it wasn't from the chill in the greenhouse. "Get busy," she scolded herself. "It's the only thing that will keep you sane."

As soon as she had the fire stoked up, she quickly set to work pricing her hope-chest items; then she placed them on an empty shelf near the front door. She had no more than put the OPEN sign in the window when the first customer of the day showed up. It was Laura Yoder, and Rachel breathed a sigh of relief when she saw that the pretty redhead was alone. The last time Laura had come to the greenhouse, she'd brought both of her children along. Barbara, who was two and a half, had pulled one of Mom's prized African violets off the shelf, and the little girl had quite a time playing in all that rich, black dirt. Laura's four-year-old son, David, had been so full of questions. The child's handicap didn't slow him down much, and like most children his age, David was curious about everything.

As much as Rachel loved children, it tried her patience when they came in with their folks and ran about the greenhouse like it was a play yard. If it was disturbing to her, she could only imagine how her other customers might feel. Most Amish parents were quite strict and didn't let their children get away with much, but Eli's Laura seemed to be more tolerant of her children's antics. However, Rachel was pretty sure Laura would step in and discipline should it become absolutely necessary.

"I see you're all alone today," Rachel said, as her customer looked around the store.

Laura nodded. "I left the little ones with Eli's mamm. I've got several errands to run, and I figured I could get them done quicker if I was by myself." She chuckled. "Besides, Mary Ellen seems to like her role as *grossmudder*."

Rachel smiled. "I guess she would enjoy being a grandmother. Let's see. . .how many grandchildren does she have now?"

"Five in all. Martha Rose has three kinner, as I'm sure you know. And of course, there are my two busy little ones. Mary Ellen's son, Lewis, and his wife are expecting most any day, so soon there'll be six."

"So I've heard."

"Since I'm an only child, my kinner are the only grandchildren my folks have, and they spoil those two something awful." Laura moved over to the shelf where Rachel had displayed her hope-chest items. "You've got some nice things here. If I didn't already have a set of sturdy dishes, I'd be tempted to buy these." She fingered the edge of a white stoneware cup.

"Guess the right buyer will come along sooner or later," Rachel remarked, making no reference to the fact that the dishes were from her hope chest. Mom hadn't been too happy when she'd learned that Rachel was bringing them here, but Rachel was relieved when she chose not to make an issue of it. Truth be told, Mom was probably praying that Rachel's things wouldn't sell and some nice fellow would come along and propose marriage soon.

"How's the flower business?" Laura asked.

"Oh, fair to middlin'." Rachel didn't feel the inclination to tell Laura that except for the need to help out, she really didn't care much about the flower business. Laura seemed like such a prim and proper sort of lady. She probably wouldn't understand Rachel's desire to be outdoors, enjoying all the wildlife God had created.

Sometimes Rachel wished she had been born a boy, just so she could spend more time outside. Even baling and bucking hay would be preferable to being cooped up inside a stuffy old greenhouse all day.

"Have you got any yellow mums?" Laura asked, breaking into Rachel's thoughts.

"Mums? Oh, sure, I think we've got several colors. Come with me to the other room and we'll see what's available."

Rachel studied Laura as she checked over the variety of chrysanthemums. Even though her hair was red and her face was pretty, she looked plain, just like all the other Amish women in their community. Except for the proper way Laura spoke, it was hard to imagine that she'd ever been a part of the fancy, English world. Rachel had only been a girl when Eli Yoder had married Laura after she'd chosen to become Amish. She had no idea how Laura used to look dressed in modern clothes or even how the woman felt about her past life. She had met Laura's fancy English folks a few times, as they'd moved to Lancaster County to be closer to Laura some time ago.

Maybe I should ask her a few questions about being English. It might help me better understand why Anna left home and what her life is like now.

She took a step toward Laura. "Say, I was wondering about something."

Laura picked up a yellow mum and pivoted to face Rachel. "What is it?"

"I know you used to be English."

"That's true. Although it seems like a long time ago to me now."

"You've probably heard that my sister Anna

married Reuben Yutzy awhile back, and the two of them left the faith and moved to Lancaster."

Laura's expression turned solemn. "Jah, I know about that."

"Except for the letters we've had from Anna, we've had no other contact with her. My daed's not one bit happy about Anna leaving home the way she did, and he doesn't want her to come here for a visit." Rachel's voice faltered, and she paused a moment to gain control of her swirling emotions. "It sure hurts knowing she's no longer part of our family."

"She's still part of your family, just not of the Amish faith anymore." Laura touched Rachel's shoulder. "I'm sure it's not easy for any of you, or for Anna, either."

Rachel's eyes filled with tears, and she sniffed. "You really think it pains her, too?"

"I'm almost certain of it." Laura released a quiet moan. "I know it hurt my folks when I left the English world to become Amish, but we stayed in touch, and pretty soon my daed surprised me by selling his law practice and moving out to a small farm nearby. He still practices law, but in a smaller office in Lancaster now." She smiled. "Even though my folks are English, they're living a much simpler life than they used to, and we get to see a lot more of them, which makes me happy."

"Do you think there's a chance that Anna and our daed will ever mend their fences—even if Anna and Reuben never reconcile with the church? Maybe even come to the point where we can start visiting each other from time to time?"

Laura clasped Rachel's hand. "I'll surely pray for that, as I'm sure you're already doing."

"I'm praying for that and a whole lot of other things."

Laura followed Rachel back to the front of the greenhouse, where Rachel wrapped a strip of paper around the bottom of the plant and wrote up a bill. Laura paid her, picked up the mum, and was about to open the front door, when Pauline rushed in. Her cheeks were pink, and a few strands of tawny yellow hair peeked out from under her kapp. "Whew! It's a bit windy out there!"

Laura laughed. "I can tell. You look like you've been standing underneath a windmill."

Pauline giggled and reached up to readjust her covering, which was slightly askew. "Sure is a good day to be indoors. I'm glad I have this job working at Grandma's Place."

Wish I could say the same, Rachel thought ruefully. Philippians 4:11, which Mom often quoted, popped into Rachel's mind: *"For I have learned, in whatsoever state I am, therewith to be content." Okay, Lord, I'll try harder.*

Pauline asked about Laura's children, and Laura spent the next few minutes telling her how much they were growing. She even told how her cat, Foosie, had paired up with one of the barn cats. Now the children had a bunch of fluffy brown-and-white kittens to occupy their busy little hands.

It amazed Rachel the way the two women visited, as though they had always been friends. She knew from the talk she'd heard that it hadn't always been so. Truth be told, Pauline used to dislike Laura because she had stolen Eli's heart and he'd married her and not Pauline. Then Pauline had gone to live with her aunt and uncle in Ohio for a time, no doubt to get away from the reminders of what she'd lost.

Rachel could relate well to the pain of knowing the man she loved cared for someone else and didn't see her as anything more than a friend. She couldn't imagine how Pauline had gotten through those difficult years after Eli had jilted her and married a woman who used to be English. It amazed her to see that there was no animosity between the two women now.

Laura finally headed out, and Pauline got right to work watering plants and repotting some that had outgrown their containers. She seemed so happy doing her work that she was actually humming.

"I was wondering if you'd mind me asking a personal question," Rachel asked when Pauline took a break and sat on the stool behind the cash register.

"Sure, what is it?"

Rachel leaned on the other side of the counter and smiled. She hoped her question wasn't out of line and wouldn't be taken the wrong way. "I know you and Laura were at odds for a while because of Eli, and I was wondering what happened to make you so friendly with one another."

Pauline smiled. "I'll admit that I used to be jealous of Laura because I felt she stole Eli away from me. It hurt so bad that I finally went to Ohio to live with my aunt and uncle. I learned a lot while I was there, and I grew closer to the Lord. By the time I returned to Lancaster County, I realized that I had to give up my bitterness and forgive Laura and Eli for hurting me. So, I apologized in a letter; then I went to their house and had a little talk with them."

Rachel's interest was piqued. "Mind if I ask what was said?"

Pauline shrugged. "Nothing much except I told Laura I was sorry for making her so miserable, and then she apologized, too. The thing was, I knew in my heart that Eli had never been in love with me. He and I were only good friends. I should have been Christian enough to turn loose of him and let him find happiness with Laura. Truth be told, Eli probably did me a favor by marrying her."

Rachel's eyebrows shot up. "Really? How's that?"

"If he'd married me, I never would have gotten to know Joe so well, and we. . ." Pauline blushed a deep crimson. "Guess you've probably figured out that I'm in love with your brother."

"Jah, and I'm sure he feels the same way about you." Rachel glanced across the room at her hope-chest items. "Say, do you think you might be interested in some things for your hope chest?"

Pauline grinned. "Maybe so. I'll have a look-see."

"I can't figure out why this stupid CD player isn't working," Reuben grumbled, as he punched a couple of buttons and turned some knobs.

Anna kept her focus on the road for fear that Reuben might hit something while he was busy looking at the CD player in his truck instead of watching out for traffic the way he should be doing.

"Everything costs a lot, but it seems like nothing ever works right," Reuben complained. "Maybe I need to trade this truck in and get a newer one."

Anna grimaced. With their tight finances, the last thing they needed was a larger truck payment. "When I went to church last week, the preacher made some good points about people putting too much emphasis on things and not enough on God."

Reuben merely grunted in reply.

"I wrote down one of the verses of scripture he quoted. Proverbs 15:16: 'Better is little with the fear of the Lord than great treasure and trouble therewith.' "

"This CD player is trouble, all right," he admitted. "Guess I'll have to learn to live without it until I have enough money to get it fixed. We've got bills to pay and groceries to buy, so having music to listen to as we drive to work every morning will have to wait."

Anna smiled. "I don't miss it, really. Having

some quiet time so we can talk is kind of nice, don't you think?"

He nodded. "With the long hours I've been workin', we don't get to see each other much anymore."

"That's true. Even our Sundays aren't spent together when you sleep most of the day."

Reuben's forehead wrinkled, and he gripped the steering wheel a little tighter. "Are you tryin' to make an issue of me needing to get caught up on my rest?"

"No, no. I just meant—"

"We can talk about this later. There's no point in you being late for work." He pulled the truck into the parking lot on the backside of the restaurant where Anna worked and stopped. "Since I'm starting work two hours later than usual today, I'll probably be working late tonight, so you'd better plan on catching the bus home."

"What else is new?" Anna mumbled, as she opened the truck door.

"What was that?"

"Nothing. Have a good day, Reuben."

When Joseph entered the restaurant in Lancaster, where he'd decided to have some breakfast, his stomach rumbled. He'd had an early dental appointment and hadn't eaten anything before he'd left home. After he'd left the dentist's office, he'd run a few errands, and now that the numbness in his jaw had finally worn off, it was time to fill his belly with a bit of food.

An English woman escorted Joseph to a table near the window, telling him that his waitress would be there shortly. As he waited, he stared out the window and thought about Pauline. It still seemed too good to be true that she was willing to let him court her, but he wasn't complaining in the least. Every chance he got to be with her was like candy in his mouth. He wished she could keep working at the greenhouse indefinitely so they could see each other more. For that matter, he wished he could quit working in the fields and work at the greenhouse, too. Maybe someday when Mom and Dad retired from the business, he could take over. And maybe if Pauline was willing to marry him, the two of them could run the greenhouse together. Rachel wasn't likely to want it.

"Can I bring you something to drink before you order your meal?"

Joseph turned at the sound of a woman's voice. It was a voice he thought he recognized. When he looked up at the waitress who stood next to his table, his mouth dropped open. "Anna?"

Her cheeks turned pink, and her mouth hung slightly open, too. "Joseph. I didn't realize it was you until I saw your face."

"I thought I recognized your voice, but I barely recognize you at all." He frowned deeply. "What have you done to your hair?"

Anna reached up to touch the blond curls framing her slender face. "I. . .uh. . .decided to try it short for a change." The color in her cheeks deepened. "Reuben likes it this way."

Joseph folded his arms and glared up at his sister. "Reuben's the only reason you left the faith, isn't he?"

Her gaze dropped to the floor. "Neither Reuben nor I have anything against the Amish way of life, but Reuben didn't want to give up his truck, so—"

"You left just to please him then—so he could have his stupid old truck?"

She shrugged. "Sort of."

He gritted his teeth. "Either you did or you didn't, Anna. Which is it?"

She lifted her gaze to meet his again. "All right then; I did leave to please Reuben, but lots of things about the English way of life I enjoy, too."

"More than being with your family? Or have you already forgotten about us?"

"Of course I haven't forgotten, but Reuben's my family, too."

Joseph sat fuming as he stared at the menu lying before him.

"I need to wait on some other customers, so what would you like to order?"

"If I place an order with you, then it's the same as doing business with you, and we both know that's not allowed."

Tears pooled in Anna's eyes, and she blinked a couple of times. "Would you like me to see if another waitress is free to take your order?"

He shook his head and pushed away from the table. "My appetite's gone, so I'll just meet up with the driver I hired to bring me to town and be on my way home. Mom or one of the sisters can fix me something to eat."

Anna took a step toward Joseph, but he moved quickly away. Seeing his older sister dressed in English clothes and wearing her hair cut short was a painful reminder that she was no longer Amish and had chosen Reuben and his fancy English ideas over her own family. All he wanted to do was get as far away from Anna as he possibly could.

Chapter 22

Daniel's back took nearly two weeks to heal, and Silas went over to the Beachys' place most days in order to help with chores and the last of the harvesting. In all that time, he never had his heart-to-heart talk with Rachel. It wasn't because he hadn't tried. He'd made every effort to get her alone, but she always made up some excuse about being too busy to talk to him. Silas was getting discouraged and had about decided to give up, when suddenly an idea popped into his head. Last Friday had been his final day helping out. Daniel had assured him that he was feeling well enough to start doing some light chores, and with the help of their neighbors, all the hay had been baled and put away in the barn, which was a good thing, since they'd had some snow since then. Silas wouldn't be going back to the Beachy farm—at least not to help. However, that didn't mean he couldn't pay a visit to the greenhouse.

He stepped up to his mother, who stood at the sink, doing the breakfast dishes. "I'm going out for a while, Mom. Should be back in plenty of time for the noon meal, though."

Her forehead wrinkled as she turned to face him. "In this weather? In case you haven't noticed, there's a foot of snow on the ground, with the promise of more coming from the looks of those dark clouds in the sky." She nodded to the window.

"I'm taking the sleigh, so I'm sure I'll be fine."

"Mind if I ask where you're going?"

"Over to the Beachys' greenhouse."

Mom gave Silas a knowing look, but he chose to ignore it. "Say, if you're heading to the greenhouse, would you mind seeing if they have any nice poinsettias? I'd like one to give my sister Susan when she comes here to celebrate her birthday next week."

"Jah, sure, I can do that." Silas leaned over, kissed his mother on the cheek, and started for the back door. "See you later, Mom."

Since none of Rachel's hope-chest items had sold yet and Pauline had decided not to buy any, Rachel thought it might be time to take them into town and see if Thomas Benner would sell them in his store. Storm clouds were brewing that morning, and Dad wouldn't let Rachel take the horse and buggy to town, saying he was worried she might get caught in a snowstorm. She had been hoping to get her things into the variety store in time for the busy

Christmas shopping season, but now she would have to wait until the weather improved. Besides, Mom had come down with a nasty cold, and it wouldn't be fair to expect her to work with Pauline in the greenhouse while Rachel went to town.

Rachel donned her woolen jacket and headed for the greenhouse. She had talked her mother into going back to bed and had left a warm pot of fenugreek tea by her bedside. Mom was resting, and Rachel would be all by herself until Pauline showed up. If the weather worsened, Pauline might not come today. For that matter, they might not have any customers. Who in their right mind would want to visit a greenhouse when the weather was cold and snowy?

Shortly after Rachel opened the greenhouse and stoked up the wood-burning stove, she heard a horse and buggy pull up. Figuring it was probably Pauline, she flung open the door. To her astonishment, Abe Landis stepped out of a closed-in buggy and offered her a friendly wave. She hadn't seen Abe since the last preaching service, and then she'd only spoken a few words to him while she was serving the men their noon meal.

"Those angry-looking clouds out there make me think we might be in for another snowstorm," Abe said when he entered the greenhouse. He wore a dark wool jacket, and his ears protruded out from under the black hat perched on his head.

Ears that are a mite too big, Rachel noticed. An

image of Silas sifted through her mind. *Abe's not nearly as good-looking as Silas, but then–as Dad often says–looks aren't everything.*

"What can I help you with, Abe?" Rachel asked, as she slipped behind the counter and took a seat on her stool.

Abe removed his hat, and it was all Rachel could do to keep from laughing out loud. A thatch of Abe's hair stood straight up. It looked as though he hadn't bothered to comb it that morning.

"I really didn't come here to buy anything." Abe jammed his free hand inside his coat pocket and offered her a lopsided grin.

"What did you come for then?"

"I. . .uh. . .was wondering if you'd like to go with me to the taffy pull that's gonna be held at Herman Weaver's place this Saturday night."

Rachel wasn't sure what to say. She didn't want to go to the taffy pull with Abe. He was a nice enough fellow, and she'd known him and his family a good many years, but he wasn't Silas. If Rachel couldn't be courted by the man she loved, then she didn't want to be courted at all. Of course, she could go as Abe's friend. Still, that might lead the poor fellow on, and she didn't want him to think there was any chance for the two of them as a couple.

"So, what's your answer?" Abe prompted. "Can I come by your place on Saturday night and give you a lift to the Weavers'?"

Rachel nibbled on her lower lip as she searched

for the right words. She didn't want to hurt Abe's feelings, but her answer had to be no. "I'm flattered that you'd want to escort me to the taffy pull, but I'm afraid I can't go."

Abe's dark eyebrows drew downward. "How come?"

She swallowed hard. "My mamm has a bad cold, and my daed just got on his feet after a painful bout with his back. I think it's best for me to stick close to home."

Abe nodded and slapped his hat back on his head. "Good enough. I'll see you around, then." With that, he marched out the door.

Rachel followed, hoping to call out a friendly good-bye, but Abe was already in his buggy and had taken up the reins. Maybe she'd made a mistake. Maybe she should have agreed to go with him. Wouldn't having Abe as a boyfriend be better than having no boyfriend at all?

She bowed her head and prayed. *Lord, if I'm not supposed to love Silas, please give me the grace to accept it. And if I'm supposed to be courted by Abe, then give me the desire for that.*

Rachel heard a horse whinny, and she glanced out the front window. A sleigh was parked in the driveway, and she recognized the driver. Rachel's heart hammered in her chest, and her hands felt like a couple of slippery trout as she watched Silas step down from his buggy and hurry toward the greenhouse. She couldn't imagine why he would be here. The harvest was done, and Dad's back was much better. Maybe he'd come to buy a plant for someone.

Silas rubbed his hands briskly together as he entered the greenhouse. His nose was red from the cold, and his black hat was covered with tiny snowflakes. Dad's prediction about the weather had come true, for the snow was certainly here.

Rachel moved toward the counter, her heart riding on waves of expectation. Silas followed. "It's mighty cold out, and I'm glad we got your daed's hay in when we did. Guess winter's decided to come a bit early." He nodded toward the door. "Say, wasn't that Abe Landis I saw getting into his buggy as I pulled in?"

"Jah, it was Abe."

"Did he buy out the store?"

She shook her head. "Nope, didn't buy a thing."

Silas raised his eyebrows. "How come?"

"Abe stopped by to ask me to the taffy pull this Saturday night." Rachel stepped behind the counter. "Can I help you with something, Silas?"

He squinted his dark eyes, and Rachel wondered why he made no comment about Abe's invitation.

"I came by to see if you have any poinsettias. My mamm's sister lives in Ohio, and she's coming to visit next week. Mom thought since her birthday's soon, she would give her a plant."

Rachel stepped out from behind the counter. "I believe we still have one or two poinsettias in the other room. Shall we go take a look-see?"

Silas followed silently as they went to the room where a variety of plants were on display. Rachel showed him several red poinsettias, and he selected the largest one.

Back at the battery-operated cash register, Rachel's hands trembled as she counted out Silas's change. Just the nearness of him took her breath away, and it irked her to think he had the power to make her feel so weak in the knees.

"Seen any interesting birds lately?" Silas asked after she'd wrapped some paper around the pot of the plant and handed it to him.

Glad for the diversion, she smiled. "I saw a great horned owl the other night when I was looking up in the tree with my binoculars. The critter was sure hootin' like crazy."

Silas chuckled; then he started for the door. Just as he got to the shelf where Rachel's hope-chest items were placed, he stopped and bent down to examine them. "These look like some mighty fine dishes. Mind if I ask how much they cost?"

"The price sticker is on the bottom of the top plate."

Silas picked it up and whistled. "Kind of high, don't you think?" His face turned redder than the plant he held. "Sorry. Guess it's not my place to decide how much your folks should be selling things for."

Rachel thought about telling Silas that it wasn't her mom or dad who had priced the dishes, but she didn't want him to know she was trying to sell off her hope-chest items. It was none of his business. "I hope your aunt enjoys the poinsettia," she said instead.

Silas gave a quick nod and opened the front door. "I hope Abe knows how lucky he is," he called over his shoulder.

Rachel slowly shook her head. "Now what in the world did he mean by that? Surely Silas doesn't think Abe and I are courting." Of course, she hadn't bothered to tell him that she'd turned down Abe's offer to escort her to the taffy pull. But then, he hadn't asked.

Rachel moved over to the window and watched with a heavy heart as Silas drove out of sight. She glanced at the dishes he'd said were too high-priced and wondered if he had considered buying them, maybe as a gift for his aunt's birthday.

"Guess I should lower the price some." Rachel felt moisture on her cheeks. She had been trying so hard to be hopeful and keep praising God, but after seeing Silas again, she realized that her hopes had been for nothing. He obviously had no interest in her. Rachel wondered if God even cared about her. Hadn't He been listening to her prayers and praises all these months? Didn't He realize how much her heart ached to be loved by Silas?

As Joseph finished up his chores in the barn, he kept going to the door and checking to see if

Pauline's buggy had shown up at the greenhouse yet. Ever since that day when he'd seen Anna at the restaurant, he'd been stewing over things, and he thought he might feel better if he talked to Pauline about it. She'd been understanding and willing to listen the last time he'd discussed Anna with her, and she had been full of good advice. Only trouble was he still hadn't found it in his heart to forgive his sister for leaving home and going English on them. It still pained him to think of Anna dressed in fancy clothes and wearing her hair cut short, and the idea of her and Reuben living in the fancy English world gave him a sick feeling in the pit of his stomach.

Joseph peered out the barn door one more time and was happy to see Pauline's buggy coming up the driveway. He slipped out the door and ran toward the greenhouse. Pauline was just getting out of her buggy when he arrived.

"Guder mariye, Joe." She offered him a friendly smile. "It's good to see you."

"It's good to see you, too." He motioned toward her buggy. "Could we sit in there awhile and talk, or do you have to get into the greenhouse right away?"

"I'm a little earlier than usual, so I have a few minutes to spare."

"Great." He opened the door on the side of the buggy closest to her and helped her inside. Then he went around and took a seat on the other side.

"Is something troubling you, Joe?" she asked. "You look upset."

He grunted. "I saw her the other day."

"Who?"

"Anna."

"Did she come to your place for a visit?"

"No. I ran into her at the restaurant in Lancaster where she works as a waitress."

"How's she doing?"

"Fine, as far as I could tell, but she doesn't look like Anna anymore."

"You mean because she's not wearing Plain clothes?"

"That, and she's cut her hair real short." Joseph gritted his teeth and gripped the buggy seat so tightly that his fingers ached.

"I'll bet she did look quite different."

Joseph sat staring straight ahead.

Pauline reached over and touched his arm. "Did seeing Anna that way make you feel sad?"

"Not sad, really. More mad, I'd have to say." He grimaced. "I could hardly stand to see my sister looking that way, and since I'm not supposed to do any business with a shunned member of the church, I walked out without letting her wait on me."

Pauline offered him a sympathetic smile. "I thought you were going to forgive Anna and move on with things."

"I can't go against the church and do business with her."

"I'm not suggesting that." She paused a moment and flicked her tongue across her lower lip. "I just think you need to forgive Anna for hurting your family and treat her kindly when you do see her."

Joseph shrugged. "Probably won't be for some time, 'cause I'm not likely to go back to that restaurant again."

"She might come here for a visit, though."

"Not if Dad has anything to say about it."

"He's still angry, too?"

He nodded. "I think it would take something big for him to let Anna come home to see any of us."

"Big, like what?"

"Like a death in the family or something."

Pauline shook her head. "Let's hope there's nothing like that on the horizon." She reached over and took hold of Joseph's hand. "I've been praying for you, Joe. Praying for all your family."

He smiled and squeezed her fingers. "Danki. I appreciate that."

Chapter 23

For the next few days, snow poured from the sky like powdered sugar, but by Saturday morning, the weather had improved some. So Rachel convinced Joseph to hitch up the sleigh and drive her to the variety store in Paradise. It was the second week of December, but there was still a chance that people would be looking for things to give as Christmas presents. She'd finally sold some towels and a few pot holders from her hope chest to a couple of customers who'd come into the greenhouse, but she needed to get rid of the dishes, the kerosene lamp, and the tablecloth.

Thomas Benner was more than happy to take Rachel's things in on consignment, although he did mention that they would have had a better chance of selling if she'd brought them in a few weeks earlier. Rachel sure didn't need that reminder. She wished she'd never started filling her hope chest.

By the time Rachel left the store and found Joseph, who'd gone looking for something to give

Pauline for Christmas, snow was beginning to fall again.

"We'd best be gettin' on home," Joseph said, looking up at the sky. "If this keeps up, the roads could get mighty slippery. I wouldn't want some car to go sliding into our sleigh."

"You're right; we should leave now." Rachel climbed into the sleigh and reached under the seat to withdraw an old quilt, which she wrapped snugly around the lower half of her body. "Brr. . .it's turning cold again."

Joseph picked up the reins and got the horse moving. "Jah, it sure is."

Rachel glanced over at her brother. He seemed to be off in some other world.

"Are you okay?"

"Sure. Why do you ask?"

"You seem kind of pensive today."

"I was just thinking about something Pauline told me the other day."

"Oh? What was that?"

He shrugged. "She's been giving me some advice lately."

"What kind of advice? Or would you rather not say?"

"I don't mind saying. It might feel good to talk more about it."

"More about what?"

"The way I've been feeling about Anna going English."

Rachel noticed the wrinkles etched in her brother's forehead. "How have you been feeling about the whole thing?"

"Not so good. Not good at all."

"I don't think any of us feels good about it, but it's a fact we can't change, so as Mom said after her last letter from Anna came, 'We must accept Anna's decision and quit brooding over it.' "

Joseph nodded. "Pauline said pretty much the same thing, only she took it a step further by telling me I needed to forgive Anna."

"Pauline's right about that. We all need to forgive Anna for leaving home the way she did—including Dad."

"I'm workin' on it," Joseph mumbled.

"Glad to hear it." Rachel smiled. "So, why don't you tell me what you got Pauline for Christmas?"

He smiled, too, and his mood seemed to brighten. "I bought her a pair of gardening gloves and a book about flowers."

"She should like that since she enjoys working in the greenhouse so much."

Joseph nodded. "She's sure changed a lot here of late, don't you think?"

Rachel bit back the laughter bubbling in her throat. "I think you've been good for her."

His dark eyebrows lifted. "You really think so?"

"I do."

"Well, she's been good for me, too."

"She's not worried about your age difference anymore?"

He shook his head. "Doesn't seem to be."

"And you're okay with it?"

"Jah."

"I'm glad." At least things were going well for someone in Rachel's family.

"Come spring, I'm thinking about asking her to marry me." Joseph glanced over at Rachel. "Don't you go sayin' anything to anyone about it, though, you hear?"

"Oh, I won't. It's not my place to be doing the telling."

"I'm sorry things didn't work out for you and Silas."

Rachel grimaced. "It wasn't meant to be, that's all. I just have to learn to be content with my life as it is. There's no point in hoping for the impossible. Job in the Bible did, and look where it got him."

"Think about it, Rachel. Through all Job's trials, he never lost hope." Joseph glanced over at her again and smiled. "In the end, God blessed Job with more than he'd lost."

Rachel drew in a deep breath and released it quickly. "I guess you're right, but it's not always easy to have hope. Especially when things don't go as we'd planned."

"Life is full of twists and turns. It's how we choose to deal with things that makes the difference in our attitudes. Take Silas, for example. . .I saw him the other day and mentioned my encounter with Anna at the restaurant."

"What'd he say?"

"He didn't seem all that affected when I mentioned Anna's name."

"Well, what could he say, Joseph? Anna's a married woman now, and there's nothing Silas can do about it." She sighed. "I'd been hoping that he might take an interest in me, but it doesn't look like that will ever occur. Truth is, not much of anything I hope for ever seems to happen."

"Our hope should be in the Lord, not in man or in our circumstances."

Rachel stared straight ahead. She didn't want to talk about Job, hope, or even God right now. She was too worried about the weather. The snow was coming down harder, and the road was completely covered. She watched the passing scenery, noting as they approached the one-room schoolhouse that the yard was empty. No Amish buggies. No scooters. No sign of any children or their teacher. "School must have been dismissed early today. Teacher Nancy probably thought it would be best to let the kinner go before the weather got any worse," she commented.

"Jah, you're probably right."

They rode along in silence until a rescue vehicle sailed past, its red lights blinking off and on and the siren blaring like crazy.

"Must be an accident up ahead." Joseph pulled back on the reins to slow the horse.

Rachel's body tensed. She hated the thought of seeing an accident, and she prayed one of their Amish buggies wasn't involved. So often, horse-drawn carriages had been damaged by cars that either didn't see them or had been traveling too fast. Lots of Amish folks had been injured from collisions with those fast-moving English vehicles, too.

Their sleigh had just rounded the next bend when they saw the rescue truck stopped in the middle of the road. Flares threw light along the highway and on a dark blue, midsize car pulled off on the shoulder. Rescue workers bent over a small figure. Several Amish children clustered around, and the sheriff directed traffic.

"We'd better stop. It could be someone we know." Joseph pulled the sleigh off the road; then he and Rachel jumped out.

They had only taken a few steps when a familiar voice called out, "Joseph! Rachel! Over here!"

Rachel glanced to her right. Elizabeth dashed across the slippery snow and nearly knocked Rachel off her feet when she grabbed her around the waist. "It's Perry!" she panted. "He was hit by a car!"

Chapter 24

Rebekah had just put a pan of chicken in the oven to bake when she heard a car pull into the yard. She rolled her wheelchair across the floor and peered out the low kitchen window. The car that sat in the driveway belonged to Sheriff Andrews. The family had met him a couple of times when buggy accidents had happened near their home. The sheriff got out of his car, glanced around the yard as though he was looking for someone, then started for the house.

Rebekah was about to head for the door to see what he wanted, when she noticed a horse and sleigh come up the driveway, with Rachel in the driver's seat and Elizabeth sitting in the seat beside her. Goose bumps erupted on Rebekah's arms. Where were Joseph and Perry, and what had happened that had brought the sheriff to their place?

Just as the officer reached the back porch, Daniel came rushing out of the barn. He stopped at the sleigh a few minutes, apparently to speak to the girls, then hurried toward the house.

Rebekah maneuvered her wheelchair over to the door and opened it quickly. The sheriff stood on the porch with Daniel. Rachel and Elizabeth had gotten out of the sleigh and were running toward the house, as well.

"What is it?" Rebekah looked up at the sheriff, then over at Daniel. "What's happened?"

Sheriff Andrews took a step toward her and bent down so he was eye level with her. "I'm sorry to have to tell you this, Mrs. Beachy, but there's been an accident on the road near your place, and I'm afraid your son's been seriously injured."

"My son? Which son?" Rebekah felt as though she were in a daze.

"Your daughter said his name is Perry."

Rebekah covered her mouth with the palm of her hand and gasped. Daniel released a deep moan.

"How. . .how bad is he hurt?" she squeaked.

"What happened?" Daniel asked at the same time.

The sheriff opened his mouth as if to reply, but Elizabeth bounded onto the porch just then. "Perry's been hit by a car!" she shouted. "I'm sure he's dead!"

The next several hours were like a horrible nightmare for Rachel, and she was sure the rest of her family felt the same way. Perry had been taken by ambulance to the hospital in Lancaster, and

Joseph had ridden up front with the driver while the paramedics tended to Perry in the back. Mom, Dad, Rachel, and Elizabeth rode with the sheriff.

When they arrived at the hospital and spoke with the emergency-room doctor, he told them that Perry was dead. The sheriff had explained how the driver of the car that ran into Perry had hit a patch of ice and swerved off the road. All the other Amish children who'd been walking home from school with Perry and Elizabeth had witnessed the accident.

When they returned home later that night, Rachel offered to fix the family something to eat, but no one was hungry. Elizabeth, who appeared to be in shock, had to be carried to bed by Joseph. Dad was busy comforting Mom, who hadn't stopped crying since she'd been given the news that her youngest son was dead.

Rachel took a seat at the kitchen table and let her head fall forward into her hands. She still couldn't believe that young, impetuous Perry, who had been making jokes at breakfast that morning and talking about the things he wanted to do after school, was gone. She felt sure her little brother was up in heaven with relatives and friends who had gone on before him, but despite the knowledge that Perry was with Jesus, she would always miss his mischievous face. She knew the rest of the family felt the same way—especially Mom, who had lost her youngest child, born just fifteen minutes after Elizabeth had entered the world.

Rachel lifted her head and moaned as her thoughts went to Anna. She needed to be told about Perry as soon as possible. After all, Anna was still a part of their family, even if she had moved away.

Early the following morning, several women came to the house with food and offers of help. One of them was Martha Rose Zook, Anna's friend.

The others joined Mom in the kitchen, but Rachel touched Martha Rose's arm and nodded toward the living room. "Can I speak with you a minute?"

"Jah, sure."

As soon as the two of them had taken seats on the sofa, Martha Rose turned to Rachel and said, "I'm so sorry about Perry, and I'd like to help in any way I can."

Rachel forced a smile. If she smiled, maybe it would be easier not to cry. "I spoke with Mom this morning after breakfast, and we want Anna here for the funeral."

"And well she should be."

"The thing is. . .we know your husband, Amon, has a phone in his place of business now, so we were wondering if you might be willing to call Anna and let her know what happened to Perry."

Martha Rose nodded. "Of course I will."

Rachel glanced toward the door leading to the

kitchen. "It might be best if you didn't say anything to my daed about this. No point getting him any more worked up than he already is."

"I understand." Martha Rose gave Rachel a hug.

Rachel found the gesture to be comforting, but having someone's sympathy made it more difficult for her not to cry. Tears had been clogging her throat ever since she'd first seen Perry's lifeless body lying by the side of the road, but she'd refused to give in to them. She needed to be strong for the rest of the family, and she knew if she started crying, she might not be able to stop.

"If Anna comes for the funeral, then Dad will just have to deal with it," she murmured.

Martha Rose pursed her lips like she was thinking the matter over. She finally nodded and said, "I won't say a word."

Joseph couldn't keep his mind on his chores. All he could think about was Perry and how much he would miss the little scamp. He could still picture the wild expression on Elizabeth's face when he and Rachel had pulled up to the accident and seen Perry lying by the side of the road. She, along with several others from their school, had witnessed the accident, and seeing Perry struck down by the out-of-control car must have been a real shock for them all. Elizabeth and her twin brother had always been close, despite their constant bickering. It would be difficult for

Elizabeth to get through the funeral, which was to be held at their house in a few days.

He ambled over to the bales of hay stacked against the barn wall and lifted one bale into his arms. He needed to feed the livestock, and other jobs waited to be done. Life didn't stop because of a death in the family, even though he might wish it could.

Joseph tried not to think of anything but the job at hand as he forked hay into the horses' stalls and filled their troughs with fresh water. He'd just finished with the last horse and was preparing to move on to the mules, when he heard the barn door open and shut.

"Joe, are you in here?"

"I'm here, Pauline." He set his pitchfork down and hurried to the front of the building, anxious to see the woman he loved.

Pauline stood near the door with a grievous expression on her face. "I'm so sorry about Perry. Is there anything I can do? Anything at all?"

He nodded and moved quickly to her side. "You can give me a hug, that's what."

She opened her arms, and he went willingly into her embrace. Tears clogged the back of his throat as he struggled to remain in control of his raging emotions. "It's not fair, Pauline. Life's not fair. God shouldn't have taken my little brother."

She patted his back in a motherly fashion. "I've never lost anyone so close to me, and I don't truly know how you're feeling, but I do know that God understands your pain, and He wants to help you through this."

Joseph tried to speak, but his words came out garbled.

"Let the tears flow, Joe," she said, hugging him tighter. "I'll cry right along with you."

He knew he couldn't fight the ball of emotions that threatened to suffocate him, so he gave in and wept until the shoulder of Pauline's dress was saturated with his tears.

Finally, he lifted his head and stepped back. "Danki for being here for me."

She nodded, as a film of tears swam in her eyes. "That's what friends are for."

"I–I was kind of hoping we could be more than friends."

She tipped her head and blinked a couple of times. "Oh?"

"I'm in love with you, Pauline, and if you'll have me, I'd like us to get married next fall."

She smiled and wiped her eyes. "I love you, too, Joe, and I'd be honored to be your wife."

Chapter 25

Anna stared out the window of Reuben's truck, watching the passing scenery yet not really seeing it. She was finally going home to see her family, only this was not the homecoming she had wanted it to be. Instead of going to a family member's birthday supper or celebrating some special holiday with them, she was going home to view the body of her little brother who had gone to heaven to be with Jesus. Would she be accepted by her family today? Would Dad, who had been determined that she not come home for a visit these past months, speak to her?

"You okay, Anna?" Reuben asked, as he reached across the seat to touch her arm.

She turned to face him and blinked against the stinging tears obscuring her vision. "I'm feeling a little uneasy about things."

"Are you afraid you'll break down when you see your brother's body?"

"I'm concerned about that, but I'm also worried

about how I'll be accepted today." She glanced down at the long, black skirt she'd chosen to wear for this somber occasion. It wasn't a Plain dress, but at least she hadn't worn slacks or a fancy dress that would draw attention to her clothes.

She reached up to touch the short curls framing her face and grimaced. "I wonder what my folks will have to say about my hair?"

Reuben grunted. "I think you're worried for nothing, Anna. I'm sure everyone will be so glad to see you that they won't even be thinking about your hair."

Anna released a sigh and pushed her full weight into the back of the seat. Truth was, even though she'd said a few times that she wished she could cut her hair, she'd only done it to please Reuben. He had wanted her to do it before they'd left the Amish faith. Of course, she would never have done anything so bold or defiant then, especially since she had already become a baptized member of the church. Even after leaving the church, she'd been hesitant to cut off her hair, but Reuben had kept insisting.

Reuben took hold of her hand and gave her fingers a gentle squeeze. "It'll be all right, Anna. Everything will work out just fine."

The funeral for Perry was a solemn occasion. Friends, relatives, and neighbors quickly filled up the Beachys' house for the service. The wall partitions had been removed so the speaker could be seen from any part of the three rooms being used. Perry's plain pine coffin had been placed on a bench against one wall in Mom and Dad's bedroom. Rachel's immediate family sat facing the coffin, with their backs to the speaker, who stood at the doorway between the kitchen and living room.

It sent shivers up Rachel's spine to think of her little brother's body lying in that coffin. In this life, she would never again have the pleasure of seeing him run and play. Never again hear his contagious laugh or squeals of delight when a calf or kitten was born. Never hug him or ruffle his hair the way she'd often done whenever he'd been in a teasing mood. It wasn't fair. Rachel wondered why God had allowed such a horrible thing to happen. Wasn't it bad enough that they'd lost Anna to the English world? Did God have to take Perry, too? She had to keep reminding herself that even though her little brother's days on earth were done, he did have a new life in heaven and was probably happier now than he'd ever been in this life.

Before Rachel had entered her parents' bedroom, she'd seen Silas and his parents come into the house. Silas had offered her a sympathetic smile, but she'd only nodded in response and gulped back the sob rising in her throat.

Rachel was miserable without Silas as a friend, and she didn't have Anna as a friend anymore, either. Even though Martha Rose had called Anna on the phone and told her about the funeral, she wasn't here, which meant she must have decided it was best not to come.

Unbidden tears slipped out of Rachel's eyes and rolled down her cheeks in rivulets that stung like fire. *If only things could be different. If only. . .*

Rachel barely heard the words Bishop Wagler spoke during his funeral message. Her thoughts lingered on her sister and how much she had hurt the family by going English. Anna had hurt Silas, too, and because of it, he had spurned Rachel's love.

The service was nearly over, and the assisting minister had just begun to read a hymn, when Rachel caught a glimpse of Anna and Reuben, who had slipped into the room. She had to look twice to be sure it really was Anna. Her modern sister was dressed in English clothes—a black skirt and matching jacket. The biggest surprise was Anna's hair. She'd cut it short, just like Joseph had said, and it made her look so "English," despite the little black scarf she wore on the back of her head.

When the service was finally over and everyone had vacated the rooms so the coffin could be moved to a convenient viewing place in the main entrance, Rachel and her family stood. As soon as the coffin had been set in place inside the living room, everyone present formed a line to view Perry's body.

Rachel knew the funeral procession to the cemetery would begin soon afterward, and she wanted a chance to speak with her sister now, just in case Anna and Reuben didn't plan on staying. So as soon as she had seen Perry's body, she sought out her sister, who had already made her way out of the house, with Reuben at her side.

Rachel had only taken a few steps when she was stopped by Silas. "I'm sure sorry about what happened to Perry." He paused, his gaze going to the casket, then back to her again. "It doesn't seem right, him being so young and all."

Rachel stood staring at him, feeling as if she were in a daze. When Silas said nothing more, she started to move away. To her surprise, he reached out and gave her a hug. She held her arms stiffly at her side and waited until he pulled back. She was sure his display of affection was nothing more than a brotherly gesture. Besides, it was too little, too late as far as she was concerned. Rachel knew she needed to weed out the yearning she felt for Silas. It would only cause her further pain to keep pining away and hoping for something that never could be.

She bit her bottom lip in order to keep from bursting into tears, then turned quickly away.

Anna and Reuben were about to step off the porch, when Rachel showed up. "Anna, hold up a minute. I want to talk to you."

As Anna turned to face her sister, her eyes flooded with tears. "Thanks for asking Martha Rose to get word to me about Perry. I–I just had to come." She glanced over at Reuben, and he took hold of her hand.

"Of course you did, and it's only right that you should be here." Rachel nodded toward the door. "I know it's kind of cold out here, but could we talk a few minutes?"

Anna looked to Reuben as though seeking his approval.

He nodded. "I'll go back inside and see if I can speak with my folks while you two talk." He gave Anna a quick hug, then returned to the house.

Rachel led Anna over to the porch swing, and they both took a seat.

"Do you think this is a good idea?" Anna asked. "If Dad sees you talking to me, he might be pretty miffed."

Rachel shrugged. "There's no rule that says I can't talk to my own sister."

Anna nodded and swallowed hard. "Martha Rose said Perry was hit by a car, but she didn't know any of the details. Can you tell me how this horrible thing happened?"

Rachel drew in a shuddering breath. "Joseph and I were heading home from town in the sleigh. As we came around the bend not far from our house, we saw the accident. A rescue vehicle, the sheriff's car, and the car that hit Perry were parked along the side of the road." She paused and swiped at the tears rolling down her cheeks. "Our little brother never regained consciousness, and he died soon after he got to the hospital."

"The roads were pretty icy, I heard."

Rachel nodded. "I'm sure the driver of the car didn't mean to run off the road. It was an accident, but still. . ." She sniffed. "Perry was so young. It just doesn't seem right when a child is killed."

Anna blinked a couple of times to keep her own tears from spilling over. "Sometimes it's hard to figure out why God allows bad things to happen to innocent people."

Rachel reached up to wipe more tears from her eyes. "Mom would remind us that the Bible says God is no respecter of persons and that the rain falls on the just, same as it does the unjust."

"That's true, but it's still hard to accept such a tragedy."

Rachel nodded.

"How are Mom and Dad dealing with Perry's death?" Anna asked. "I only saw them from a distance, and I wasn't sure if I should try to talk to them right now." She glanced away. "From Mom's letters, I'd have to say that she's forgiven me, but I think Dad must still hate me for leaving the faith and all."

Rachel shook her head. "He doesn't hate you, Anna. He and Mom are disappointed, of course, but you're still their flesh and blood, and if you were to come back, they would welcome you with open arms."

Anna flexed her fingers, then formed them into tight balls in her lap. "I won't be coming back, Rachel. Reuben's happy living the modern life. He likes his painting job, and I–I'm content to work as a waitress."

"You could have done those things and still remained Amish."

"I know, but Reuben really needed a truck to get him back and forth to work, not to mention traveling from job to job."

Rachel merely shrugged in response. She probably didn't understand how important Reuben's vehicle was to him, Anna figured. Maybe he did put too much emphasis on worldly things, but Anna didn't think it would be right to discuss that with Rachel. At least not right now.

"How are things with you and Silas these days?" Anna asked, feeling the need for a change of subject.

Rachel gave no reply other than a brief shrug.

"Are you going to tell me about him or not?" Anna pried. "I can see by the look on your face that you're in love with him."

Rachel shook her head. "There's not much to say. Silas and I are friends, nothing more."

"Has he taken you anywhere or come calling on you at the house?"

"We did a few things together for a while there, but it didn't mean anything to him, I'm sure."

"That's too bad. I was kind of hoping that, after

I left home, Silas's eyes would be opened and he'd see how good you are for him."

Rachel stared at the porch, and Anna's heart went out to her. If there was something she could do to make Silas see how good Rachel was for him, she surely would.

"You never really said–how's the rest of the family taking Perry's death?"

A fresh set of tears pooled in Rachel's eyes. "It's been mighty hard–especially for Mom and Elizabeth. Perry was still Mom's little boy, and even though Elizabeth and her twin argued sometimes, I know she still loved him."

Anna was about to reply, but Joseph stepped out the door and headed their way. She hoped he wouldn't make an issue of her being here. Maybe he wouldn't speak to her at all.

Joseph tromped across the porch and stopped when he got to the swing. "Hello, Anna," he mumbled.

"Hello, Joseph."

"I came out to tell you two that everyone went out the back door and they're climbing into their buggies already. We need to head for the cemetery now."

Rachel stood, but when Anna didn't join her, she turned back toward the swing. "Aren't you coming? You can ride with me and Joseph."

Anna stared down at her clasped hands,

struggling with her decision. "I'm not sure I should. Some folks might see it as an intrusion."

Rachel shook her head. "How could they? You're part of our family. You have every right to be at Perry's burial."

Anna looked up at Joseph, obviously waiting to see what he would say.

He nodded and reached out to touch her arm. "You and Reuben are welcome to ride in the buggy with me and Rachel."

Anna's chin trembled as she smiled up at him. "Thank you, brother Joseph."

"You're welcome." A feeling of relief flooded Joseph's soul, as he and Rachel stepped off the porch, and Anna went back into the house in search of her husband. Joseph really had found forgiveness in his heart toward his sister, and for the first time in many weeks, he felt a sense of peace.

A horse-drawn hearse led the procession slowly down the narrow country road, with the two Beachy buggies following. Behind them, a long line of Amish carriages kept pace, and Silas Swartley's was the last. He felt sick to the pit of his stomach, thinking how it would feel to lose one of his brothers. Even if they didn't always see eye to eye, they were kin, and blood was thicker than water.

At the cemetery, everyone climbed out of their buggies and tied their horses to the hitching posts.

Perry's coffin, supported by two hickory poles, was carried to the open grave and placed over it. Relatives and friends gathered near.

Silas stood near his own family, directly across from the Beachy family. He was surprised to see Anna standing between Rachel and Joseph, and Reuben nearby with his parents and younger sister. Silas's heart stirred with strange feelings when he saw Anna wearing modern clothes. Her hair was cut short, and it looked like she might be wearing a bit of makeup. Such a contrast from the Anna Beachy he'd known as a child. She no longer resembled the young girl he'd fallen in love with so many years ago.

Silas glanced over at Rachel. Her shoulders drooped, and tears rimmed her eyes. She looked exhausted. His heart twisted with the pain he saw on her face. If only she hadn't shut him out, he might be of some comfort to her now.

Maybe it was best this way. She didn't trust him anymore, and he wasn't sure she should. What had he ever done to make Rachel believe he cared for her and not her sister? The truth was, until this very moment, he'd never truly seen Anna for what she was—a modern woman who seemed more comfortable dressed in English clothes than she did the Plain garb she'd grown up wearing.

Silas forced his attention back to the graveside service. Long straps were placed around each end of the coffin, and the pallbearers lifted it with the straps, while another man removed the supporting crosspieces. The coffin was then slowly lowered into the ground, and the long straps were removed. The pallbearers grabbed their shovels and began to fill the grave. Despite the snow they'd had a few days ago, at least the ground wasn't frozen; that made the men's job a little easier. Soil, mixed with snow and gravel, hit the casket with loud thumps, and with each thump, Silas noticed Rachel's shoulders lift and fall back.

When the grave was half filled, the men stopped shoveling. The bishop read a hymn, and the grave was then filled the rest of the way. The service was closed after everyone had silently said the Lord's Prayer.

Silas's heart went out to Rebekah Beachy, who sat in her wheelchair, audibly weeping. She clutched her husband's hand on one side, and her youngest daughter stood on her other side next to Joseph. Elizabeth sobbed hysterically, and when family members turned from the scene and moved toward their buggies, Joseph lifted the little girl into his arms. It was time to return to the Beachys' for a shared meal.

Chapter 26

Since so many people attended Perry's funeral, they needed to eat in shifts, so some went outside to the barn while they awaited their turn for the meal.

Rachel knew Anna would not be welcome to eat at any of the tables with her Amish friends and relatives, so she set a place for her and Reuben in the kitchen at a small table near the fireplace.

"That's okay," Anna said with a shake of her head. "I'm not really all that hungry."

"You've got to eat something," Rachel argued. "You're already skinny enough, and we can't have you losing any more weight."

"We'll both eat something," Reuben said as though the matter was entirely settled.

Anna finally nodded and took a seat at the table. It was obvious to Rachel that her sister was ill at ease, but even so, she was glad Anna and Reuben had come. She just wished Dad would say something to Anna instead of looking the other way whenever Anna came near. It pained her nearly as much as losing

Perry to see her flesh-and-blood sister being treated that way. And for no good reason; Dad didn't have to give Anna the silent treatment. Shunning didn't require silence, so Dad was just being stubborn and spiteful, as far as Rachel was concerned.

When the meal was over, Rachel returned to the kitchen, hoping to speak to her sister before Anna and Reuben returned home. Reuben was nowhere in sight, but she spotted Anna and their mother sitting at the small table where Anna and her husband had eaten their meal. Clearly Mom had been crying, for her eyes were red, and the skin around them looked kind of swollen.

Rachel slipped quietly away, knowing that Anna and Mom needed this time alone.

She scurried up the steps and went straight to her room, realizing that she, too, needed a few minutes by herself. She'd been so busy helping with the funeral dinner and trying to put on a brave front in order to help others in the family who were grieving that she hadn't really taken the time to mourn.

As Rachel stood in front of the window, staring at the spiraling snowflakes that had just begun to fall, her thoughts kept time with the snow–swirling, whirling, falling all around, then melting before she had the chance to sort things out.

Oh, God, why did You have to take my little brother? Why did Anna have to hurt our family by leaving the faith? Rachel trembled. *And how come Silas has to pine away for Anna and can't see me as someone he could love?*

Deep in her heart, Rachel knew that none of these things were God's fault. He had allowed them all right, but certainly He hadn't caused the bad things to happen. God loved Perry and had taken him home to heaven. Anna hadn't left home to be mean. She'd only done it because of her love for Reuben. Love did strange things to people; Rachel knew that better than anyone. Look how she had wasted so many months hoping Silas would fall in love with her and trying to gain his favor. It wasn't Silas's fault that he couldn't seem to get over his feelings for her sister. Anna had hurt Silas badly by running off with Reuben, and he might always hunger for the love he'd lost.

Rachel had to get on with her life. Maybe God wanted her to remain single. Maybe her job was to run the greenhouse and take care of Mom and Dad. It was a bitter pill to swallow, but if it was God's will, she must learn to accept it as such.

Rachel walked to the corner of her room. Maybe Anna would like to take something from her hope chest. Surely she could put a few of the things to good use in her new English home.

Rachel opened the lid and removed some hand towels, several quilted pot holders, and a few tablecloths—all things she was sure Anna could use. Next, she lifted out the beginnings of a double-ring wedding quilt. Its colors of depth and warmth, in shades of blue and dark purple, seemed to frolic side by side.

Rachel's eyes filled with tears as she thought about her own hope chest, now empty and useless. She had never started a wedding quilt, and the few items she'd stored in the chest had either been sold or were on display at Thomas Benner's store. Rachel had no reason to own a hope chest anymore, for she would probably never set up housekeeping with a husband or have any kinner of her own. Maybe her destiny was to be an old maid.

Shoving her pain aside and reaching farther into the chest, Rachel discovered an old Bible and an embroidered sampler near the bottom. Attached to the sampler was a note, and a lump lodged in her throat as she silently read the words.

Made by Miriam Stoltzfus Hilty.
Given to my mamm, Anna Stoltzfus,
To let her know how much
God has changed my heart.

Rachel knew that Miriam Stoltzfus was her great-aunt Mim and that Anna Stoltzfus was her great-grandmother. She noticed a verse embroidered on the sampler:

A merry heart
doeth good
like a medicine.
–Proverbs 17:22

A sob tore at Rachel's throat as she read the words out loud. She clung to the sampler as if it were some sort of lifeline. The yellowed piece of cloth gave her a strange yet comforting connection to the past.

Rachel's gaze came to rest on the old Bible then. She laid the sampler aside and picked up the Bible, pulling open the inside cover. Small, perfectly penned letters stated: "*This* Biwel *belonged to Anna Stoltzfus. May all who read it find as much comfort, hope, and healing as I have found.*"

Rachel noticed several crocheted bookmarks placed in various sections of the Bible. She turned the pages to some of the marked spots and read the underlined verses. Psalm 71:14 in particular seemed to jump right out at her: "*But I will hope continually, and will yet praise thee more and more.*" Rachel had been reciting this same verse for several months. Was God trying to tell her something?

Rachel was about to turn the page when another underlined verse from Psalm 71 caught her attention: "*For thou art my hope, O Lord* GOD*: thou art my trust from my youth.*"

Hot tears rolled down Rachel's cheeks as the words of verse 5 burned into her mind. All this time she'd been hoping to win Silas's heart. She had praised God for something she hoped He would do. Never once had it occurred to her that the heavenly Father wanted her to put all her hopes in Him. She was to trust Him and only Him, and she should have been doing it since her youth. Instead, she had been trying to do everything in her own strength, because it was what she wanted. When Silas didn't respond as she'd hoped he would, her faith had been dashed away like sunshine on a rainy day.

Rachel broke down, burying her face in her hands. "Dear Lord, please forgive me. Help me to learn to trust You more. Let my hope always be in You. May Your will be done in my life. Amen."

Rachel picked up the precious items she'd found in Anna's hope chest and turned toward her bedroom door. The Bible belonged to Anna's namesake, and she should have it. The sampler belonged to Great-Grandma Anna's daughter, Miriam, and Anna should have that, as well.

"It's so good to see you again, Anna."

Tears welled in Anna's eyes as she sat at the table beside her mother. "It's good to see you, too."

"We've missed you, daughter."

"I've missed you, as well."

"You can still come home, you know." Mom reached for Anna's hand.

"I can't, Mom. My place is with Reuben now."

Mom's eyes swam with tears. "I'm not asking you to leave your husband, but I'm hoping Reuben will want to return to our way of life, too."

Anna shook her head. "I don't think he'd ever

be willing to give up his truck or the TV programs he enjoys watching."

Mom stared at the table. She obviously didn't know how to respond.

Anna moistened her lips with the tip of her tongue, wishing she knew how to express everything that was on her mind. "I must admit I've come to enjoy some things about the modern way of life, too."

"Like wearing short hair?" Her mother's wounded expression and mournful tone of voice let Anna know that Mom disapproved of her new look.

Anna reached up to touch a wayward curl. "It was Reuben's idea that I cut my hair. He thinks I look prettier this way."

Mom clicked her tongue, which Anna knew meant she was very displeased. She was about to explain things further, when her father stepped into the room.

"Some of our guests are leaving now, Rebekah," he said, nodding at Mom. "Might be good if you went into the other room and said good-bye."

Mom sat for a few seconds as though she was contemplating his suggestion. Then she motioned to Anna and said, "Aren't you going to say hello to our daughter, Daniel?"

He grunted and gave his beard a quick pull. "Not much to be said, is there?"

Anna's heart felt as if it would break in two.

Why couldn't Dad find it in his heart to forgive her? Why couldn't he at least try to talk things through?

Mom maneuvered her wheelchair away from the table. "I'll tell you what, Daniel. I'll go say good-bye to our guests, and you can visit with Anna awhile."

Dad blinked a couple of times as if he couldn't quite believe what Mom had just said, but to Anna's surprise, he pulled out the chair across from her and sat down.

Mom gave Anna a quick wink and promptly wheeled out of the room.

Anna drew in a quick breath and prayed for the right words to say to her father. "Dad, I–"

"Anna, I want you to know–"

They'd spoken at the same time. "Go ahead, Dad," Anna said.

He shook his head. "No, you started speaking first."

She swallowed hard as she stared at his face. Was his pained expression from losing his youngest son, or was her being here today what had caused Dad's obvious agony? "I–I just wanted to say how sorry I am for hurting you and the rest of the family. I know it was wrong to hide the fact that I'd been seeing Reuben secretly, and I know it was wrong for us to sneak off and get married the way we did."

Dad sat stoically, apparently waiting for her to continue.

Anna swallowed once more, hoping to push

down the lump that had lodged in her throat. "Reuben and I won't be returning to the Amish faith, but we do want to keep in contact with our families—come here for visits and all."

Still nothing from her father. He remained silently in his chair, wearing a stony expression.

"I know you don't understand, but I love Reuben so much, and even though I probably wouldn't have decided to leave the Amish faith on my own, it's what he wanted. If I was going to be with him, I knew I had to make a choice."

He nodded slowly, and tears gathered in the corners of his eyes. "Love does that to people. Fact is, it can cause 'em to make all kinds of sacrifices." He glanced toward the door leading to the living room. "Your mamm and I had a few problems when we were young and some misunderstandings that nearly kept us apart."

Anna gave a quick nod. She'd heard from Mom about some of her courtship with Dad and knew they'd almost not gotten married.

"For a time, your mamm thought I only wanted to marry her so I could get my hands on the greenhouse. But I finally convinced the silly woman that it was her I loved and not her business." Dad shifted in his chair. "I even offered not to work there if she'd take me back. Said I'd spend the rest of my days workin' at my daed's dairy, though it wasn't my first choice." He stared right at Anna and offered her a smile. "So you see, I do understand in some ways what caused you to move away. You wanted to be with Reuben so much that you were willing to give up the only way of life you'd ever known."

Anna nodded, and tears rolled down her cheeks.

"I'm still not happy about you and Reuben goin' English, mind you, but I am trying to understand." He extended his hand toward her. "And I do still love you, Anna."

She clasped his fingers, feeling the warmth and strength and reveling in the joy of knowing she was still loved. "I love you, too, Dad."

Anna wasn't in the kitchen when Rachel returned, but Mom sat at the table with her head bowed. Not wishing to disturb her mother's prayer, Rachel slipped quietly out the back door. She found Joseph and Pauline sitting side-by-side on the porch. They looked so good together. Rachel was happy Joseph had found someone to love.

Joseph turned when Rachel closed the screen door. "Oh, it's you, little sister. Nearly everyone's gone home, and we didn't know where you were. Anna was looking for you."

A sense of panic surged through Rachel. "Did Anna and Reuben leave already?"

Joseph shook his head. "Naw. She said she wouldn't go without talking to you first."

"Reuben's still inside talking with his folks, but Anna said something about taking a walk down by the river." Pauline removed her shawl and handed it to Rachel. "If you're going after her, you'd better put this on. The snow's let up now, but it's still pretty cold."

Gratefully, Rachel took the offered shawl. "I think I will head down to the water and see if Anna's still there. I've got something I want to give her."

Rachel started out walking and soon broke into a run. The wind stung her face, but she didn't mind. Her only thought was of finding Anna.

The rest of Silas's family had already gone home, but he wasn't ready to leave just yet. He wanted to hang around and see if he could offer comfort to Rachel. She hadn't looked right when he'd seen her earlier, and after lunch he'd gone looking for her, but she seemed to have disappeared. He figured she must be taking Perry's death pretty hard, and it had pained him when she hadn't even responded to his hug. She'd felt small and fragile in his arms–like a broken toy he was unable to fix. It was as if Rachel were off in another world today–in a daze or some kind of a dream state.

He remembered hearing his mother talk about her oldest sister and how she'd gone crazy when her little girl drowned in the lake. He didn't think Rachel would actually go batty, but she was acting mighty strange. He couldn't go home until he knew she was going to be okay.

Silas decided to walk down to the river, knowing Rachel often went there to look for birds. Just as he reached the edge of the cornfield, mottled with snow, he spotted someone standing along the edge of the river. His heart gave a lurch when he saw the figure leaning over the water. Surely, she wasn't thinking of—

Silas took off in a run. When he neared the clearing, he skidded to a halt. The figure he'd seen was a woman all right, but it wasn't Rachel. It was her sister Anna. He approached slowly, not wanting to spook her.

She turned to face him just as he stepped to the water's edge. "Silas, you about scared me to death. I thought I was all alone out here."

"Sorry. I didn't mean to frighten you. I was looking for—"

"I used to love coming down here. It was a good place to think. . .and to pray." Anna dropped her gaze to the ground. "Sorry to say that since I left home I haven't done as much praying as I should. I have started going to church with a friend, though, and I've come to realize that the only way to deal with life's problems is to walk close to the Lord."

Silas nodded. "Praying is good. I think it goes hand in hand with thinking."

Anna smiled and pointed to the water. "Look, there's a big old trout."

"Rachel likes to fish." Silas couldn't believe that even a silly trout made him think of Rachel.

Anna grinned. "I think you and my sister have a lot in common. She likes to spend hours feeding and watching the birds that come into the yard."

"I know. I bought Rachel a bird book and a pair of binoculars for her birthday."

"I'm sure she liked that."

"I thought so at the time, but now I'm not sure."

Anna touched the sleeve of Silas's jacket. "How come?"

He stared out across the water. "She thinks I don't like her. She thinks I'm still in love with you."

Rachel stood behind the trunk of a white birch tree, holding her breath and listening to the conversation going on just a few feet away. She'd almost shown herself, but when she'd heard her own name mentioned, fear of what Anna and Silas were saying kept her feet firmly in place. Was Silas declaring his love for her sister? Was he begging her to leave Reuben and return to the Amish faith? Surely Silas must know the stand their church took against divorce.

"But you're not in love with me now, are you, Silas?" Anna asked.

Rachel pressed against the tree and waited for his response. She was doing it again—eavesdropping. It wasn't right, but she could hardly show herself now, with Silas about to declare his love for Anna. Her thoughts went back to that day many months ago when she'd heard Silas say to Anna, *"When you're ready, I'll be waiting."* Was he still waiting for her? Did he really think they had a chance to be together?

"I used to love you, Anna," Silas said. "At least I thought I did." There was a long pause, and Rachel held her breath. "Guess maybe we'd been friends so long I never thought I'd fall in love with anyone but you."

"Have you fallen in love with someone, Silas?" Anna asked.

Rachel chanced a peek around the tree. Silas stood so close to Anna he could have leaned down and kissed her. He didn't, though. Instead, he stood tall, shoulders back and head erect. "You were right when you told me once that Rachel is good for me. I love her more than anything, but I doubt we'll ever be together, because I don't know what I can do to prove my love to her."

Feeling as if her heart would burst wide open, Rachel jumped out from behind the tree. "You don't have to do anything to prove your love. What you said to Anna is proof enough for me!"

Silas jumped back. His foot slipped on a patch of snow, and he nearly landed in the water. Rachel raced forward and caught hold of his hand. "Be careful now. You'll get what I have for Anna all wet," she said, as he pulled her close to his side.

Anna stepped forward. "What have you got for me, Rachel?"

She lifted the sampler and their great-grandmother's Bible. "I found these at the bottom of your hope chest, and I thought maybe you'd like to have them."

Anna's eyes flooded with tears. "Great-Aunt Mim's sampler and Great-Grandma's Bible. Mom gave them to me for my hope chest several years ago, but I'd forgotten all about them."

Rachel handed the items to her sister. "I read some passages I found in this old Bible and was reminded that I need to put my hope in the Lord and keep trusting Him, not hope for the things I've wanted or try to do everything in my own strength." She looked over at Silas. "I thought I'd have to learn to live without your love, but now—"

Silas placed two cold fingers against her lips. "Now you'll have to learn to live as my wife. If you'll have me, that is."

She nodded. "Jah, I'll have you, Silas."

He leaned down to kiss her, and Rachel felt as if she were a bird—floating, soaring high above the clouds—reveling in God's glory and hoping continuously in Him.

Epilogue

One year later

Rachel stood on the lawn, her groom on one side, her brother and new sister-in-law on the other. Two weeks ago, Joseph had married Pauline, and today the young couple were offering their congratulations to Rachel and Silas. Both couples had received double-ring wedding quilts from their mothers, and today Rachel's heart held a double portion of happiness. The only thing that could have made her day more complete would have been to share it with her older sister. But apparently Anna and Reuben hadn't been able to come, for Rachel hadn't seen any sign of them during the wedding ceremony.

On an impulse, Rachel glanced across the yard and was surprised to see Anna and Reuben walking toward her.

"Excuse me a minute," she whispered to Silas. "I need to speak with my sister."

Silas nodded and squeezed her hand. "Hurry back, fraa."

Rachel smiled and slipped quickly away. She drew Anna off to one side, and they exchanged a hug. "It's so good to see you. I was hoping you had received my invitation to the wedding and that you would be able to be here today."

"I'm sorry Reuben and I didn't get here in time for the ceremony. He had a little trouble with his truck this morning, so we were late getting started. I did want to wish you well and give you this, though." Anna handed Rachel a brown paper sack.

"What is it?"

"Take a look."

Rachel opened the bag, reached inside, and withdrew a sampler. At first she thought it was the same one she'd given to Anna a year ago, but when she read the embroidered words, she knew it wasn't:

> *"For thou art my hope, O Lord God:*
> *thou art my trust from my youth."*
> *–Psalm 71:5*

"I thought it would be something you could hand down to your children and grandchildren." Anna placed her hand against her stomach. "That's what I plan to do with the Merry Heart sampler Great-Aunt Mim made all those years ago."

Rachel's eyes widened. "You're in a family way?"

Anna nodded. "The baby will come in the spring."

"Do Mom and Dad know that they are going to be grandparents?"

"I told them a few minutes before you came outside." Anna smiled, and her eyes filled with tears. "Dad and Mom want me and Reuben to come visit more often after the baby is born." She glanced around the yard as though someone might be listening. "I'm sure a few in our community still might exclude us from some things, but as long as we feel welcome within our own families, that's what counts."

Rachel hugged her sister. "I'm glad things are better between you and Dad."

Anna nodded. "Reuben and I had a long talk awhile back. We decided that we both want to stay English, but we're attending church together now, and we're reading our Bibles and praying every day."

"I'm happy to hear that, and I thank you for coming today." Rachel held the sampler close to her heart. "I'll always cherish this, and every time I look at it, I'll not only be reminded to put my hope in Jesus but I'll think of my English sister, who is also trusting in God."

Anna pulled her fingers through the ends of her hair, which she had let grow long again. "That's so true."

"Well, I'd best be getting back to my groom, or he's likely to come looking for me," Rachel said with a giggle.

Anna nodded. "Tell him I said to be happy and

that he'd better treat my little sister right, or I'll come looking for him."

Rachel hugged Anna one last time; then she hurried toward Silas. She was glad she had opened her sister's hope chest last year, for if she hadn't, she might never have found Great-Aunt Mim's special sampler and Great-Grandma's Bible, so full of hope found only in God's Word.

When Rachel reached her groom, he pulled her to his side. "I love you, Rachel, and I pray we'll always be this happy together."

Rachel leaned her head against his shoulder. "If we keep God at the center of our lives and put our hope and trust in Him, the love and happiness we feel today will only grow stronger." She smiled and looked up. "The Lord is truly my hope, and I pray that all of our future children and grandchildren will put their hope and trust in Him, too."

Rachel's Ribbon Salad

Ingredients:

3-ounce box of lime gelatin
3 cups boiling water, divided
3 cups cold water, divided
1 small can crushed pineapple
½ cup chopped walnuts
3-ounce box of lemon gelatin
8-ounce package cream cheese
¾ cup whipped cream
3-ounce box of raspberry gelatin

Dissolve lime gelatin in 1 cup boiling water. Add 1 cup cold water, crushed pineapple, and nuts to the gelatin, then pour into an 8x8 pan to make the first layer. Chill in the refrigerator until set. Dissolve lemon gelatin in 1 cup boiling water, then add 1 cup cold water. When the mixture becomes cool, add the cream cheese and whipped cream. Pour this mixture over the first layer of gelatin that has already set. Return to refrigerator and let set again. Dissolve raspberry gelatin in 1 cup boiling water. Add 1 cup cold water and mix well. Pour over the top of the first two layers, return to the refrigerator, and chill until set.

About the Author

Descended from Anabaptists herself, Wanda E. Brunstetter enjoys writing about the Amish because they live a peaceful, simple life. Wanda's interest in the Amish and other Plain communities began when she married her husband, Richard, who grew up in a Mennonite church in Pennsylvania. Wanda and Richard have made numerous trips to Amish Country and have many Amish friends, living in several communities. Wanda hopes her readers will learn to love the wonderful Amish people as much as she does.

Wanda and Richard have been blessed with two grown children, six grandchildren, and one great-grandson. In her spare time Wanda enjoys beachcombing, ventriloquism, gardening, photography, knitting, and having fun with her family.

Wanda has written over 60 books, as well as hundreds of stories, articles, poems, devotionals, and puppet scripts.

To learn more about Wanda, visit her website at www.wandabrunstetter.com.